Debasements of Brooklyn

Debasements of Brooklyn

IKA GOLD

THE PERMANENT PRESS
Sag Harbor, NY 11963

For information, address:
  The Permanent Press
  4170 Noyac Road
  Sag Harbor, NY 11963
  www.thepermanentpress.com

Library of Congress Cataloging-in-Publication Data

Gold, Ira, author.
  Debasements of Brooklyn / Ira Gold.
  Sag Harbor, NY : The Permanent Press, [2016]
  ISBN 978-1-57962-443-9
    1. Gangsters—Fiction. 2. Couples—Fiction. 3. Domestic fiction.
  4. Brooklyn (New York, N.Y.)—Social life and customs—Fiction.
  I. Title.

PS3607.O4355 D43 2016
813'.6—dc23   2016002728

Printed in the United States of America

*For H—whom I hope will one day tell me
the other letters of his name*

Part I

1

Lovers' Quarrel

These basic facts come direct from Pauli Bones. About everything else I extemporize.

Scrunchy Cho, a pawn, a nobody, runs down Avenue V and East Nineteenth Street. It's midnight in Sheepshead Bay, as it is everywhere in this part of Brooklyn. In the houses—two family stuccos and stubby brick apartment buildings—not one person is looking out the window to see if Scrunchy can evade his pursuers. He gulps air and sweat oozes from the clogged pores of his parchment skin.

Ever hear of wrong place, wrong time? Well, that isn't Scrunchy's issue. Scrunchy has stabbed one of our whores. Yes, she had lifted a bill and a half from his stash when he made the mistake of falling asleep in her bed for ten minutes. Had Scrunchy not been such a cautious man things might have turned out better. But he wakes with a start, wearing a sleeveless undershirt and smudged white underpants. Melissa Apple, aka Candi Apple, a twenty-year-old from Parched, Arizona, who has worked for Vinnie Five-Five for four years, lies next to him on the bed, her eyes closed: perhaps asleep, probably not.

Scrunchy doesn't disturb her when he puts on his pants. A beanpole with a mean face, lined as an accordion, Scrunchy counts his money a dozen times a day, more when he's nervous. Fingering his cash calms him.

So he knows by his roll's weight that he's short, even taking into account the two bills he gave to Candi. When he sees that a dear fifty and a precious hundred have also gone missing, he pulls Candi up by her hair and smacks her face. She starts shouting. Scrunchy has only a few seconds to get his money or his revenge. Candi curses and swears that she has taken nothing, so Scrunchy cuts her face and sticks her in the breast. Then he jumps out the second-floor window just as the guys burst in. They take off after him. Pauli Bones and Garlic Pannetto race out on foot, while Benny Double-Down gets the car.

Scrunchy's half-block head start might have held up if he hadn't tripped in front of 1670 East Nineteenth. Garlic and Pauli Bones close in quick. Scrunchy memorizes the address in case he ever has the opportunity to initiate a suit for the broken sidewalk. Then he streaks down an alley. Hopping a fence, he dashes onto Eighteenth Street just as Double-Down turns the car onto the street.

Scrunchy is hard to miss, as he's the only creature on the block running for his life. Double-Down, a terrible blackjack player but a decent thug, cuts onto the sidewalk right in front of Scrunchy. Because he keeps glancing over his shoulders, Scrunchy crashes into the chrome bumper with such force that he dislocates his right kneecap. Double-Down, a man of some heft, bulls out of the car clutching a tire iron, just as Bones's wiry frame comes into view. In the rear, Garlic arrives as Scrunchy bleeds out from a half-dozen orifices, some of them created just for this occasion. More importantly, Pauli Bones kicks Scrunchy into the once-in-a-lifetime experience of a cerebral hemorrhage. Garlic doesn't bother to get his loafers bloody on an already unconscious Scrunchy. All three, however, lend a hand tossing the corpse into the trunk where Double-Down keeps a spare tarp for just such an eventuality.

In less than five minutes, they are back in the house, wrapping Candi in a sheet for disposal. The knife has nicked her aorta.

Double-Down, laconic as always, eulogizes, "Fuckin' shame."

"Nice fucking girl," Garlic, the expansive one, growls. "Good ho."

Bones, the conscience of the group, intones, "Told her a hundred times about rollin' these animals."

None fear any sort of investigation connecting them to either murder. Anyone who may have loved Candi or Scrunchy would consider their disappearances as both a biological and a karmic inevitability. Candi has a young son back in Parched living with her own mother, a forty-year-old ambulance driver and itinerant meth addict who would raise the boy with as much care and devotion as she raised Candi/Melissa.

The furthest thought from each man's mind is war. Justice has been served; things are even. The only issue left to negotiate, perhaps, is the money that Candi lifted from Scrunchy that rightly belongs to his next of kin, if he has any. For safekeeping, they divide it evenly, along with the contents of Scrunchy's cherished stash.

2

A Canticle for Scrunchy

The war, in fact, surprises everyone in Vinnie Five-Five's orbit. For one thing, Scrunchy's passing, while unmourned, does not go unnoticed. Scrunchy's superiors, of whom he had many, meet in a small, decrepit apartment below a strip club on Eighth Avenue and Fifty-Third Street, also in Brooklyn.

There, Crazy Bo Moon of Sunset Park and Wuhan Prefecture Penitentiary, along with his sociopathic underboss U Li, a Burmese of Chinese descent who trained in prison conservatories all over Southeast Asia, agree that the Italians have been in decline ever since a brief flowering during the *Cinquecento*. They posit that the whole crew should have been knocked off at the end of the Renaissance. It is time for the East to rise and to take over south Brooklyn. Scrunchy's murder is no skin off Crazy Bo's back. (He, in fact, blames Scrunchy for craving white-devil pussy when the best girls in New York live in houses right there in Sunset Park.) But it gives the Chinese boss an excuse to finish the job on the Italians that assimilation and a low birthrate started.

Before the war can begin, however, the Chinese need to make a deal with the Russians, whose territory lies on the ocean side of Sheepshead Bay, in Brighton Beach. For years the Russians and Italians skirmished. The Italians, in part because the younger generation moved to Jersey and points west, had their territory shrink to the Gravesend area on the F train and the Sheepshead Bay stop on the Q and B lines. It doesn't take long for Crazy Bo and U Li to contract the job of taking out the small Italian crew that controls such an insignificant principality to Vlad the Impaler. Scrunchy Cho must be avenged.

Sensing opportunity, the Russians readily agree to undertake the bulk of the annihilation.

So with the energy characteristic of American immigrants since the early European arrivals set about exterminating the native population, Vlad initiates the slaughter with the same conscientious devotion to detail.

Double-Down, slow and heavy, is the first casualty. His body is found in a van on Ocean Parkway and Avenue S, in front of a very large Orthodox yeshiva. Pasty-faced boys in black hats and white shirts crowd around the yellow police tape and watch as the ambulance pulls the bullet-riddled corpse from the vehicle. These unworldly innocents titter when they realize what hangs from his mouth is not the stub of a cigar but a chunk of penis. (In the Sicilian tradition, genitals in the mouth mean the victim violated some sexual taboo. Something must have been lost in the Russian translation, for Double-Down spent all his energy losing at cards.)

A day later, sanitation workers uncover Garlic's body stuffed in a hefty bag, actually three different ones, under the elevated on McDonald Avenue.

Garlic and Double-Down had helped run Vinnie Five-Five's two houses. Of Sicilian descent, they both dreamed of becoming made men, which even in this debased age amounts to a license to mint money providing you avoid assassination.

Pauli Bones still exists. Despite his attention-deficit jumpiness, it will be harder to whack him. He thinks like a stone killer during those times he's not actually being a stone killer. He's also a great earner (though a lousy spender) who Vinnie would be forced to avenge. As for me, I'm just a stringer, half-Italian, half-Jewish, half-asser who kicks upstairs no more than a G a week. My main gig is in the sleepy backwater of selling weed. Besides my clients from this territory, I have hooked up with the supers in the Brooklyn neighborhoods where the people actually know shit about Brooklyn. They retail to the social media types who populate the gentrified one-bedrooms in Carrel Gardens and like to think they're cool and tough because they don't live in Gramercy Park.

At the gym, I have acquired some bulk on my six-three frame. So I work security, do collections, and provide muscle wherever needed for Vinnie. Easy gigs for an autodidact.

Actually, I hate my job, I hate my colleagues, and I hate Vinnie Five-Five most of all. The homicidal pip-squeak lusts for every penny I kick up. Worse, Pauli Bones has hinted that certain associates, maybe lusting after my little business, have intimated to Vinnie that something about me is not right. This, coupled with my semiobvious lack of commitment, has awakened in Vinnie a murderous suspicion. Nothing more dangerous than a gangster who wants out of the gang. The Feds can flip a guy like that as easily as they can a light switch. Every day I sense that Vinnie's loyalty to my dead father, his old bookkeeper, diminishes.

Ah, I find my whole crew to be no better than the barbarians on Wall Street, the tenure-fuckers in academia or the scum in Washington. Money, pussy, respect. The more people desire these things, the less I want them. Why? I don't have a clue. I never considered myself a contrarian. Probably I'm cracking up. But all I crave lately is freedom from historical imperatives. Fuck history. Is that too much to ask?

Adding to my woozy sense of dislocation is this fiery desire to do nothing but read this collection of books I inherited from my dad. Why? It makes no sense. Not since I attempted suicide nearly eight years ago had a train hit me so hard. I used to like getting laid.

In fact, most people as pedigreed as I—my father laundered every dime of Vinnie's money for decades—would want to make the most of the endless opportunities for graft. One can even get high on the threat of getting clipped. But I want out. I never enjoyed head banging. In the ten years of doing this and that for Vinnie, I beat up maybe two-dozen people. I may intimidate with my size, but Bones, with his quick fists and crazy eyes, with his psychopathic mannerisms and sharpened kitchen knife, always finds himself in situations where serious violence occurs. Cautious people avoid me; only the insane mess with Pauli Bones.

Maybe it's a phase. Maybe I'm reading too many of dad's Penguin classics. I really wish that money, pussy, and respect still held my interest. But I find myself thinking of a million other things, including how the pursuit of money, pussy, and respect has brought me little in the way of contentment.

If I just disappear, vanish, I'll never be able to return. Like many CEOs today, Vinnie believes his lowest-level workers have no right to retire. I could be a danger floating around on the outside. Yes, this neighborhood indeed sucks—savage people, hardly any green space—but the only ones whom I love are here.

3

Favors

Though a serial killer, Pauli Bones is solicitous. "Lay low. Vinnie's working on a sit-down with Crazy Bo and He Lies. Who the fuck calls his kid He Lies anyway?"

"U Li." I correct and then speculate, "That might not be his given name."

"Asshole." Pauli Bones eyes me with enormous malice. "Every time you open your mouth . . ." Bones is so antsy that he rarely finishes a sentence while hopping from foot to foot and eyeing the tables hoping for some trouble. The poor maniac mourns his friends. "Double-Down was a degenerate gambler, but Garlic didn't do nothin'. The lazy shit didn't want to get blood on his shoes."

Pauli Bones and I are working Vinnie Five-Five's poker room on West Third Street and Avenue X. It is a 1,200-square-foot second-floor apartment where the interior walls have been removed to create a functional open floor plan that fits a dozen round, green-felt tables. It's a slow night. Only five tables are taken. We're standing near the door.

In the crew, Pauli's the only one I hang with. We sometimes drink and get high at an after-hours club on Fourth Avenue in Bay Ridge. Pauli's best stories concern hospital workers—doctors, nurses, orderlies—who are his main suppliers of prescription drugs. He likes to say that the medical profession is ripe with sick motherfuckers.

"Look dickwad . . ." I wait for Pauli Bones to gather his rather simple thoughts. "The Chinks and Vlad are going to split Vinnie's territory. They don't give a Peking duck who did Scrunchy. Probably glad the ugly mutt's dead."

"Vinnie's not going down without a fight. One call to Tony D . . ."

Insanity again eddies from Pauli Bones's fevered brain and smokes his black eyes. "You think Tony D gives a rat's cunt about Vinnie? Vinnie's been on the shelf for a year."

I am an idiot. Why didn't I know this? I know that Tony D—the New Jersey boss of our gerrymandered Brooklyn family—is unhappy with the money Vinnie kicks his way. Our shrinking territory has cut into our profits. Either earn or lose protection. Or maybe Tony thinks that Vinnie is holding out. Still, it's hard to believe that Tony D will allow the Russians to take over. "They're first cousins."

"You're a moron and every book you read makes you more stupid. I can't talk to you for five minutes before I want to kill you."

Pauli Bones recognizes my dissatisfaction, knows that I am not the goon I intermittently attempt to be. Luckily, however, he finds my burgeoning inner life a source of amusement and a good entrée for abuse and insult. I sense, if not respect, at least tolerance.

"I'm sorry, Pauli. The political winds shift so fast—"

"Don't be an asshole. I'm telling you the motherfucking *emmes*. No reinforcements. If the negotiations fail, just a slaughter." Emotion can overcome even the toughest lunatic. Pauli Bones sits down in the chair, unusual for a man with his unstable energy.

It is entirely possible that somewhere in his traumatized psyche Bones grieves not only for himself but for his friends and for our doomed way of life. I take a few steps toward him and put my hand on his shoulder.

"Get your fucking hands off me." Then, with heartfelt sincerity, he pleads, "You got a couple of bills I can borrow?"

By this Pauli Bones means *give me 200 you stupid fuck*. But like most of Pauli's deepest desires since childhood, this one too would go unfulfilled. I take out my wallet and open it. I show him the empty billfold. "Nada."

And then, suddenly, I reconsider. I have little enough for my own war chest, but Pauli destroys money in the crematorium of financial idiocy. Everything he buys he can't afford, despite a large, tax-free income.

In the end, something compels me to pull out a couple of hundred dollars and wave it in front of Pauli's face. He jerks his head away, but I see a flicker of surprise and gratitude before he snatches the money from my hand. "Find a place to hide. I just saved your sorry-ass life."

I don't know how to take Bones's warning. I can see how paranoia might be one of his issues. On the other hand, they did decapitate Garlic.

4

Origins

Do I need to worry about this war? Until an hour ago, I thought only Vinnie would ever consider me worth whacking. After all, I am Mr. Small-Time. Dr. Insignificant. My existence is of interest to no one. I'm not fully Italian so I can never be made. My father's name, and consequently mine, is Fenster. Dad was a numbers man, an accountant and a horseplayer. But he made his nut no matter what. And his interests soared beyond the neighborhood, sometimes even beyond the ponies. The seeds he planted when I was young have blossomed into a beautiful garden that dazzles me as it illuminates my misery.

My mother, on the other hand, had been a Gugliani. Outwardly, I resemble her. My tribal marking confirms my membership as a fully paid-up Guido: the slicked-back hair, the focus on my musculature, my fascination with an outdated and seedy underworld dying here in Sheepshead Bay.

My dad had tried to protect me. He insisted on naming me Howard, hoping, thinking magically, like a gambler, that such a name would keep me out of the life. But I lost "Howard" and any hope of living straight the moment I translated my surname from the Germanic for my future crew which included Vinnie's twin sons—Gus and Julius. This life-changing event occurred in third grade. I have since learnt to keep my mouth shut.

So today they call me Windows. *(Fenster* in German.) Unlike emaciated Pauli Bones, or even Vinnie Five-Five, who got his nickname forty years ago when he was the tiny (five foot five) starting point guard for the Lincoln High basketball team, Windows says nothing about my anatomy or personality. If anything, I am opaque. You cannot look through me and see my soul, even those silly enough to believe one exists. Today, Vinnie's nickname still works, for he's five foot five in diameter, having put on some girth since his basketball days. My nickname, like my half-breed status, has descended like a supernatural visitation, foisted upon me by a universe whose workings make little sense to the casual observer and no sense at all to the deep thinkers.

From my mother I inherited an attachment to this aging neighborhood and its people, a loyalty returned with painful conditions. Other than great books, my father bequeathed an aversion to regular work, which I still consider my healthiest instinct.

One thing. Dad's love of the artistic and intellectual never included an affinity for educational institutions or their overseers. His fiery contempt for schoolteachers' small-mindedness informed my childhood. "Read for yourself," he counseled in the manner of the towering humanist Erasmus. My mother, a shy and conventional Italian girl when she first met my father and a shrewd, practical, and disappointed woman afterward, wondered what the hell I did in my room all day. Never a scholar herself, she couldn't comprehend how I spent hours reading and still did lousy in school.

My mom and her family reviled all educational institutions, not for their intellectual narrowness but as a general waste of time. After forgiving my mother for marrying a Jewish schlemiel, my cousins, nearly all of them named Sal, took me under their wings as we gangbanged here and there, finding it more and more difficult because of the steadily declining ethnic tensions that existed in Brooklyn. (The action, of course, was in those neighborhoods closer to Manhattan, but instead of Italian, Irish, and African Americans kids fighting with bats and chains, developers battled it out with residents at zoning board meetings.) Physical culture always interested me. Never one for team sports, I took up street fighting and Pilates.

5

Stalking Memory Lane

Rosy-fingered dawn arrives even in this blighted neighborhood. By six A.M. Pauli Bones and I are the only ones left in the place. He glares at me with untamed hatred, maybe because I only fronted him 200, maybe because he is a psychopath. You can't talk to him when he gets into a homicidal state, so I volunteer to lock up the poker room and tell him to go home or wherever he plans to escape being murdered.

Without saying another word, he flees the building as if pursued by howling demons. A brief stab of anxiety pricks, seeing Bones so terrified. Normally, he welcomes mortal violence.

I lock up. Vinnie Five-Five never keeps a room open two days in a row. He rotates the game from one of his four apartments using an algorithm I can't fathom, though the gamblers gather together as if directed by a heavenly call. Me, I get a phone call an hour before my shift starts. By switching the rooms around, Vinnie keeps the chance of being hassled by the police and other gangsters to a minimum.

It has been a tepid, rainy April, punctuated by winter chills. But sunrise brings a crispness that wakes one into life and ignites hopes of rebirth. I cross Ocean Parkway, a wide boulevard bordered by grass, service roads, and the oldest dedicated bike lane in the country. I usually cherish this mile-long stroll, from East Third Street to East Twenty-First Street where I live in my sister's (half sister, my father had an earlier, even unhappier marriage) basement apartment. It is a cozy place, with the windows peeking up to the driveway where I have a wonderful view of the radial tires belonging to my brother-in-law's Civic.

So I walk the streets familiar from my earliest childhood and recognize every tree, ancient yet skinny as crackheads. I prize the old wood-framed houses that rest cockeyed on their foundations. Mostly, though, attached row houses with high stoops and narrow porches line the street. This part of Brooklyn contains many retired plumbers and Mafiosos—all suffering from irrelevance and waiting for death.

On Coney Island Avenue I pass the store where I used to buy candy and baseball cards. On East Seventeenth Street, quieter than the other blocks, I, the Five-Five boys, Bones, others, played punchball using the parked cars and manholes as bases. These childhood markers might oppress some with thoughts of underachieving. Me, I'm a sentimentalist. The crap and unrealized goals I let slide, while the loving care and good times take on a numinous glow. My mind flies across time and space when I read my father's books, but my body feels most comfortable in the neighborhood that I know from infancy. Nothing really bad can happen to me here.

6

Basement, my basement

This morning, however, my heart races with every passing car. Adrenaline courses through my body whenever I notice someone in the gloaming. I'm nervous as shit.

Pauli Bones has spooked me. I spin around as I hear voices. Nothing there. I fight against breaking into a run. Sweat drips down my forehead and my hair stands on end.

I quicken my pace. Just because I'm a flunky does not mean that I'm exempt from the iron laws of war. My lowly status might even make me more of a target. Killing me would annoy, but not enrage, the powers that reside both here and in Jersey.

Besides, I am not totally unknown. My pot-selling operation has expanded as I meet more and more building workers. I am also friends with a goon named Ivan Rachmaninoff, a fifth cousin of the composer. We sometimes play handball, this Ivan and I, at the Manhattan Beach courts. He happens to have a deep interest in Russian literature. He's the only gangster I know who has a strong opinion on the Turgenev/Dostoyevsky debate. He agrees with Dostoyevsky that Russia has a Slavic, not a European, soul.

This cocksucker knows where I live.

I finally make it home. I go in through the side door and walk a half-flight down.

Here, my setup comforts me. This single-wide room has served as my crib for five years. Strategically dotted around the space are a queen-size bed, some chairs, and a small kitchen table. In an unfinished area near the boiler I have my bathroom. The sink, stove, and fridge are up against the staircase wall where a washer/dryer used to be. (Judith moved them into a converted pantry upstairs.) On the back wall, warped wooden bookcases hold my father's sacred library. If Pythagoras infused souls into beans and the Hindus transform cows into deities, why shouldn't my father worship Penguins? He would reach nirvana while reading every word of every masterpiece—no matter how boring and disappointing the wisdom of the ages proved to be.

Ah, my father was a sick man, suffering from cruel compulsions. Had he enjoyed sci-fi or mystery rather than Swift and Von Kleist he might have escaped his gloominess.

And now, as if his soul possessed mine, as if the curse of the esoteric passed from generation to generation, I too have become fixated on these orange-sheathed, compact, and easy-to-carry volumes. Each word I read in them makes me more of an outcast.

I lie on my bed. After work, my body usually switches off in a minute but today I quiver with nerves. My apartment might look secure on this quiet street in this out-of-the-way neighborhood, in a house with sturdy doors and bars on the ground-floor windows. Yet a determined adversary, a killer, could easily penetrate the perimeter and slit my throat. I sure would not be the first to go this way.

Still, I need sleep. I think of the catatonic effect of reading *The Faerie Queen*. This might work, but I can't bear a single line. So I go to my medicine cabinet and swallow an Ambien and, for good measure, a Benadryl. As if conked on the head with a mallet, I sleep for six solid hours.

At noon, I awake struggling with a faceless figure, a phantom who has escaped from one of my nightmares and attempts to suffocate me with a pillow.

7

Stateless in Brooklyn

Dazed with the drugs and exhaustion, I go upstairs. My sister, Judith, sits on a stool at the kitchen island drinking coffee and watching *The Price is Right* on a small television. Except for the grating TV noise, this presents a homey scene. Judith keeps a neat kitchen, with copper pans hanging from hooks and dozens of spices resting on a rack. A cookie jar and toaster stand side by side on the granite countertop. The sun pours in from a window above the sink. Judith, with a seven- and a ten-year-old, girls, works hard keeping house. Until last week she also cashiered at Key Foods three days a week before they gave her a choice of full time or nothing. Child care would have eaten up every penny of her pathetic earnings so she is forced to take nothing. This adds more financial anxieties to an already worried woman.

But she is always happy to see me. She comments, "The price is never right." And with that she presses the remote.

I don't know why Judith feels so loyal. Growing up we rarely saw each other as her mother pulsed with radioactive hatred for our father. Neither of us understood why. Dad was a mildish man, given to rages only when drunk. And he drank rarely—New Year's Eve, July Fourth, Halloween, a few points in between. Enough, I guess. My own mother, used to brutal and unpredictable men, appreciated the reliability of my father's violence. By keeping careful tabs on him, she knew how to strategically withdraw, to keep me out of his way, as soon as he poured his third drink. If we were out, she'd simply take me home. If we were home, she would tell dad that if he took another sip, she'd spend the night and maybe the rest of her life somewhere else. Dad would look at my mom, would look at his glass, tortured by a terrible dilemma. Then, he'd tell her to take a hike. Because my mom caught him early in the bender, he never sounded nasty. On the contrary, he was concerned for our well-being, offering to drive us as far away as we wanted to go, perhaps into the Atlantic where our carcasses could feed the fish and thus serve a useful purpose. We always took public transport.

I don't think Judith's mother had the diplomatic abilities of my mom. Her mother came from a more typical Jewish family where men, when dealing with frustrations, likely numbed themselves with cake and coffee and attacked those nearest with sarcasms that left them feeling pleased with their wit. My mom, a full-blooded Sicilian, saw the women of her family defend themselves with threats, posturing, and, if need be, heavy frying pans. If shove came to shove, I always suspected that my demure mother could take my father, no problem. He could have suspected the same thing, for while sober he never raised his voice and while blasted he never raised his fist.

Judith, meanwhile, had loved our dad. She could care less about his drunken interludes or his compulsive gambling. He never missed his child support and was always kind to her, shooting her extra money whenever he could. And Judith was strong minded enough to ignore her mom's assault on dad's character. Especially in high school, when Judith's mother became more and more isolated and estranged from the world, Judith would come to visit us after class, welcomed not only by dad, but my mom, who took pity on this unhappy girl.

Judith, ten years older than I, sometimes babysat. She kept these meetings secret from her mother, but they increased in the years before our father died.

Judith, tall and sturdy like I am but with much softer eyes, married a handsome dope who barely makes a living as a roofer and is equally unsuccessful pursuing extramarital affairs. After my mom died, Judith offered her basement to me until I found a new place. Truthfully, my search, never aggressive, petered out as soon as I moved my books in. Perhaps I lack ambition. Perhaps I recognize a good thing when I have one.

I do what I can around the house. My most important chore is keeping John from beating Judith. She always used to have a story, but the black eyes and swollen lips told a different truth. Luckily, John, a cauldron of frustrated ambition, had been careless enough to smack Judith soon after I moved in. I don't know what they were fighting about, but I ran up the stairs in time to see him bring Judith down with a backhand to the nose. I broke his wrist and would have killed him if Judith hadn't jumped on my back. Paradoxically, this act of near fatal violence convinced John of the value of nonviolent resolutions to domestic disputes. At least until I move out. Meanwhile I have earned his eternal hatred, though he happily smokes my pot.

Judith slumps on the stool. "I have to talk to you."

These words, of course, always precede bad, no, terrible news. Whether it's being fired or dumped or any other everyday horror that causes suicidal despair, the words and, even more, the tone cannot be mistaken. I don't need more tsuris, but one cannot choose one's time of death.

"You know I lost my job," Judith continues.

I wait.

"John, too. Business has been real slow."

I have a few bucks and a brick of weed secreted in the dropped ceiling. I deeply regret the dough I burned on Pauli Bones. "Do you need some money?"

Judith hears the crack in my voice, and she, too, chokes up. "You're paying what you can, but John says we can get twice as much or more on the open market."

John, though a total failure as an engine of wealth creation, has always had an unbending belief in the free market even as its unforgiving machinery destroys him and his family.

"How much is he asking?" For a second I think I might be able to swing a higher rent. Maybe I can get in on a couple of truck hijackings.

"John says 1,200."

Being a half-assed gangster never pays well, and with the war my prospects dim further as business gets put on hold. When I have it, I give Judith 600 a month. When I don't, I live for free.

Judith is crying. "Judith."

"You can stay in the guest room until you find a place."

How Judith turned out so wonderful given her crazy mother, our feckless father, and the overall barbaric attitudes of all who surround us, I don't know. Her charity is the one random, undeserved gift destiny has granted me. To lose this hurts all the more. "I should leave anyway."

Judith picks her head out of the well of her coffee mug. "Why?"

"Some problems at work."

No idiot, this alarms Judith. "With Vinnie Five-Five."

"No. Not exactly."

"With one of the boys?"

"Not our boys."

Judith relaxes when she finds out that no one in the neighborhood is after me. She has no idea of the genocidal ferocity the murder of Scrunchy Cho has unleashed.

She notices my expression and retreats. "We can manage for a bit longer if you—"

"No. I'll go underground and take the danger with me."

"I'm so sorry, Howard. I wish—"

"Don't wish nothing. I'm not a baby."

"Keep your stuff here until you find a place. Do you have enough money?"

"Of course!"

"How much do you need?"

My finances are complicated. That is I have little actual money. Cash flow goes into inventory (the brick), and is used for kickbacks and kickups.

My few hundred bucks would barely get me beyond city limits. Yet I can't take anything from Judith—who has two kids, a lug of a husband, and no job.

Judith leaves the kitchen and comes back with her hand in the pocket of her housecoat. She approaches and slips some bills into my hand, holding on to it for a second.

She probably just handed me her last spare penny. "I can't take this."

Judith rearranges herself on her stool and grips her cup again. "You have to stay alive. That's the most important. Now get out of here before John comes back. If he knew that I just . . ."

I hug my sister as if we are separating for life, but she gently wiggles out of my grip. "It's all right, Howie. You're going to make me start crying."

I go downstairs and pack a gym bag with clothes. At the last minute I put in a pair of brass knuckles I have owned since I'm fourteen. Hidden in a remote panel of the dropped ceiling I have stored a beautiful cadmium-handled Glock 9, the best weapon I ever owned and the well-wrapped kilo of weed. These I will leave until I find a place to stay. I'd like to have them on me, but wandering around with them is a risk.

I count the money Judith gave me. Six hundred dollars. Not only that. The bills look familiar. One of them has a tear in the top right-hand corner. On another, someone has blotted out Benjamin Franklin's homely face, as if the vandal had a particular wish to insult the only man to sign the Articles of Confederation, the Declaration of Independence, and the

Constitution. These are the same bills I had given Judith the last time I paid the rent.

Like a mother, like poor housewives of all eternity, Judith has kept the money I paid her in escrow in case I needed it. Her concern for me, so baffling, overwhelms and I collapse on my beloved bed, maybe for the last time. My mother had not cared for me more.

But I don't stay for long. I can't. My sister needs the apartment. The Chinese and Russians are gunning for me and I'm putting Judith in danger by being here. So I leave through the side door and walk down the driveway having no idea where I might go. I'm a man without a neighborhood.

8

A Clean and Well-Lighted Escape

The elevated train's rusted, bolt-infested girders shade East Sixteenth Street. Hidden way above the tracks is a giant blue sky and a spot of yellow sun, stuck in the center as with Velcro.

It is just past one on an almost-summer Tuesday afternoon. April should be crueler.

In the beginning, a century ago, pushcarts rested at the bottom of the subway, selling everything from apples to undergarments. Then stores spread, offering cheap clothing, fruit, flowers, meat, fish, baked goods, whatever one might need on the way back from the garment factories that crushed the soul. Today, an equally oppressed working class populates the dilapidated buildings near the train.

Into this morass where people are ground to pulp by work and, more, by the lack of it, a café named *Stamm Tisch* (Regular's Table) opened in a storefront twenty feet from the stairway leading to the Q/B platform.

The vast majority of the commuters have little energy to sip lattes while watching hungry people stagger home. Why? You need to glimpse the kids before they go to bed. You can't miss your favorite show. Some may even want to exchange a few tired words with a spouse.

In the more northerly parts of Brooklyn, cafés spread like the pest. Along with wealth, they crept southward. Yet, on the whole, they remained miles from Gravesend and Sheepshead Bay, unable to cross the cultureless moat of Midwood and Flatbush, miles and miles of desolate landscape peopled mostly by savage tribes of Orthodox Jews and roving bands of the low net worth individuals.

Yet somehow downtown had planted a flag, miles from its nearest outpost. Rickety wooden tables of various sizes filled the café's interior. One could get a chessboard from the barista. A few books, maybe the only ones in the neighborhood, lay neatly stacked on built-in shelves. *Stamm Tisch* brings all the claims of middle-European intellectualism to the grandchildren of people who despised it when they lived there.

When I had first seen the place, I laughed. Here is not Manhattan where the redundant hold off panic with cappuccino and meds. Did this dinky joint, with its fey pretentions, with its four-dollar espresso and its sprout-filled wraps, expect to make it in a neighborhood where bodegas earned fortunes by selling Colt 45 to twelve-year-olds, where connected Italians would firebomb the place rather than order its morning-glory muffin? In fact, Vinnie Five-Five debated this very issue. He has a piece of a popular Italian café on Avenue U that serves rock hard biscotti and overstuffed cannolis. *Stamm Tisch* presents a challenge to the ethos of all people who care about the substantive and the traditional. It is a perfect example of style over substance, theory over *praxis*. "It sucks cock," Vinnie pointed out.

I love it.

In the end, Vinnie Five-Five, like me, thought that the joint would choke on its own silliness. No one in their right mind would sit at tiny tables two inches apart so each word you uttered to an associate could be heard by every sniveling punk in the neighborhood.

Vinnie had sneered at the very thought of having a conversation there. "Might as well invite the Feds to a meeting. Forget about it. I give it two months."

Ah, people adapt too slowly for the pace of change these days.

I, much to my shame, often drink the overpriced coffee and gobble down the skimpy, bland turkey and Brie sandwiches. If I need to get a slice afterward, so what? This place guarantees me one thing. I will never run into my crew. I have enough of them at work, at the club. Here I can read without someone commenting on my masculinity or my sanity.

Today I don't plan on going in. A person fleeing for his life should not stop for a macchiato. I have left my car behind, but the subway is inches away.

Yet I enter. The interior exudes peacefulness. What can happen at the calm center of civilization? The young, its target market, avoid it. But other people, elderly, ancient, who had been on their last legs a decade earlier and now go about on stumps, held up by canes, walkers, and in one case, by a wheelchair with a chin strap, occupy the tables. They sit happily with cookie crumbs on their shirts and coffee dribbling down the sides of their mouths. A Jamaican aide to the woman in the wheelchair laughs uproariously into her cell phone, speaking in patois while her charge mumbles numbers—thirty-two, thirty-three, thirty-five—into her paper cup.

Only one table is taken by a patron under eighty. Layers of light brown hair shield her face for she is reading a book, an unusual enough sight that it catches my attention. So, as if pulled by magnets, I head to the counter where the pastries glow with ethereal light. A round, layered carrot cake of burnished mahogany—an architectural marvel of carrots, cream cheese, and walnuts—rests in the center of the counter, a perfect Oldenburg that gives a timeless dignity to this out-of-place haven.

Though the entire Mongol horde be after me, though General Zhukov himself plots my defeat, I will sit in this place for a bit, right next to the attractive woman and pretend that I am in the midst of other battles, ones fought in journals and monographs, ones whose weapons are hot tea and cold schnapps, coffee, and cigarettes. These battles pitted Leibniz against Spinoza and Popper against Wittgenstein, where hurt feelings and academic positions rather than crushed testicles and slit throats lay in the balance. Such a world had indeed been stomped to death by the Nazis in the name of Aryan supremacy, and, on our shores, by the marketers who suffocate thought in a barrage of bullshit under the guise of business.

I take the empty table to the right of the girl.

She looks up when she senses my presence and I say, "Hey."

She nods.

I used to pick up chicks like I breathed, with an effortlessness that was the only thing my friends envied about me. But not lately. Lately, I have lost interest. Don't know why. But for some reason this girl I can't resist. "Good book?" I make sure to ask this in a way that indicates I have no interest whatsoever in the book and am solely concerned with picking her up.

More bafflement than fear registers on her face. She does not expect a palooka like me to notice her book.

Without saying anything she shows me—*The Valley of the Horses.* Not a Penguin classic. On the cover is a picture of a blonde Amazon riding a horse bareback.

"You like it?"

She reacts as if under interrogation, with monosyllables. "Sure. Good."

She does not want to speak to me. Either that or there is something shameful about reading *The Valley of the Horses.*

By the counter is a box with newspapers. I want to get the *Times* but I only see a *Post.* As I return to my seat, I study the girl. Like me, she flounders somewhere in her early thirties. Unlike me, she wears thick black tights and a short black skirt that show off tasty legs. She looks good—petite, intelligent eyes, nice rack. She brushes her hair behind her ears with an innocent, schoolgirlish gesture. She strikes me as serious and demure. What she is doing in the ass end of Brooklyn I have no idea.

I move my eyes to the café's picture window. On the street a few people hurry toward the subway. I glance back at the girl. A small dimple clefts the point of her chin. My mind, racing, imputes all sorts of vulnerable charm that she possesses. Not for her the bored, glazed, and depressed expression that so many beautiful women cultivate.

She glances at me again, not hostilely but quizzically. She's uncertain about my intentions, which she very well should be. Yet . . . could she be intrigued?

I don't want to scare her so I continue to stare out that front window.

Ivan. Goddamn it. He's across the street walking with a friend, a whippety little guy half Ivan's size. I don't know him but I instantly make the judgment that he has the strut of the extra special sociopaths who too often inhabit this diseased world of ours.

I worry Ivan recognizes me. I don't know if he has homicide on his mind, but I can't stay to find out. I take my gym bag and slip into the bathroom. I feel the woman's eyes on my back.

Besides the actual commode, this toilet's greatest feature is a window, the glass slathered in thick white paint. It opens onto a small cement courtyard containing nothing but large trash cans that are dragged down an alley every Tuesday and Friday.

I hear, "You see big man sitting here?" Ivan must be questioning that lovely woman.

Now I will find out how truly lovely.

I hear no response. Maybe she's terrified. This Mutt and Jeff team of monsters would intimidate tougher-looking cookies than that girl.

"One minute before," Ivan's voice rises, and I realize whatever our relationship had been, whatever we had shared, our long conversations over whether the Russian soul is indeed unique in its sensitivity to the celestial realms, Ivan, given the chance, would whack me.

A voice, tremulous, rightfully nervous responds, "I don't remember seeing anyone."

So I fall in love as I drop my gym bag out the toilet window and follow it. In a second Ivan will start his own search and the first place he'll check is this sanctuary. I hop the chain link fence separating the yard from the building opposite and I scurry onto the next block.

I'm not 100 percent certain that Ivan has murder on his mind. It could be that he wants to continue to debate literary matters. But why take chances? From the other end of the street I watch the café. Before long Ivan and his little friend come out and head in the direction of Brighton Beach.

9

Sand Castles

I slip down the block and reenter *Stamm Tisch*.

The woman's eyes pop wide when she sees me.

I approach her, a serious expression hiding my laughing mind. "Thanks."

She's paler than when I first saw her. But after a second blood floods her cheeks and she lights up as if on fire. "Who were those men?"

"Friends."

She clears her throat. "Friends?" Her voice trills light and high. "What did they want?"

"Did not want to fucking find out." I split the infinitive with the unnecessary participle because I believe she expects a taste of rough trade. I sense her delight in meeting someone from another world, the underworld. How disappointed would she be if she discovered I was just another know-it-all asshole who mentions *The Valley of the Horses* is a sequel to the much superior but still schlocky *The Clan of the Cave Bear?* No doubt she had her fill of those types.

"They checked the bathroom. You're lucky you . . . escaped."

I see that my half-finished coffee still rests on the table next to hers so I sit down in front of it as if I never dived out the toilet window.

She's eager to talk now, but I nonchalantly examine the paper, the *Post*. It's a rag, yet its every fatuous headline testifies to man's bottomless capacity for cruelty. No aspect of human achievement is exempt. Scientific, educational, commercial, judicial, political, theological, martial—each institution abuses its power, causes untold suffering against individuals and the environment, fails to show an iota of compassion, serves only itself, excuses the worst sadism in the name of principle, exhibits no shame, and relies on the fear and ignorance of a disoriented populace to maintain a hold on power.

The front page shows a picture of the Hefty bags containing Garlic. Since neither Candi's nor Scrunchy's bodies are found, nor are they reported missing, the article errs by assuming that Italian families are waging fratricidal war. No one mentions the clash of civilizations predicted by Samuel Huffington *et al.* The police do not want to frighten the citizens by suggesting that Asiatic hordes are once again attacking the remnants of the Roman Empire. Besides, nostalgia for the original Mafia is quite an industry.

I turn to the story inside. "I knew that guy."

The woman cranes her neck and sees a photo of two cops holding the two bulging trash sacks, posing as if they just caught a giant fish.

"Which guy?"

"It's only one guy. They put him in two bags."

Even against her will, this intrigues the woman. She does not hide the top to bottom examination she gives me. Her head bobs slightly, as if already regretting her compulsion to continue this conversation. "There's a man in that bag?"

"Garlic, because he loved garlic more than he loved his mother. He thought it would protect him from colds. No one warned him about hacksaws. Now, there's a war."

I look over and see how the cute chick is taking this. She's white again, colorless as a dress shirt, but asks, "Who's warring with who?"

With whom. Instead, I say, "The Triads, who contracted Vlad the Impaler. They plan to divide Vinnie Five-Five's territory."

At the mention of Vlad, she begins to tremble. She recalls the two Russian soldiers who just accosted her. But she pushes forward. "Why?"

"It started over a poor dead whore."

I regret immediately uttering this last word. Women resent the term, take it personally. Much better to use "sex worker." But "sex worker" fits neither the sentence nor the sentiment.

After another second's hesitation, she asks, "What whore?"

I have her. She wants to just connect. Though shy, murder turns her on. "Candi Apple. She rolled that weasel Scrunchy Cho so he stuck her. The bros took care of Scrunchy. Ah, we're yesterday's news. The Chinese, the Russians, they know it. All Vinnie wants is to survive in the rackets until he qualifies for Medicare. Then it's Julius and Gus's problem. His sons." I fold up the newspaper. "The real bloodbath begins when Crazy Bo hits Vlad."

She comprehends enough to nod, "Sounds like a movie Scorsese should make."

"Nothin' new under the fuckin' sun. You have a name?"

She hesitates only for a second. "Ariel."

"My friends call me Windows." I hold out my hand and she responds as if touching a bloody animal lying on the roadside.

It's a start.

"Windows?"

"Howard Fenster. Fenster is German for window. Howie if you want."

She's getting over the surprise of being in the middle of a gang war. "Are you going into town, Howard Windows?" This is a natural question since the café's proximity to the tracks makes it a way station for travelers to and from Manhattan.

"Sure," I decide. "I gotta get out of Brooklyn. You know, to avoid certain people."

Our eyes lock and we laugh. A shared private joke is as good as shared nudity in the development of any horizontal relationship.

"If you have nowhere better," Ariel volunteers, "I'm going to the Met."

I figure she means the museum, not the opera, but my face must have shown some confusion, so she explains, "The big museum on Eighty-Second and Fifth. It's one of the best in the world."

I go infrequently but I know its collection pretty well, even if the place mostly oppresses me. Like culture itself, I imagine the Metropolitan Museum a sand castle. A single evil breeze would bring the stones crashing down onto the heads of the oblivious patrons. I mostly liked the medieval rooms, where tapestries, Holy Families, crucified Christs, and sculptures of heavily draped saints tilt toward heaven and yearn for the eternal in a refreshingly unironic way. Once artists figured out perspective, subjectivity and thus doubt crept into their work. Occasionally, one yearns for an unambiguous attitude toward transcendence. Medieval art allowed me such contemplation. To the girl I say, "What do you like in the museum?"

She gets a kick out of this, because again she titters, "The art."

What I mean, of course, is what period she favors. I again begin to wonder what would happen if I talk less like an ape and more like a human being. "Fuckin' this," "fuckin' that"— is this really necessary? With my crew, maybe, I need to sound like a cretin to fit in, to assure that I'm one of them. But with a woman who no doubt landed in this benighted neighborhood through some personal cataclysm, I might build a narrow bridge to connect my internal with the external.

She encourages, heedless (or perhaps quite heedful) of the consequences. "Why not? Going to a museum with someone else is more fun." Again, her face flares crimson: "And probably the people after you won't even think of looking there."

True enough. I know no one alive who ever expressed the slightest interest in high art. Even my sister, lovely and sensitive as she is, limited her exposure to a fifth-grade field trip to the dinosaurs at the Natural History. Had she lived with my father, it might have been different. But her mother saw leaving the house for any reason as a dangerous waste of time.

Because I don't answer directly, Ariel prods, "Have you ever seen a Rembrandt self-portrait?"

Here my heart leaps. Other than the Fra Angelicos, Rembrandt's vision of himself as an aging man moves me, terrifies me actually. In fact, the self-portraits have the unfortunate effect of making other paintings, other masterpieces, melodramatic and false. That Ariel mentions this particular work excites me as much as her luscious breasts and tight body. I almost open up to her, explain that I have interests beyond getting laid. But no doubt she has a college degree, has probably junior-yeared in Europe. I cringe to think of what she would make of my childish insights concerning art.

Besides, I think she gets a kick out of leading me. "I'll give it a fu— a shot."

She drains the last of her tea. "Let's go."

10

A Brief History of Her Time

Every time I take the B, I remember my father believed his greatest accomplishment was to live at an express stop. He pitied those who needed to switch for the local, and he barely contained his contempt for those who lived in places where you need to take a bus to the train. He'd point to the weary, bedraggled commuters forming a line in front of the bus stop and warn, "Poor schmucks. If I teach you nothing else, remember: live near the express."

The train pulls in, sounding its barbaric yawp over the roofs of the neighborhoods—Midwood, Flatbush, Prospect Park, Fort Greene—and then underground toward DeKalb Avenue. I feel freer with every passing stop. Also, Ariel starts talking. We sit side by side and Ariel's leg brushes against mine. It doesn't take much prodding "You look like a fu—, not like the girls who live around here. What brings you to Gravesend?"

And the story comes tumbling out.

She had escaped Avenue Z and East Third Street by attending Tufts in Boston and then held a series of jobs in public relations. She started three master's—in education, history, and business—unable to finish any as the work got more boring and pointless with each passing course. Then she got stuck in digital marketing, sending out e-mails and Facebook updates for dubious health aids and for-profit college scams. She got canned because she wrote a resignation letter calling her boss a thief. A brain freeze, as she describes it, caused her to leave it on her desk when she went out. When she returned to the office, the letter was gone. Her boss had found it. "After I got fired," Ariel finishes with that story, "I regretted not making it even more insulting."

It's here that I first detect the grit and edge that Ariel hides under a shy and modest front.

She continues, telling me about a breakup, an exciting but disastrous fling, subletting the co-op she had bought with her life savings to move back with her mom until the job thing worked itself out. "I'm okay for a while, but I'm losing my subletter in a couple of days. I'll move back in for a bit. Living with my mom is impossible. If all else fails, I'll become a teacher."

Certainly she could teach people how not to finish what they start. I listen to her carefully while imagining her in panties and bra, the fabric straining artfully against her chest and backside. I think she would enjoy my body too—my abs cut from years of crunches, my legs muscled from daily runs.

By now we've rattled across the Manhattan Bridge and pulled into Grand Street. I let Ariel know that I live not far from her, in my half-sister's house. Then we discuss how to get to the Upper East, for the B runs on the West Side.

"Let's get off on Eighty-First Street and walk across the park," Ariel suggests.

I nod but wonder if a stroll across Central Park may be a little too romantic for a first meeting.

11

Confessions

For the past two years, I have not pursued pussy.

This after spending most of my adulthood as a horndog. The club scene in Bay Ridge attracted me from the time I was sixteen. I sometimes went into Manhattan, but mostly I stayed in Brooklyn and hooked up with local talent.

I'm thirty-two but never dated a woman for more than six months.

The girls, for the most part, were not sorry to see me go, especially after the initial excitement wore off. Some complained that I never expressed a single emotion, that I was inarticulate to the point of muteness.

To this charge I said nothing.

Some criticized my strange hours, disparaged my unsavory friends, noted my ambivalent allegiances. Each one pointed out my poverty and lack of both prospects and ambition.

One girl, Gina, offered to facilitate my entry into the civil service, into a much-coveted job with the sanitation department where her father worked as a supervisor. Though tempting—union job, good wages, great benefits—I decided against a garbage-collecting career. This I consider one of the biggest mistakes of my life.

The truth is I never cared deeply for anyone.

I'd often assure the girls that I lacked a gene for love and that they'd be better off with almost anyone else. Not a one argued with me. During the last years I believed this to be true.

Celibacy, meanwhile, fed on itself, devouring the rest of my libido. I don't know why. My drinking and drug use remained stable. I avoided tobacco but smoked organically grown, hothouse weed from my own inventory. The more my sex drive diminished, the more healthfully I lived. I practiced aikido for business and pleasure. I checked full-length mirrors for accumulating fat or for muscle deterioration. I delved deeply into my late father's library. Yet, nearly overnight, I stopped trolling for pussy. The lassitude that characterized my career aspirations spread to the one area in life in which I previously exhibited significant initiative.

Other than her well-maintained body, Ariel is not typical of my past paramours. She doesn't tease her hair. She goes easy on the makeup. She finished high school, had done graduate work. If she is to be believed, she owns an apartment in the city, had lived there for years. She visits museums for fun. She reads books. The last woman who I definitively knew read a book was my fourth-grade teacher who enjoyed reciting *Tom Sawyer* in a cornpone accent.

Ariel could become more than a lover. But I tell myself to just try and get laid so as not to scare her off. But could I frighten her? There's something strange in the way this girl so fearlessly embraces me and my bullshit. Actually, I think she's buzzed, drunk.

"I once tried to kill myself," I blurt, apropos of nothing as the train pulls into Seventy-Ninth Street. "Right here at this station."

Ariel suddenly clams up.

We emerge from the underground and enter the park. An intimacy rises between us as we walk down the path. I imagine that for a moment we commune over shared anguish.

But the comfortable silence stretches into awkwardness. Shit, why open with the suicide attempt? Some girls will hold it against me. I try to put it in context. "My father had died and I got really fucked up at this club. It was three in the morning. You know, when the trains come once an hour. Even the cops laughed when they dragged my ass back onto the platform."

This sort of suicide, they claimed, must be done at rush hour.

"Were you so drunk that you just fell on the tracks? I hear that happens a lot."

I tense, then breathe out. "Maybe."

She probably thinks I never had enough of an inner life to experience hopelessness. But I always had difficulty finding intrinsic value in existence, or in my own existence. After being kept under observation, they diagnosed alcoholism and agitated depression and let me go on the condition I take Seroquel. *Agitated depression* my ass. I had even lacked the energy to argue.

"What about love?" Ariel asks.

Has Ariel ever attempted to off her own self? "What about it?"

"Love is an absolute good. All you can think about is someone else, how to make them happy. You get out of yourself. When I get really down, I remember the people I love."

While easily admitting my suicide attempt, I am ashamed to say that I have never been in love. When I don't respond, Ariel murmurs, "Yeah, the deepest feelings are not always reciprocated."

I fill in the blanks. Breakup, job loss, depression, Brooklyn. My situation mirrors hers except for the breakup and job loss.

In the end, we agree that everyone is entitled to one suicide attempt. The wolf of despair sits on your chest, holding you in place while the world spins faster and faster. When let up, disoriented, one's neighbors, school friends, coworkers have sprinted off. No amount of running allows you to catch up. Once in a while you amble by one of these runners, injured at

the side of the road—divorced, estranged, unemployed, ill—
and go a ways together before one leaves the other behind.

Our pace slackens further. The sun causes the grass to
glow green. The breeze shakes the leaves on the trees. We see
no reason to rush. Art is forever, the day is short.

The hands at our sides sometimes touch.

"In high school," Ariel continues our conversation with
another non sequitur, "I played the lead in an adaptation of
Jane Eyre. During the production I floated a hundred miles
above the earth. I had one other big role, as Anne Frank's
mother. But the girl who played Anne forgot her lines and
the first time the Nazis entered, some clown in the audience
yelled, 'She's in the attic!' "

Ariel sounds still mortified. "After that, the cast quit, and
we didn't mount another production. The rest of high school
was just unbearable. I wish I kept going with the acting."

For some people, the four years of high school loom as
large as a stay in a concentration camp. But because of my
detached intellectual interests and eagerness to punch people
in the face, no one bothered me much. No. My troubles,
along with my education, came later.

"These days I feel like I just graduated college," Ariel says.
"At loose ends. With nowhere to go. At a crossroads."

I offer, "In my business, we're at a crossroads every ten
minutes."

Ariel shoots me a puzzled look, as if those words should
not have come out of my mouth.

12

Chance Encounter

Right before the park's Eighty-First Street exit, a fat man, huge, blocks the path.

We both stop, confused, wondering if we are about to be mugged by a guy who would find it difficult to make a speedy getaway.

"Wassup, homie?" A rubber band holds his brown hair in a topknot.

Just as the adrenaline hits my brain, I recognize the guy. He's a fence and a contract killer. Once, in the Dunkin' Donuts on Avenue U, we had discussed the cinnamon cruller special.

"Hey." After this initial burst of greeting, the conversation flags. Without the reassuring presence of pastry, we find little common ground.

"How's the old neighborhood?" he asks. "Find any more headless torsos?" He laughs a deep unhealthy laugh that ends in a hacking fit. His hands pat a black tracksuit that billows around him and he pulls out a pack of cigarettes. He recovers himself after he inhales. Waving the cigarette, he growls, "This is the only thing that helps my cough."

The fat man is Frankie Hog, who works for Vinnie Five-Five as an all-around dangerous muffin who enjoys ripping off burglars fencing their goods. A long time ago we did a few jobs together—busting into a jewelry store, hijacking a tractor trailer loaded with stereo equipment. He's a cool cat, missing the neurotransmitters necessary for satiation and fear. I never expected to find him strolling around Central Park.

Then again he too requires the anonymity of the city. He must lay as low as his spongy blubber allows. The park is the only spot large enough to contain his bulk.

He wheezes before he chokes out, "Vlad got the contract on Vinnie Five-Five. Take my word for it. The average Russian is crazier than the craziest Italian. Hug the ground, bro. My problem is, I always get noticed." And he pats his giant stomach as if it were the world itself. "Vlad's boy, Dmitri, that bullet-headed fuck, told me he was going to make sausage out of my guts and sell it in Primorski's delicatessen. Those animals are fucking cannibals."

A lot of punks like to think they have a contract stuck to their ass when all they have there is a piece of shitty toilet paper. But I can see that Frankie Hog might piss off the wrong people. He boosts shit off bad guys. He kills people. He's sarcastic.

I turn to see what Ariel thinks of my friend. She gives nothing away. Or just those semaphore spots of blush high on her cheeks.

I advise Frankie Hog without caring one way or another, "So get out of the city. Hide in the Himalayas. Take the train to Long Island."

Frankie Hog looks this way and that. He takes his hands off the sides of his girth and waves at the trees around us. "This is as deep into the country as I get, *paisano*. Forget about it. Vinnie will need us. You think he won't fight? Be available, pussyman. I hear you read books by foreigners, illegal immigrants. Jerkoff. You better be around when Vinnie calls."

Frankie Hog may have his good points. He may have talents other than moving stolen laptops and shooting people from behind. But I can't imagine what they would be. So I like reading in translation. So what? While I don't give a shit what he thinks, I must respond to the insinuation that questions my loyalty. "Of course I'm available for Vinnie, you fat fuck. And listen, if you're trying to hide, you might want to wear something less conspicuous."

He looks down at his tent-like covering. "What are you talking about?"

"Lose the elephant suit. Know what I mean?"

His eyes narrow to murderous slits. Fuck him. What could he do, sit on me? "Sorry about Candi," he purrs. "I know she used to give you a discount." Frankie Hog flashes Ariel a rotten-toothed smile. "A small discount for a *small* . . . Know what I mean?"

I don't flinch, nor do I take my eyes off the Hog, a treacherous beast who for no good reason I have riled. I, too, got a big mouth, even if I don't say much.

Could his spotting me here, now, with Ariel be pure coincidence? Could Vinnie's doubts about my dedication have caused him to tell Frankie to keep an eye on me? Is he the one talking shit behind my back to Vinnie? And I really don't like the way he's eyeing Ariel.

Frankie Hog finally waddles toward the wild, northern reaches of the park, but before getting out of earshot he releases a stream of gas that cracks the air like machine gun fire. Ariel's face first shows surprise and then she begins giggling. She tries to stop herself and puts her hand on my shoulder. "Sorry, sorry," she's doubled over. She catches her breath. "Who was that?"

"A friend," I say.

"You keep funny company." But I can see that this nonsense excites her.

13

Rembrandt's Hat

We reach Fifth Avenue.

Here, the elegant buildings with their casement windows, their carved wooden doors, their gargoyle lintels, their marbled foyers, their perfectly proportioned doormen dazzle. Moguls, movie stars, heiresses own these apartments, the cheapest of which could feed a sub-Saharan country for a year. Can an Upper East Side ever exist in an equitable world? Hard to imagine.

Still, one needn't reach the topmost sphere of heaven to be satisfied. Like the Athenian philosophers in Dante's cosmos, the higher levels of hell will do fine, better, because of the more interesting company. Dante himself, exiled from his beloved Florence, never escaped his living hell. But in the hell of his imagination he managed to find happiness by hanging with a proud and defiant crew consisting of those who told Christ to get stuffed. Chatterboxes all. Dante may have rented in heaven, but he would have bought in hell.

The massive palace finally rises before us. Despite my ambivalence for its content, the Metropolitan Museum impresses at first sight. It is a temple fit for a god, more than one god. Each god has its own wing.

These, however, are not living gods. The museum mummifies everything it collects, even those artifacts that remain most vital. No artistic movement is allowed to rest in peace.

I keep this to myself, for I see that Ariel feels at home in this necropolis of cultures. She bounds up the steps like a young doe. Only when she reaches the top does she look back to see me carefully climbing as if the bone-white stairs are a sheer rock face.

"Come on," Ariel encourages. "Don't be scared." Virgil tells Dante something similar at the portico of Dis. The museum looms in front of me like a huge, hungry animal. I approach the doors as if they contain sharpened teeth. I enter with the dread of one being swallowed forever.

Who the hell thinks this about a museum? No wonder I daren't say much to Ariel.

She waits for the guard to check her bag.

He barely glances at it, while he glares at me as if I carry chaos in my pockets, the whirlwind in my gym bag. He digs through my clothes. It's a good thing I left the gun behind.

I trail Ariel to the coat check, where she checks her gauzy white sweater and I my bag. I keep my leather jacket; if I am going to spend a couple of hours looking at art, I want all the protection I can get. For the Goyas I'll want a Kevlar vest.

Ariel joins the line to get a little sticker that marks you off as a retard every time you leave the museum with it still attached to your shirt.

While waiting behind the tourists who always pay the full suggested price, the dizziness and the nausea that rips into the pit of my stomach every time I come here attack anew.

I stagger away without alerting Ariel to my distress.

She finds me a couple of minutes later prostrate on a lobby bench. She pasted her sticker to a lovely spot above her left tit.

Her smile fades when she intuits that something might be wrong. "Are you okay?"

"Fine," I gasp. I can tell that she's happy. One second she's drinking tea and wondering how to kill a few hours. The next she's in the middle of a gang war. How lucky can you get?

Anyway, the dizziness passes. Before I know it, we are standing in front of the Dutch seventeenth century, a period where everyone seemed to eat well. The peasants' meager dinners look far more luscious than the cornucopia of processed rubbish that inundates our grocery freezers.

I let Ariel lead me around. She points out that during the 1600s the Dutch had created neither religious nor secular paintings. Rather they infuse spiritual significance to the most mundane events and objects. "Right here. This is why I come."

We are stopped in front of the portrait of an old man with a spiteful, rutted face and a swollen, pocky nose. A hideous beret flattens his head. Wattles of flesh eddy off the neck and disappear into the ether of the background. The eyes glance sideways, as if catching the viewer in an embarrassing act, like staring unashamedly at an ugly, decrepit old man. *Look in your own mirror*, I can hear him cackle. Though not ancient, the guy has reached the second asexual stage of life, no more gendered than an infant despite the straggly hairs spidering off his chin. Fury, however, fills his eyes as they rail against the pointless, inexplicable suffering that went into the making of such an unpleasant *punim*. Rembrandt. A self-portrait.

Ariel says softly, the voice of reason and pity, "Slowly dismantled by time and the destruction of illusions. It's not pretty, but the honesty gives us courage."

I can barely tolerate life *with* the illusions. Why would such a man want to go on? Then I glance over at Ariel and the painting takes on a less disgusting cast. Pleasure exists too. The painter, for example, takes a great pride in his ugliness. He revels in decay. For example, he didn't have to wear that hat, a pancake of putrid cloth that threatens to melt into his face. In no time or place could that hat have been cool. Its very repulsiveness suggests that broad, universal standards of beauty might exist.

What I really want to tell Ariel, however, is that the power in the painting lay not in its honesty nor in its technical mastery. Its power lay in its contempt for the viewer. This man did terrible things. He looks like shit. But the portrait declares with a full force of vindictive rage, *Fuck youze.* I know people like him, free from the manacles of societal pieties and dangerous as chain saws. I'm glad I have my jacket on. Still, I shiver. Should art terrify? Embrace transcendence, it says, but watch your back.

Ariel moves closer to my side. "You look like you're about to faint." She slips her arm into the crook of my elbow. "Maybe we should go up to the roof for some air."

It takes awhile to find the right elevator and along the way we pass through medieval Europe, the Roman Empire, and classical Greece—a journey so perfectly backward in time that I think Ariel plans it. A vase depicting Odysseus in Hades talking to the shade of Achilles arrests us. Ariel remembers what Achilles says to the man-skilled-in-all-ways-of-knowing. "Better to be a slave living on bread and water than king of all the exhausted dead."

Ariel is trying too hard to impress.

The elevator opens onto the roof. As we emerge from the dimness of the past, the sun's rays slice into us like blades. The air smacks us with a rush of pure oxygen. From this height, the glory and horror of New York spreads before us. Looking west, the trees of the park give us a chlorophyll high. Eastward, the jagged towers of glinting glass blind us. We also encounter brightly colored sculptures by someone who thinks blowing up everyday items to gargantuan proportions—paper clips, staples, forks, condoms—constitutes a breakthrough in human consciousness. A half dozen of these pointless monstrosities dot the rooftop.

Like everyone else we gravitate toward the roof's edges. The guardrail reaches my neck. With my eyes, I measure the distance I'd need to get a running jump and leap over it. That would be a pretty spectacular way to go. Flying over the Metropolitan Museum, making my own statement about the restorative power of art. But at that moment Ariel asks, "Feeling better?"

I nod and peer east. What does she want? She's lonely as Gilgamesh after Enkidu's death, cut loose from the everyday, not knowing if she should go here or there, wondering about the point of life in a death-filled cosmos.

I turn back from the brink. Would it kill our budding relationship if I spoke more than one syllable at a time? As far as I know, she's fallen in love with my inarticulateness.

"Are you getting hungry? I know a luncheonette on Eighty-Third Street that makes the best BLT sandwich in the city. The best."

Every time I look at Ariel, she appears prettier. This phenomenon has happened with only a few of the girls whom I dated. These are the women who end up hating me the most.

I should get out now. Today of all days is not the time to start something. A single need dominates: disappear. Go to the Port Authority and get the bus to Atlantic City. Stay with my friend Johnny Nickels who works the tables at the Taj. Or go to Grand Central and take the train to Nyack where my father's old track buddy, Milton Buchsbaum, is living out his widowerhood in a one-bedroom overlooking the Tappan Zee. He knows the score. Before he died, my dad warned him that trouble would follow me like a grateful mutt. At my father's funeral, he told me that if I ever needed a place I should come up.

"So. Food?"

I shrug. "Sure."

14

Baked Fries

On the way to this diner, Ariel tells me more of her life story. The great shock, one that "sent her on a spiral" as she put it, has been her mother's recent revelation that Ariel's father might not be her father. Rather, some hippie who moved to Colorado could have impregnated the young Mrs. Hirsch with what became her eldest daughter. I listen with half an ear, keeping alert for dangers popping out of doorways or screeching to a halt in black cars. But it's unlikely the Russians would mount a manhunt outside of Sheepshead Bay. They'd pick off low-hanging fruit, killing those in the neighborhood who do something really stupid like go to the fruit store.

"Here it is."

Yes, Ariel has led us to a throwback. The place still has the original green Formica counter and old signs with line drawings of frothy glasses of egg creams.

We take a booth. Ariel says, "You really remind me of this guy I used to date."

I pay even less attention. Meeting Frankie Hog truly worries me. Why would that pile of blubber with feet find sanctuary in the loveliest spot in the city? He spends most of his time in Bensonhurst bakeries, hooked up to a cannoli drip. South Brooklynites rarely come to this part of town. Maybe he suspects I'm a rat, that I'd wear a wire. More. What if he now thinks that Ariel is my handler? She could easily pass for a Fed. And why else would I squirrel away in some stupid museum with a lady I'm not banging? What is he going to tell Vinnie?

Is Vinnie hesitating out of loyalty to my dead father?

"My other boyfriend," Ariel continues in her melancholy nasalness, "also said little. What is it with you guys? You must be thinking *something* when we talk, when we converse. Aren't you? Or do guys not even articulate in their heads?"

I would speak more freely, but it would certainly change the dynamic, and perhaps not for the better. "It's the war."

Ariel bends her head toward me and lowers her voice. "So why can't you talk about it? I won't think less of you. We all have our fears."

What can I make of this? Is being caught in a battle between two homicidal gangs a topic to take up in couples' therapy? Does she think that if I admit my fears Crazy Bo and Vlad would disappear into the ether like a grudge over a raised toilet seat? Would she chalk up their butcheries to my intimacy issues?

The waiter comes over and, before he says a word, Ariel orders a Heineken. I get one too.

Ariel then apologizes. "How can I even talk to you like this? We met, what, an hour ago?"

Half the girls I slept with I knew for less time.

I look at the menu, printed on cardboard. Even the font is old-fashioned. Only the prices (eighteen dollars for a tuna-fish sandwich) add a contemporary touch.

"Everything here is made on premises. The shrimp salad sandwich, by the way, is fabulous."

I drop the menu on the table. "Sounds good."

"They *bake* the french fries."

Everyone loves an oxymoron, especially one that sums up the main dilemma of life: how do you get what you want without destroying yourself? Ariel drinks her beer, which instantly reignites the flames in her cheeks. She's enjoying herself. More. She's excited, almost happy.

But by the time the waiter takes our order, Ariel regrets building up my hopes. She tries to manage expectations. "The food here is good but simple. Everything is fresh, they use fine ingredients. It's better than your average diner."

"I like this place," I assure Ariel, "no matter what the food tastes like."

Ariel laughs. "I get nervous whenever I suggest a restaurant because my old boyfriend was such a snob. To him, the salt needed a pedigree or he wouldn't touch the meal." She pursed her lips and turned snooty, "*This is the same salt that Julius Caesar used to pay the Roman Legion.* He'd think a place like this as boring as a prison cell."

"Your man never spent a second in a cell," I say.

"No. Have you?" Her face turns ever redder.

At that second my phone rings. *Unknown Number* pops onto my screen. It's Vinnie Five-Five. I debate picking up. It could only be bad news. But if I ignore his calls, he'll kill me.

"I should take this," I apologize to Ariel. I'm already moving out of the booth and into the street. This conversation is for nobody's ears, not even mine.

"Where the fuck are you, you fucking punk?" Vinnie starts out calmly. "Get your ass over to the club. We have a situation."

My next sentence could be my death sentence. "I'm not in town. I have some business."

"I'm your fucking business! You jump ship when I need you and I swear you won't see tomorrow if I have to come back from the grave to rip your balls off."

This speech is the longest I heard Vinnie Five-Five make in a long time. He breathes deeply from his efforts. Me, I can take a hint.

"Ninety minutes, Vinnie. I need ninety minutes . . ."

He hangs up without another word.

By the time I get back to the luncheonette, the sandwiches and the baked fries have come. Also, a fresh bottle of beer stands in front of Ariel.

Yes, Ariel is hammered. That continual flush, the reckless intimacy has happened not because she is at loose ends or is a victim of love at first sight. She's been drinking. She had a few before she came to *Stamm Tisch*. And watching her take a healthy swig explains much since.

Her BLT remains untouched in front of her. "More trouble?"

"I got to go." I stay standing.

"Now?" She can't hide her disappointment. "But your lunch . . ." Then she lifts her sandwich to her mouth but puts it down before biting into it. "What's going on, Howard?"

That is the first time Ariel calls me by my name.

"Business in Brooklyn." I look at my sandwich as if it is my bitter enemy. After a second, I plop down and chomp large bites into it. I might never eat again. Tasting not a thing, I say, "That was delicious." I throw some money on the table.

"That's too much," Ariel protests. She pushes one of the twenties back in my direction.

We stare across at each other.

Finally, Ariel speaks for the both of us. "This is so weird." She chugs her beer.

We should never have spent an idyllic day of park, museum, restaurant. Each luminous moment now sticks us with pointed regret.

Ariel says, "I have a really bad feeling about you going back to Brooklyn."

This feeling is not difficult to understand considering that she has seen Ivan and the picture of the garbage bags containing Garlic.

"Yeah," I murmur.

Ariel chokes with alcoholic emotion. "You're not a killer. You're not a real gangster, even if you have the verbal wherewithal of an orangutan."

She has me down after just two hours. I sell pot and do some chores for the guys in the neighborhood. My main goal has always been to avoid nine-to-forever work. And while this ambivalence makes me lovable to Ariel, Vinnie will clip me if he thinks I'm too weak a link. A soldier must be ready and eager to do the captain's bidding.

Melting into the wide world is a legitimate tactic in times of trouble. Only when the negotiating stops and the shooting starts does melting turn into running and running into a death sentence.

Ariel walks me outside. I hail a cab because a subway delay will get me killed.

She holds onto my left arm. The heightened color which paints her face transforms into a deathly pallor. She asks, "Am I going to see you again?"

I shrug. Do I want to see her again? My God! In her nude body I envision my own redemption. My brain steams with desire to protect her, to get naked with her, to make her happy. Strange. Inexplicable.

Our lips touch and I slide into the cab. She raps on the window. The cabdriver presses it down and she gives me her phone number. "Call me when . . . anytime. Just tell me you're safe."

I hope she sees me nod as the cab speeds me to the war.

15

Signifying Nothing

No traffic. I get to Vinnie's club in under an hour.

It used to be a popular spot called Shorty's, with music, dancing, and a decent southern Italian kitchen. But Vinnie closed it down because it had attracted too many Mafiosos. The place became a liability. The Feds bugged it. The health department wouldn't leave it alone. So now he plots an occasional crime there. Today, for example, it's conspiracy to commit mass murder.

The metal grates cover the front. A goon named Joseph O'Neal, whom we call "IRA" because of his extraordinary talent in pointless slaughter, guards the front door. A bulky, stringy-haired maniac, IRA is a *mischling*, a mixed-race mongrel like I am, but he's much more tightly connected to Vinnie's inner crew. At times he calls himself "Joey Spoleto," as in Vinnie "Five-Five" Spoleto. IRA pretends to be Vinnie's third son and gladly does the dirty work. He loves planning hits and is Vinnie's principal strategist. Unfortunately, he's also something of an idiot, and his elaborate plans often backfire, with both comic and tragic results. Yet having graduated top of his class in psychopathy school, IRA is a good man to have at a time like this.

"You fucking made it," he sneers.

"What does that mean?"

"It means that we don't kill your sister." He leers. "We would let her two little angels go even though they're almost ripe." At times like these, IRA affects a brogue. He seems to think that an Irish accent makes him sound more unhinged. A glimpse into his dead blue eyes, however, tells the whole story—from his animal-mutilating childhood to his recent purchase of an extra freezer to keep human body parts fresh.

Besides, Vinnie is old school. He doesn't go after the family. Sisters, wives, kids have nothing to do with this, other than the assets are kept in their names. I just wish the Russians had the same attitude. But for them, killing whole families is the heart of their business model.

I could have replied sharply to IRA's instigation. But that would have meant one of our deaths. So I walk into the club and would have seen, if not for a cloud of smoke as thick as those blanketing Asian cities, Vinnie, Frankie Hog (of course), Pauli Bones, and Vinnie's two fireplug sons, Julius and Gus. I'm also introduced to two men I don't know. One, whose tiny features look marooned on his giant round face, Vinnie calls Jack the Jew. The other, a hulking linebacker in sunglasses and a baseball cap, does not mind being introduced as Moron. I can tell little about him other than he is smart enough to rip the head off your neck at the slightest provocation.

On the table are three innocuous-looking M16s and two placid mini Uzis that Vinnie Five-Five keeps in the club's basement and only breaks out for the most festive occasions. Vinnie sits at the head of the rectangular table covered with a dirty white tablecloth. Julius and Gus sit on each side. The others all stand, almost at attention.

When he sees me, Vinnie taunts, "Such loyalty touches my fucking heart."

Anything touching his fucking heart would be instantly poisoned.

To respond out loud to Vinnie's sarcasm would simply reveal overwhelming anxiety and net serious trouble. So I just square my shoulders in a way that indicates I can take it.

The group pulls itself closer toward Vinnie.

"Windows, get IRA."

As soon as the half-Irishman sees me, he glances down the street in both directions and slips inside, bolting the door behind him. He stands to the right of Vinnie's chair.

"So here's the story," General Five-Five begins. "We make the fucking gooks and those Russkie bastards think that a war with us is a war with Dellacroce and Tony D. We take the fight to their kitchens and whorehouses. Surprise them." He looks to IRA, the idiot mastermind. "Joey will give you your assignments."

Though Vinnie Five-Five is as violent and vicious as any gangster, he lacks imagination, the vision, so necessary to keep a thriving underworld empire going. He has struggled ever since he inherited the position of captain from his brother Gregory, who died of a heart attack induced by the stress of being shot in the eye. We never found out who ordered the hit. In truth, Greggy Boy's diabetes would have killed him just as dead. Being a wise guy does not protect one from the ravages of obesity. Vinnie himself has gone on countless diets, which he announces loudly. He once rubbed a pear tart into Frankie Hog's face as Frankie ate a third one in the presence of the dieting Don. After that, all sweets were off-limits at the club until pastry returned to Vinnie's good graces.

IRA takes over and describes his plan, simple yet brutal.

"We got two cars outside. You," he points to Frankie Hog, "drive one. Me and Pauli goes with you. And Gus."

Julius, Vinnie's favorite and heir apparent, nods. Like his father, Julius has turned into a man broader than he is tall, with a pug nose and raisin eyes glinting with the same anarchy and puzzled stupidity as Sarah Palin's. But compared to his brother, Augustus, he's another da Vinci. Gus, the tallest of the Five-Fives at five foot six, appears to be of normal intelligence. But his entire vocabulary consists of only a few words: "I," "fuck" (and variations such as "motherfucker"), "shit," "cunt," "whore," and "money" along with a few articles and linking verbs. ("I fucked the cunt," or "Fuck the cunt," being sentences he uses in all sorts of situations.) Certainly, he keeps whatever IQ he may possess under tight wrap. He defers to both his father and his brother. At everyone else, he just barks obscenities. Both of Vinnie's sons are close childhood friends of mine, though as I've become disenchanted with the life, we've grown apart.

"You," IRA glares at me and uses his thickest Irish lilt, "drive one car. Jew, Moron, take the other two big guns, and Julius gets the Uzi. At five o'clock," again he points to me, "you will pull up in front of 559 Brighton Fifth. That's where Vlad has his most profitable house. It's full of whores from Moldova, supposedly the best skanks in all of Europe. There will be three men downstairs. Blow them away. I don't care what you do to the whores. Scare them. Shoot up their rooms. Break their legs if it don't take too long. Collateral damage. Shock and awe. Then you get out of there. Don't take a fucking thing, no matter what's lying around. This is not about money. It's about respect. You don't chop my soldiers into five pieces and think that's fucking okay. And you guys," he speaks to those who will go in Frankie Hog's car, "are going to 2022 Fifty-Third Street between Third and Fourth Avenue. Same deal, except the Chinks, because labor is so cheap in their neighborhood, have five assholes downstairs. Just blow them away and run. Don't even go near the whores, who are all from Guangdon Province and are the toughest birds in the coop. They might be packing themselves and no one is more dangerous than a whore with a gun."

Vinnie examines his crew, checking mostly for indecision, reluctance, but maybe for signs of intelligent life. I see a glimmer of disappointment, even of despair, shadow his gaze.

Me, I feel sick. I dislike murder and I hate driving. Both Vinnie and IRA know it. I've been peacefully working criminal enterprises my whole life, getting into fewer violent situations than a frat boy at a state college. Even Vinnie knows my limitations. He uses me to watch his gambling rooms and to intimidate degenerates into paying what they owe. And he takes 50 percent of my marijuana profits. For now, he tolerates my ambivalence. But he'd whack me in a second if he decides that I might buy my way out of the rackets by cutting a deal with the Feds. Double crosses are common. Everyone in the life exists under a constant veil of suspicion. Vinnie plays no games with potential rats. And I'm now positive that Frankie Hog has been whispering sweet nothings into his ear about me.

So another thing. By including me in this slaughter, he makes a deal nearly impossible. The authorities hesitate to let killers walk.

I then try to put things in perspective. We're attacking other killers, revenging the gruesome murders of Garlic and Double-Down.

This helps only a little. While I am not one to grant the state a monopoly on violence, this is further than I want to go. Maybe I'm more sensitive than others in my position. I recognize that among my potential victims are men who find themselves in situations in which there is no way out. Like in any high-stress situation, one wonders how things have become so aggravating and unsustainable.

Vinnie must have noticed something. "Windows!"

He wiggles his finger, leading me to the far corner of the club. "You have a problem?"

"No. I'm cool."

Vinnie has my number. He shoves me against the wall. "I want to explain something."

I let him continue.

"Drive to the building, wait for them to come out, and drive away. I don't even want you to speed. *Capisce*? A few cocksuckers gone. Who cares?"

How can I explain that my reluctance revolves not around getting caught but around participating in the crime? How do I explain to Vinnie that I don't believe in retaliatory murder?

"Me and your family go way back." Vinnie appeals to old ties. "Your father worked for my brother before he worked for me. We can't let these new fucks from countries that have no respect for tradition come into our homes and pillage us without doing fuckin' nothin'."

"Fuck no," I agree.

Vinnie waxes nostalgic. "We used to control the whole of South Brooklyn—Flatbush, Brighton Beach, Bensonhurst, Gravesend, Sheepshead Bay. Millions of people depended on our whorehouses and crap games." Vinnie hitches his pants and adjusts his groin. He winces as he cuts a fart. "When Brooklyn was a wasteland, we operated dozens of bookie joints. We had more money on the street than JPMorgan Chase. We have a right to be in the place that our ancestors civilized. Don't you want your nieces to grow up on the same streets like you?"

I can do nothing but continue to agree. It's always these beautiful, sentimental visions that lead to total destruction. Sentimentality is the hydrogen bomb of stunted lives.

"We got to wipe these animals out. For our people. We focus on pleasure. Gambling, sex. The Russians, the gooks, don't care who gets hurt. Look at what happened in China when the gangsters took over. Forty million people starved to death."

Vinnie surprises me with his allusion to Mao's genocidal policies. In fact, his range of references—the appeal to history, to family, to a stable social order—impresses me. It doesn't make me want to go out and murder anyone, but I understand his point. Retreat or, worse, assimilation doesn't occur to Vinnie, as it does not occur to the Russians or to the Chinese. Instead of a brotherhood of the bloodthirsty, the nation-state paradigm holds. Religion, language, culture, style of whacking people all serve to unite the most violent elements of each society, whether these go by the name of Mafia, Crips, or marines.

Vinnie concludes with a gentle exhortation. "If you fuck up, Windows, I'll slice your balls off and stick 'em up your ass. Your dad was a genius but that goes only so far."

We return to the table. IRA fondles his automatic weapon, licking and kissing the narrow barrel, to the girlish delight of Gus and Julius. Even Moron is smiling.

"I love you, I love you," IRA's tongue darts into the hole, "you beautiful ho——."

"That's enough," Vinnie growls. "Get ready. Don't forget. You kick in the door, take care of business and get out. Frankie . . ." Vinnie throws him a chain with a car key that Frankie Hog snatches out of the air with the darting suddenness of a frog's tongue catching a fly.

"A red Odyssey parked down the block on this side of the street," Vinnie informs.

So Frankie lifts his massive butt off the chair and waddles to the door, a fat goose with a gaggle of gangsters behind him: IRA, quiet now, followed by Gus and Pauli Bones. The guns they hide under their jackets.

We wait a minute and then Vinnie places another set of keys on the table and shoots them at me. "It's a blue Explorer parked right in front."

My head pounds. I start to sweat. I walk in a quagmire, stuck in the tar, swallowed by quicksand. If I struggle I will only sink faster.

Ah, maybe Vinnie's right. The *Federales* won't waste many resources on busted-up whorehouses. But I want none of this. The deaths of Double-Down and Garlic are a tragedy, almost exclusively for them, but they might have had loved ones. This escalation of hostilities will accomplish nothing but to hurry our own demise.

I reach the car and begin to hyperventilate. Sweat now pours freely down my face. I begin heaving the remains of lunch. Even looking at the black mess reminds me of Ariel, her lovely face, her hammered sweetness, her civilian naïvetés, her love of Rembrandt, her excitement over a sandwich, our afternoon together.

"If you can't do this, fuckhead," Julius says with great sympathy, "then get the hell out of here. I'll drive."

I almost hand him the keys. But Vinnie expects me to drive. If I pull out of the operation now I'll be considered nothing less than a traitor and a deserter.

My chest tightens. I recognize the classic symptoms of a panic attack.

Julius, this menacing troll, clenches his fist. I pull myself together. My stomach settles. The sweating stops. Only the tightness in my chest remains.

My memory of what follows has the lightness of a dream and the dread of a nightmare. Up until now, I had been an idiot about many things. Whenever I think back, my actions mortify. I have humiliated myself on innumerable occasions. But never have I committed an act that would pursue me across my life. There's no statute of limitations on murder, neither for the cops, nor for your conscience. Just when you think all is forgotten—twenty years have passed; you've picked up a wife, a kid, a mortgage, the whole catastrophe—and someone talks, someone cuts a deal, and boom, at two, three in the morning they kick down your door. Or you wake up with a terrified start and imagine they do.

But contingency overpowers thoughts of the future. I drive in a daze. The streets look familiar yet blurry, as if shrouded in fog. The adrenaline wears off. No one says anything more. I pull up across from the targeted building, a gruesome construction of cracked stucco broken only by a grey steel door. Boards cover the windows of the houses on either side.

I grab a parking spot right across from the building. What luck. We sit there for a second before Julius starts shouting, "What are you doing? Circle, circle you motherfucker! Do you want them to make us?"

"We'll lose the spot."

Julius takes out a .22, and places it against my temple. I put the car in drive.

"Circle until 4:57," Julius orders.

The dashboard clock reads 9:10. I pull out my phone to check the right time, which I hope a cop won't see and think I'm texting while driving.

I turn left then right then left. Finally, Julius suggests, "Head back, asshole."

I do, while trying to think of a literary equivalent to my predicament: a relative innocent dragooned by circumstances into an immoral, life-altering event. Of course, millions of such novels exist, but under the pressure of the situation, I can't think of any. I am totally alone.

Back at the bordello I see that, as predicted, someone has taken the great spot. I am about to taunt Julius with this but think better of it. Not finding parking may sound like a minor issue, but it causes a serious problem. Where will I wait for the crew? The cops are not particularly vigilant about preventing murder, but they ferociously patrol these streets to nab double-parkers.

"Where are you going?" Julius cries, too aggravated to add an obscenity.

"I'm looking for a spot."

"Stop. Now. Asshole." His short, sharp tone spits so much venom that the car's interior turns toxic.

So I slam on the brakes. I hate this. Double-parking functions as a magnet for the police.

The Jew, Moron, and Julius pour out of the car and move toward the building. I keep my eyes on them in the rearview mirror. They get to the steel door. Moron, unknown in this neighborhood, rings the bell as if he is a customer. Julius and the Jew press up against the wall of the building. When the door opens they plan to enter shooting.

But the door does not open. Moron rings again. He then pounds on the front of the door.

Nothing.

The street, full of dilapidated houses, is quiet. The local population knows trouble brews.

Julius shoots the lock. I think this ludicrous and worry that a ricocheting bullet will kill someone. Then with the force of a mule, Julius kicks at the door until it flings open. The men plunge into the building and I can hear the pop, pop, pop of the weapons. The band wrapped around my chest squeezes so tight that the black spots do an encore dance before my eyes.

While concluding that this is no panic attack but an actual cardiac event, I see Julius and the others flee the building. They tumble into the car and a sudden surge of power pulses through me as I floor the accelerator. The tires shriek like tormented souls.

Julius bellows. "Slow down, slow down, you fucking idiot."

A short stop jolts the guys in the backseat onto each other. Julius, riding shotgun, grabs the dashboard. No one says anything until Julius starts banging the passenger-side window.

I turn my head and look at the Jew and Moron. At first, their faces remain inscrutable, but then Moron smiles and the Jew starts laughing.

Julius, his face dark and combustible, turns. "Shut up."

As if waiting for this punch line, the two thugs in the back explode in hilarity.

"What's so fucking funny?" With my heart attack still in progress, I can't imagine what set off these two humorless tarantulas.

"No one there," the Jew hiccups between giggles. "You should have seen Julius, shooting up a chair as if it was about to jump him."

Relief stands behind this merriment.

"Did someone tell them?" Julius muses. "They fucking expected us."

The laughter dies down. If we have a rat in our midst, everyone is suspect. Ferreting out a double agent is a messy business and the upstate lakes teem with the bodies of both the rightly and the wrongly accused. But I have a feeling that IRA, the genius who planned the hit, had bum information. The whorehouse probably moved months ago.

16

Westward No

We ride the rest of the way in silence. A half-dozen blocks from the defunct club, we abandon the stolen car. Each of us walks to HQ by different routes.

I arrive last. Vinnie had set up a long table in the darkened room and the others are eating: pasta, meatballs, bread. IRA gulps wine like Sicilian peasants. "The skull," he chews and loudly recounts his exploits, "blew into a million . . . remember when Letterman would drop watermelons from the roof. That's what this guy's head did. Brains in every fucking direction. I wish I could see that in slow mo."

Vinnie notes that the newly arrived group is not as bubbly as IRA.

IRA, too, shuts up now and gazes at us with his usual mixture of contempt and hate.

"You do it?" Vinnie Five-Five asks.

"No one there." Julius sits in a chair at the other end of the table, directly across from his father. "Place was empty. Maybe the Russians knew we were coming."

The empty house may have been a coincidence. Then again, if the Russians had known something, it's interesting that they never told the Chinese. Maybe this is a first shot in the larger war the Russians planned to fight. Let the Wops take down a few Chinks to save trouble later on.

Vinnie points to the food. "*Mangia, mangia.*" D'Angelo, a restaurant down the block, has sent everything over in giant serving dishes.

I sit and IRA watches as if roaches just pulled up chairs. "You guys are losers."

"Shut the fuck up," Julius snaps. "This was your plan, your info."

Since IRA sucks up to Vinnie, he doesn't directly confront the son. But I can see fratricide in his glare. "Our part went perfect," he uses the broadest brogue. "We scared the living Christ out of them, too. You should have heard. Crying for his Chinese mama."

I keep my eyes on IRA as if he is pointing his weapon at me. He's so insane that I don't like being in the same room as him. He makes Pauli Bones seem as sagacious as Pitt the Elder. For one thing, Pauli Bones possesses enough brains to keep his mouth shut here.

IRA talks, Julius talks, and then the others chime in. The Jew repeats, with less amusement, Julius blowing away the chair. Frankie Hog eats without stop, though he interjects that he nearly killed a woman pushing a carriage when she crossed right in front of them during their getaway. "I could already see that baby flying like a football."

Images of Eisenstein's carriage scene in *Potamkin* pop into my mind and comfort me.

When the spaghetti is passed to me, I put some on my plate because not to would have attracted attention. My chest still hurts, but not quite as badly. Time regains its normal speed.

Vinnie waits for Julius to devour two plates of food before he says to him, "Come here."

They head toward the back room of the club. Vinnie turns and looks in my direction. Once, Julius points his thumb toward me. I am certain I will not leave the building alive.

While this pounds through my mind, I again begin sweating. This is disastrous. If I am to have any chance of survival I need to appear innocent—pure, without sin, eager to massacre anyone who never did me wrong. But this thought, instead of forcing me to relax, causes me to shake. Salvation now rests in the toilet, where I can stick my head under the faucet.

I manage to walk to the bathroom without even a glance at Vinnie or Julius.

In the restroom, I splash water on my face until I feel the blood recede from my cheeks. I piss and rub more water on my face. I calm down sufficiently to die with dignity.

I rejoin my friends with a steady gait. Vinnie and Julius have returned to the table.

IRA continues to give his considered opinion, "We need to kill every single one. Wipe them off the fucking earth. Now. Before they hit back."

Everyone at the table nods except Pauli Bones and Vinnie.

"We wait," Vinnie says. "They kill two of ours, we kill three of theirs. If they want war, they got it. But before we go all in, I need to talk to Jersey."

Through some arcane Mafia politics, Vinnie got made in a New Jersey family and has been a captain since Greggy Boy's demise. He answers to Tony D, who thinks Vinnie is holding out on him. In truth, the whores, gambling, and loan-sharking have all suffered from competition by the Russians and Chinese. Vinnie makes a living, but he closed the club and even his funeral parlor is barely breaking even. And customers there are steady as the rain in Seattle.

Ah, we're a legacy here. Every day there are fewer of us. Vinnie wants to pass the business to Julius, but the kid believes it may be time to start anew in a place where immigrant energy is not such a force. Julius has proposed setting up in the Southwest.

But Vinnie, hard-headed, stone-hearted Vinnie, spins fantasies. "I think Vlad will make peace if we push him hard enough. We can go after the Chinks together. The cops hate Chinatowns because it's fucking Chinatowns."

My eyes pierce into Vinnie. Is he referring to the greatest film noir ever made? If so, why doesn't a fondness for cultural allusion contaminate Vinnie's soul in the way it does mine?

But it's funny. Vinnie is as attached to this neighborhood as I am. What sentimentalists we gangsters be. Are we just in a rut, or are we loyal to a vision that has little currency in our rootless society? It's a strange thing. Some people can't wait to run from here. Others would rather be murdered in their beds than live decently in foreign lands.

Julius argues, "Pop, we're not dealing with men of honor. The Russians only know the knife and gun. They don't sit-down like men. They kill cats, dogs, families. They don't share business. We can expand out west, maybe into Arizona like Sammy the Bull. He'd still be there if he didn't join a Nazi biker gang."

Vinnie bangs the table and everyone, even IRA, jumps. "We ain't selling the business," he shouts. "This neighborhood is getting rich from those cocksucking Russians and those Syrian Jews who would fuck a goat as long as it isn't their wife. They need our whorehouses. Would Warren Buffett sell his company for $200 billion? He understands potential, the real value of his thing. And I know the value of Our Thing."

First Mao, then Polanski, and now Warren Buffett? At an initial glance, Vinnie seems such a dope. But then you get shocked by a reference here, a deep thought there. It gets so you can't make nasty generalizations about anyone.

Of all of them, I probably would benefit most from a change in climate. Though not exactly flinty, my body, hardened by training, suits the desert. I have never needed much water. But this life grips you by the gonads and you can't move without your balls being torn from their sack.

Besides, who would protect Judith? What would happen to the doormen who resell my pot to the hard-working, ambitious kids who make New York New York? Even my colleagues, psychos and murderers to a man, are familiar ghouls. Before the stress of war, I got along fine with Pauli Bones.

You can have a simple conversation with him. And Gus and Julius have been my friends since childhood. We frequented the clubs, fought each other and strangers, shared women. The homies of one's youth can never be replaced by friends made later in life. The protective ghost of my father hovers above *this* neighborhood.

But no amount of wishing can keep things from changing. Vinnie Five-Five glowers at the head of the table. Maybe he considers his sons ungrateful for not appreciating the risks he takes to keep his kingdom in place. "We stay and fight," Vinnie snaps. "We secure our territory here first. No one pushes Vinnie Spoleto out of his home."

Vinnie Five-Five speaks heroically, channeling every great general in history. He also sounds delusional. At best Vinnie Five-Five fights a rear-guard action. In this way Vinnie and I are alike. We yearn for dead worlds, a fatal mistake in any business.

Vinnie stands. His stomach sticks out less than usual. The bastard has been losing weight. I wonder if this is due to anxiety or to a diet. "All of youze, be available but stay off the street." He heads for the back door. Julius and Gus follow him. He stops before he disappears into the storage area and turns. "Pauli, lock up. For now, keep out of sight."

The rest of us remain frozen until Pauli Bones says, "Get the fuck out of here."

In another second we find ourselves on the street, exposed to every passing hit man. Vinnie and his sons are Vlad's primary targets, but the Russian would happily whack anyone.

Frankie Hog waddles down the street without a word. He walks with the confidence of a man who has secured a safe situation. At least his bulk protects him from any self-doubt.

IRA grins and pulls a Beretta from his waistband, checks the chamber. He does the same for the Magnum he keeps holstered under his leather jacket. "I'm ready." He moves his head like a rooster. "Maybe I'll go to Brighton for some Russian food." With that he saunters off, and I imagine him wiggling his tail in an attempt to attract an assassin's attention.

"Man's crazy," Moron the mercenary says.

I examine this Moron. He's as Irish as IRA, though he has none of the Irish madness of which Auden writes so movingly. Heavy bags hang in crescents under his eyes, as if he hasn't had a good night's sleep in a decade. Gray stubble covers his face. With his hooded look, he appears dangerous but not unreasonable.

I am tempted to ask where he is heading, but he'd never tell me. He waits, as if he, too, wants to talk. But then he crosses the street. I watch as he gets into his car and drives off.

Where am I to go? I cannot chance bringing death and devastation on Judith and the kids. Nor can I vanish and ever hope to return, for Vinnie has been unequivocal about staying local.

Pauli Bones walks out of the club. He nods at me and goes into his pocket. My bowels loosen. I think he's going to whack me right here. But he pulls out his money clip and peels off a couple of bills. This shocks me so that I don't even reach for it.

"Take the money," he orders.

Being a made guy, he could take advantage and forget to pay back small debts to an associate like me. But this is not the first time Pauli Bones has acted decently. I glimpse into his eyes and they reflect nothing, not even insanity. This is as kind and benevolent as Bones will ever get. "Thanks, Pauli," I say.

"Get the fuck out of here. No hanging around the club."

17

A Café Runs Through It

For no reason, I walk north.

I turn the first corner and stop. I'm at a loss. A second ago I had a crew, people who I might have killed for and, more reluctantly, died for. Now I'm trapped in a deadly maze. I smell the Minotaur's foul breath as it seeks to devour me. I need to get off this stinking street.

The day started one hundred years ago, but it's only seven o'clock. Exhausted, I still schlep the bag I packed that morning. But with nowhere to go, I am condemned to schlep for eternity.

Only one place, one safe haven, occurs to me—*Stamm Tisch*. I can't resist even though a person of normal instincts should avoid such places whenever possible. One prefers even the failed corporate bonhomie of a Starbuck's to the independent coffeehouse that attempts to resurrect the intellectual spirit of pre-war Vienna or 1950s Paris, not to mention the earliest Rationalist gathering places of Baroque Europe. But *Stamm Tisch* has one advantage. In Sheepshead Bay, such a place had all the cachet of a smelly, demented poet.

Yes, I remember that Ivan thought he had seen me there. But that was a freak occurrence, not to be repeated. He left convinced that even I, despite all my interests, would not be gullible enough to fall for *Stamm Tisch*'s tricks.

The joint, however, soothes. My father would have loved the atmosphere. Everyone else I know shuns *Stamm Tisch* as he would any place not directly related to sex, violence, or money. Outside is Islamabad. Inside is as safe as a cave in Bora Bora.

The half-dozen-block walk to the café keeps me on high alert. I duck into alleys if I sense a car slowing. I sniff the air for toxins and run when the street clears of people. Thus, I arrive at the café puffing.

The barista, a chunky woman with dyed blonde hair and dangling pearl earrings, notices nothing amiss. She is this place's one Lower Brooklyn touch. Sleek, bright-eyed actress types staff Manhattan cafés and size up each patron with the accuracy of seasoned hookers. They stay alert for those in the entertainment industry who might save them from their glamourless existence.

This barista sees me at the counter and decides this is the perfect moment to bus tables. I wait and think of another advantage of *Stamm Tisch* besides its unholy attachment to the life of the mind that so repulses the local inhabitants. It's rush hour. The subway disgorges a thousand people every ten minutes. The street becomes so crowded that a carload of gunmen would be hard-pressed to open fire without killing scores of bystanders. Even Vlad does not want the aggravation that would ensue from such a massacre.

The woman finally draws a cappuccino. I take it to a table near the counter, farthest from the window. I wish for some heavy-duty Motrin to stanch the throbbing above my right eyebrow and hope that a shot of caffeine relieves the migraine pain.

Settling in, I begin to believe that I have found the best hiding place of all of Vinnie's crew. This neighborhood anomaly provides the obscurity accorded to all things even marginally intellectual. Unfortunately, it closes at eight. I have an hour to think of something.

I pull out the book that I grabbed from my shelf—*Persian Letters* by Montesquieu. Why not? Long ago, my father—never one to talk about his business, gambling, or scholarly interests—mentioned this work as one of his favorites. So I have long been curious to find out why.

I won't bore the reader with the genius of this book by one of the most erudite Westerners who ever lived, who gave the world the concept of governmental checks and balances, who obsessed over notions of liberty and tyranny with the same force of mind that people today use to strategize about snagging a spot on alternate-side days. He critiqued the vanities, delusions, and pretentions of his society with the satirical force of a Petronius or a Rabelais. I won't get into his advanced ideas on the rights of women, on economic justice, on limiting the role of religious intolerance (and hence religious leaders) in public life. I can just say that this book is quite appropriate to read in the context of everything else going down. "Letter 48," for example, suggests *taking men as you find them, and when people are said to be good company, often the reason is simply that they have the more civilized kind of vices.* Civilized vices. Sweet. Quaint. I need those. Not the savage crushing of the weak, the surprise bullet in the neck so prevalent today in all walks of life. Drunken debates, gregarious gluttony, sordid sex, luscious sloth. Our hyper materialism and focus on the buck makes us lose touch even with simple hedonism.

Montesquieu is my only companion. After reading for about thirty minutes, the pressures of the moment force me to close the book. I need to plot my next move.

I look around. A coed with heavy glasses and earphones chews on a sandwich while she watches something on her iPad. An old lady sips from a paper cup with a raised pinky. And at the table nearest the door, a hard-looking, heavily painted woman reads a newspaper.

I zero in on her. She has dyed her hair albino white and covers her cheeks with so much rouge that it looks as if someone has slapped her around. Her sleeveless gray blouse displays wiry arms and a tattoo of a mushroom (or a mushroom cloud) and I see that she's not actually reading the paper. She gazes intently out the window, as if expecting someone.

I tell myself not to worry. People use cafés for meeting places all the time. People naturally scan the horizon.

Who is this woman? The rackets, though not on the cutting edge, do reflect the culture at large. Thirty years ago a woman's only career option would be to run a whorehouse. But today a few have set themselves up as jewel thieves, drug runners, and even hit people.

It takes a great deal of energy to tamp down panic. Even in this neighborhood, with its dearth of bloggers, screenwriters, and social-media types, the café attracts a certain clientele, mostly the very old and students from Kingsborough Community College. Economic necessity forces these women (always women) to live here, and this place alerts them to the world beyond. Their well-proportioned hair and unadorned faces mirror the style of the more naturalistic world to which they aspire.

This woman exudes a Vinnie Five-Five ethos, where a hard, almost shellacked, surface protects her from the vicious blows that injure the naive and unsuspecting.

My nerves tingle. She has fingered me. I had been wrong about Ivan. He hadn't just wandered by earlier in the day. He had come looking for me. He knows my weakness for *Mitteleurope*. He sent this woman to watch for me. I need to bolt. Fuck Vinnie Five-Five with his warning to stay close. Away from all this, I stand a chance. Here I'm a dead man.

I am about to charge out the front door and leave Brooklyn to the thugs and yuppies vying for its control.

Then Ariel enters the café.

I want to melt into the walls. Why bring her further into this mess? She grew up here, but she has no part in the action. Maybe her father had pointed to a family down the block and claimed with a sagacious nod that they were *connected*. Men of his narrow ilk often mistook a Sicilian heritage with membership in the Cosa Nostra.

Few, in actuality, can make it as a mobster. To be a gangster takes perfect self-regard combined with ruthless cruelty and a willingness to annihilate anyone who crosses your path. Only when these conditions are met does a person have any chance to rise in an organization that, like most institutions in our winner-take-all-society, provides a rich and adventurous life to those who climb the ladder and little but heartache to everyone else.

I, in truth, lack the above-mentioned qualities. Ruthless mainly on myself, I loathe my ambivalence. Why hadn't I left the rackets years ago? I regret not finishing high school. I could have opened a dojo and taught martial arts. I'm good with my hands. Instead, I'm a gangster who vomits at the prospect of real violence. Instead, ashamed and trembling, I cower in my chair, hoping a harmless woman will not notice me.

But Ariel sees me attempting to slither under the table. Her forlorn expression morphs into a delighted smile. She approaches. "Here again? What are you doing? How did it go with, with . . ." She stutters to a stop. She has had another beer or two since I left her. Then she falls into the chair across from me and asks directly, "What's going on?"

If I tell her about my afternoon, she would crumple in horror. Still, I debate opening up. She's buzzed and anyway not the judgmental type. And she'd be delighted to hear me speak in sentences like a normal person. I consider a second longer and then answer. "Fuck."

"You're such a chatterbox." She speaks with the abruptness of the oblivious. She seems to have forgotten the situation I've gotten into. Or maybe she thinks that since I'm sitting in a café like nothing happened that nothing happened. Alcohol stops the inexorable forward motion of time and fate. She asks me that since I skipped lunch, if I want to have dinner.

Meanwhile, I imagine my slashed and bloody torso resting, headless, in a box.

She stands over me. Will she make a scene if I tell her to get lost? I gulp down the rest of my coffee. "Let's get out of here."

On the way to the door, we pass the tattooed woman who doesn't even glance our way. Outside I'm unable to accept being utterly wrong in my reading of the woman's intention; I peek into the café's window hoping to catch her talking angrily into her phone, reporting the arrival of Ariel and my leaving the café without being killed. But she does nothing. Ah, if my certainties have no basis in reality, where does that leave my speculations and educated guesses?

Ariel, in a voice a touch too loud, chirps, "So where are we going?"

I shrug.

"Are you hungry?"

"No." This bit of truth comes out angry and dismissive.

Ariel finally stops. "If you don't want company, just say so. Maybe . . . another time."

Ignoring this, we continue to walk side by side. Even I don't understand my problem. I like Ariel. More than that. I'm in the mood for her. She's from another world, one I just know from books. Being sick of women who get off on their connection to the connected had been the first symptom that I was tired of the business. Not to mention that I'd like to fuck Ariel into unconsciousness. I believe this feeling mutual.

Ariel stops in front of a house that lies midway between Avenue X and Avenue Y on East Third Street. The houses on this block, attached and identical, all have high stoops with garages under the porches. Construction workers, small shop-keepers, and lower-level civil servants without the means to escape to Staten Island live here.

"So this is my place. My mom's place. Thanks for walking me."

My vision of Ariel's home differs from the inelegant pile that looms over us. I imagine her in a chic Village brown-stone, an Afghan prayer rug covering her floor and a mural painted by an artist friend enlivening her walls. Colorful pillows on her futon add the final touch. This vision comes to me unbidden. Maybe I should have been an interior designer.

Ariel breaks me out of my reverie when she lunges for an awkward hug. Her head tilts up and my lips graze hers.

She reacts by tightening her grip and squashing her breasts against my chest. Her mouth desperately seeks mine. One of my eyes scans the street for danger. The other I keep on Ariel, who loses herself completely in the smooch. She rubs against me. Our tongues meet, attempt to knot. All this would have been more pleasant if I weren't afraid of being gunned down.

I pry her legs apart with my thigh. It rests at the base of her crotch until the heat of my flesh penetrates her jeans. She moves her lips away from mine and moans.

Then she softly reengages by standing on her tiptoes and licking my cheek and chin before suctioning against my mouth again.

After a minute I pull away and whisper, "I'll call you."

Ariel watches me take two steps before she orders, "Stop. Come inside."

"Your mother lives here."

"So?"

"She'll take one look at me and call the cops."

As if reluctant to be detained, I take another quick step before Ariel offers, "I'll let you in the side door. Go to the basement. It's finished. Mostly. There's a bed and a bathroom."

I make no move.

"Since her knee replacement, my mother never goes down, not even to do the laundry." Ariel speaks urgently, intent on selling me.

I manage to appear undecided.

"She's also hard of hearing. I use the basement as my office, so she won't be suspicious if I spend hours down there."

I come toward her and she grabs my hand and leads me to the side of her house. "I'll come around and let you in."

Just being in the alley makes me feel safer. I marvel at the coincidence of meeting Ariel on this day of all days when it has been years since I have met a woman I like. And it's been forever since an attraction has been this mutual.

Suddenly, the side door flies open. Ariel stands on a landing above a narrow, twisty staircase. I follow her down.

Ivan and the Russians would have no idea. True, Frankie Hog saw her, but he would never believe a woman like Ariel could live on Avenue X. I am safe here. I imagine emerging after years of living underground and finding the whole of Sheepshead Bay a smoldering ruin.

18

Dark Sanctuary

The room is long and low. My head brushes the dropped ceiling. The varnish on the pressed wood panels has faded, giving the walls a yellowish tint. Immediately to the left of the staircase is the washer/dryer. The office that Ariel talked about consists of a desk sandwiched between a deep chrome sink and the closet-sized toilet. Next to that is a stall shower with black and white tiles, cracked and filthy. The room opens into a wider but almost totally empty space. In one corner are some bowed bookcases with rotting paperbacks. In another corner is a bed, its mattress bare.

"When I was a teenager I thought I'd move down here," Ariel says. "Mostly to escape my younger sister."

"It's comfortable."

"It's depressing."

The mind makes a heaven of hell. To me this decrepit cellar smells sweetly of sanctuary. It reminds me of Judith's basement apartment. I throw my bag on the floor and go to the bed.

Ariel grimaces as I stretch out. "That mattress is kind of grimy."

I sit up.

"Listen, do you want a drink or something? We have Diet Coke. Or beer? I think I finished the last one. But I can run out. I also have a bottle of vodka in the freezer."

"Anything."

She takes the steps two at a time. Her eagerness to please baffles me. I am an inarticulate punk, on the run from professional punks. Does she perceive life and excitement in this grubby story? What would happen if I started talking? Or worse, if I started discussing the waning of the cultures in which we both live, throwing in a quote or two? I'd lose every bit of dangerous allure. Besides, old habits are hard to break. Refined conversation is like a language I understand perfectly but cannot, or am afraid to, speak.

While she is gone, I explore the basement further. I check out the bookcase. I'm always a little surprised by books that aren't Penguin Classics. They all seem, somehow, flimsy. Mostly there are mysteries with a smattering of texts that Ariel probably did in school—*Oliver Twist, Huck Finn,* a collection of Wallace Stevens's poetry. A pocket-sized paperback of "Howl" catches my eye. *I saw the best minds of my generation destroyed by madness.* It might be an indictment of the society, but Ginsberg is also congratulating himself for knowing the best minds. I'd like to see what kind of poetry he would write concerning the minds of Gus Spoleto or IRA.

I go back to the bed, which is the only place to sit down other than in Ariel's desk chair.

More minutes pass. Did her mother find out about me and tell her how stupid she is to harbor a man hunted by a pack of killers?

War sucks ass. The assassins themselves need to be disgusted by the bloodshed before it stops. That takes awhile. I pace and worry that the tread of my shoes can be heard upstairs.

So I tiptoe over to Ariel's computer. No password is needed so I get online and start to read the financial news. My father gave me a few shares of this and that, which I've added to now and then. Every quarter I collect 200 in dividends. Even gangsters retire. It's a start, even if it's a lousy start.

GE down a quarter point. Why, why get out of bed? The market fucks with you worse than the Mafia. Better stick with loan-sharking and drug dealing. Less risk. Still, I read the Bloomberg home page. For making money, stocks hold my interest like nothing but drug dealing.

Footsteps finally sound on the stairway. I push away from Ariel's computer and hide in the shower. I close the ancient curtain just in case it's her mother.

"Hello?"

It's Ariel. I rip the plastic sheet aside and she screams.

"Sorry, shit, sorry."

From upstairs, a cry, "Ariel!"

"I'm okay, Mom." She motions for me to freeze. "I just almost fell down the stairs."

"Be careful," a wobbly voice calls.

"Okay. I'm okay."

Then Ariel looks at me. "Why . . ."

"I didn't want your mother . . ."

Ariel stares at me with both anger and relief. "I told you. My mom never comes down here. You have nothing to worry about."

"What took so long?"

"I got some beer. Also some Jack Daniel's. You can chase it with the beer or Coke."

She has bought Budweiser, probably believing it to be my favorite. I prefer Pilsner but now is not the time to say anything. I pop a Bud but turn down the bourbon.

Ariel herself cracks the Jack and swigs straight from the bottle. Her eyes are alight with mischief when she apologizes, "Sorry. I always wanted to do that." Belatedly abashed, she mutters, "I'll get myself a glass."

She opens her desk drawer and removes a short, wide cup with the word *Chivas* embossed in gold. "I usually drink vodka. But today, for some reason . . . I'm just in the mood . . ." She holds her drink up to the fluorescent light and the liquor shimmers. "My mom is going to a friend's for dinner in a few minutes. Then I'll bring down your bedding."

She is very anxious about this bedding.

"I'm fine with the bed the way it is," I say.

"But I'm not."

Ariel smiles and I smile back. No point in wasting time. She sips her drink and joins me on the bare bed. She has lovely lips, thin but soft. Our tongues touch, and this brings all sorts of muscle slackening. She pushes me down on the dirty bed, and lies on top of me. The heat of our bodies increases with the friction of squirming against each other. Her shirt rides up and I touch her smooth back where it slides into the jeans. She wears red panties with lace trimming. I stick my hand down the back of her jeans. She squeezes her hand between her chest and mine and pinches my nipple. Her other hand unzips my fly. Grimy mattress be damned. Her fingers graze my penis and I'm ready to rip every piece of clothing off her body.

She jumps off me.

"What the hell . . ."

"Don't move, you gorilla." She rushes from the room as if the building is about to collapse. My dick is so hard that I think it will shred my underwear.

The longest, strangest, most pressurized day telescopes to this moment. Nothing matters but Ariel. My eyes tear. Water pools at the bottom of my sockets and starts to leak down my face.

Shit. I think of Odysseus tossed about the seas by an angry Poseidon. We are all at the mercy of powers greater than ourselves. But what's not mentioned is that Odysseus is an ass. "Man blames the gods for his fate," Zeus points out to Athena, "but man's stupidity doubles his suffering."

I think of my life. No individual decision sticks out as particularly idiotic. Society offers not much to a guy like me. Years and years of drudgery. Why shouldn't I take advantage of my bulk and sit at the door of a poker room? Why shouldn't I collect a debt or two? Why not sell pot? I never really hurt anyone. Pauli Bones kills. IRA carries lethal violence in his paunch. They bring me along for show. When I scowl, people pay up.

I should never have dropped out of school. If only so much of it weren't a waste of time, obsessed with monkey work and peopled by teachers more ignorant than rocks and dirt. I enjoy my freedom from tedious labor. I do small jobs and fulfill low expectations. For years all had seemed sensible, with a healthy balance between doing nothing and getting laid.

But I was foolish to think that I'd skate. I might not have taunted the gods as Odysseus had done, but I played fast and loose with reality. When you hang with murderers, whether state supported or freelance, bad things happen.

What I really need is a complete change. That can be accomplished. It just depends how many people get killed, who kills them, and if I'm one of the dead.

Ariel whooshes into the room at the same speed she left. "My mom's gone, so I grabbed these." She holds a pile of linen that would furnish a small B&B. She grabs my shirt and pulls me off the bed. "Come on. Come on. Hold these." She thrusts the bedding at me.

She works furiously. "I brought two sheets because the bed is so dirty."

I watch her tuck in a pale blue bottom sheet. She then flaps open the second and does the same. Maybe she has worked in a hotel. Or maybe she brings guys down here all the time. She certainly knows the drill.

She rips some pillows out of my hand. With the same dexterousness that she has dealt with the sheets, she puts on the pillowcases. I'm left holding a thick, pink quilt. Ariel must have thought that I looked at it askance because she says, "It's the only extra one."

"Fuck it."

"Oh, you and your *fuck it.*" She grabs the blanket and drops it on the edge of the bed while I grab her and drop her in the middle of the bed.

We lay side by side. This time she doesn't worry about touching the dirty mattress. First, she bites my lip, a love nip. I don't realize she draws blood until I swallow something salty. A drop of wine dark blood even stains Ariel's upper lip. I brush it away.

"What are you doing?" she asks.

In answer I pull her shirt over her head. Telling Ariel that I've bled into her mouth would just break the mood. I see that along with the bedding Ariel has brought a couple of condoms serrated to each other. Pillows, sheets, condoms. Like Noah, Ariel has carried down two of everything. My eyes roam around the basement, my ark. Could this flimsy cellar protect me from the coming storm?

I can't spend any more time thinking about this as Ariel, maybe feeling underdressed in just her orange bra, is taking my shirt off. I wear nothing underneath and Ariel starts running her nails up and down my chest.

She shifts her back as I unclip her bra. Her compressed breasts, larger and rounder than I imagined them, spring free. Ariel then straddles my waist, her tits waving in front of my face. A pink nipple dangles close enough to my mouth that I lift my head and swallow it.

She freezes. I suck gently and sidle my tongue over her areola. She slowly lowers her chest, pushing her other breast into my eye. I worry that she'd smother me so I release her nipple. She instantly jumps off me and orders, "Pull down my pants."

To save time I also grab her panties. But she stops me. "No. Just my jeans."

So I yank just the jeans. Next she tells me, "Now you stand up. I want to take down your pants."

I laugh. Before I stopped fucking, I fucked a lot. It never went like this. It wasn't always the same, but it was never like this.

So I stand. And Ariel strains as she gets my pants down, leaving the underpants. So I'm in the same state of undress as she.

"Touch yourself," she commands.

"What?"

"Pull your penis out of your underpants."

I obey.

"Wow," Ariel gasps. She reaches for her glass and downs what's left of the Jack.

So I am literally standing there with my dick in my hand. And I can tell you, the man who coined the expression knew from experience how awkward this can be.

I clear my throat, but Ariel seems mesmerized by the cock resting in my palm. She finally commands, "Pump it like you're trying to masturbate."

I frankly don't know the etiquette of the situation. Certainly, if I do as she suggests, I'd come all over her clean sheets. And I mean come. Never in the history of the Mafia did someone need release more than I do.

Ariel does not repeat her request. She seems happy enough to stare until, as if in a trance, she reaches over and touches it herself. The result of this is instantaneous. I yank down her panties. She stepped out of them like Venus from her clamshell, and lies back down on the bed. I tear the condom package with my teeth.

"Lie down," Ariel regains her authoritative voice. "I want to get on top."

She really has a wonderful body, trim, but with hips and a great tapering behind. Her thighs are thick but muscled. As I'm rolling off her, I hear an enormous crack, almost like a gunshot. I blink and realize that Ariel has smacked my ass as hard as she could. "How does that feel?"

Is this chick nuts? Furious, humiliated, I barely hold myself back from cracking her head open.

"How does it feel now?"

I concentrate. "Not bad," A warmth had spread across my butt.

"Kind of nice?"

"Yeah."

"Lie down."

I do. Ariel straddles my midsection with her behind pointing at my face. She begins licking the shaft. I reach between her legs and rub the side of my index finger along her slit. Her pubic hair is sticky. "Lick me," she orders and pushes up to make herself totally available. I stick my tongue into her. Her mouth encircles the tip of my penis. I cry, "I'm going to come."

Her head shoots up. "Don't you dare!"

She takes the condom from the open pack and rolls it down. Then she slowly impales herself. I shudder with every vibration as she slides herself on. She controls her vaginal walls like a maestro, doling out sweet music with each iteration of her muscles. She sways on top of me as if dancing. Her eyes close and her head tilts toward the ceiling. She speeds her rocking but a little. I can hear the waves of pleasure crashing through her midsection. I follow her gyrations, the heat and wet increasing with every motion. Then she stops. She grabs my neck and presses me so deep inside her that I come with such explosiveness that I knock us both off the narrow bed. On the floor she still holds on for dear life, her breathing fast and rhythmic. We lie together, she on top of me, until her hyperventilating returns to mere panting. Only then does she release her death grip on my neck.

19

Gorilla Dreams

Ariel holds the base of the condom as she frees herself. I'm nearly as hard as before.

"You're amazing," she says.

We climb back onto the bed, sweat dripping from both our bodies.

She lies back, spent. I go to the bathroom. When I return, Ariel says, motherly, "I got to get you slippers."

"Why?"

"The floor's kind of dirty. Didn't you notice?" I sit back on the bed and Ariel rests her head against me. "What else do you think you'll need?"

"I don't need nothin'."

"Nothin'? You're sure?"

Of course I'd need things if I stay down here. I'd need food. Every day would be best. I'd need reading material. I'd need toilet paper. I might do without cable, but I'd want Internet. And I wouldn't be getting to the gym regularly so some weights would be nice if she wants me to keep the edge on the body that she so fancies.

"Do you know what you're getting into?" I ask her.

"Sure I fucking know." Ariel makes her voice deeper as she rakes her nails over my back. "Do *you* know what you're getting into? You're going to be my prisoner." My silence goads her to continue. "Don't worry. I'll be a kind master."

I don't want to mention money. "You need some money?"

"No. Don't be silly. I might."

"I got about 500 on me. I can get more."

"Don't worry about that now."

No. No point. I try to calculate how long the war might last. There are so many variables. They could knock off Vinnie Five-Five right away and that would be that. If they kill the captain, his soldiers will capitulate. Julius and Gus would indeed move away, believing that tough guys from Brooklyn could make it anywhere in the country but Brooklyn. Good-bye and good luck.

But if the boys in New Jersey think the organization would be better with Vinnie than without, that would prolong things. If Jersey imports a few more Morons and Jews, we have another Iraq on our hands, an unwinnable slog perpetrated mostly by distant monsters who never glimpse the blood of the slaughtered.

Yet even if they hang Vinnie Five-Five out to dry, that would not be the end. In his small neighborhood Vinnie is a big player. He has resources to put up a fight. Besides gambling, sports betting, and loan-sharking, he owns a busy funeral parlor and a catering hall on Ocean Parkway. He runs all the whorehouses and gets kickbacks from three Italian restaurants, a cheese shop, and a storefront that sells fake designer accessories. I remember my father had admired the little Italian marooned in a sea of enemies. "Assets won't protect you from a bullet," Dad said, "but it never kills you to have a few."

Maybe this was dad's way of telling me to get my act together. Don't be a putz. My father had the old Jewish habit of storing money in a thousand places, of being a man of many pockets. He had fourteen bank accounts, eight brokerage accounts, and three safe-deposit boxes. He also had a Swiss account that had sixty-eight dollars in it. Tiny amounts of money well hidden everywhere. He had been a brilliant accountant, but a lousy handicapper.

What was left of the decimated fortune my mom got. When she died, I got what was left from her. She didn't play the ponies, but she had relatives more pathetic than her son. One brother got eight years for hijacking a trailer of canned tuna fish. Canned for cans. When I heard tuna, I thought, well, okay. Sushi grade bluefin. In Tokyo, a prize specimen goes for $350 a pound. And this Uncle Louis was supposedly connected in the fish markets. Some connections. He left three hungry mouths. Due to his incompetence at just about everything, his captain warned him to do no more hijacking. So he got precious little help from his associates when he went to "college." My mom paid his wife's rent while he lived courtesy of the government. He got out a few days before my mom died. For the funeral, he didn't even have money for a decent bouquet.

"What do gorillas dream about?"

"What?"

Ariel still prone on the bed, rephrases, "What are you thinking?"

"Tuna fish."

She bolts upright. "Are you hungry? I knew you were hungry." Ariel blushes because she sounds like a Jewish mother. But then she adds, "We can get some sushi. The only problem is that the rice has to be warm for the sushi to be really good. Take-out rice is always cold."

Ariel is so damn cute, so excited about everything—the sushi, the war, me. And I don't care a whit about the temperature of the rice. The quality of the fish is what counts. Of course, the rice should not be ice-cold.

Ariel drapes herself over my shoulders. "You can teach me about crime and I can teach you about . . . other things."

I nod.

"Maybe I can teach you how to talk."

"Maybe." So she does like this game.

I pull a couple of beers from the ring and give Ariel one. "I better not," she says.

"Why?"

She takes the beer and admits, "I'm drunk. You think I always act like this?"

No. Sober, she'd have to be nuts to harbor and sleep with a goon like me. And for this I'm grateful.

I ought to be, however, on the other side of the world by now. Yet I have only traveled down the block, via Manhattan and mass murder.

"My mother is going to get back soon," Ariel says. "I should go upstairs." She hugs me around the waist. After a second she comments, "Your heart beats really slow. That means you're in good aerobic shape."

I run my fingers through Ariel's hair. "Or maybe I'm dying."

"I briefly dated a cardiologist," she explains, sounding tired. "You know, the last guy I went out with didn't talk much either. The guy before him, the one who kept breaking up with me, couldn't shut up. But the cat's got everyone else's tongue."

I would like to respond to Ariel more fully. The strong, silent type never impressed me. Babbling, it's true, indicates uncontrollable anxiety, but silence often signals a vacancy upstairs.

In the best scenario, Ariel probably chalks up my reticence to some old country notion of *omerta*, or a profound respect for secrecy. I don't think she would have gone this far with me if she suspected my skull contained *no* gray matter. But she certainly enjoys having more gray matter than I have.

I stay silent for one other reason: to keep Ariel out of trouble. She has no obligation to report a crime if she has no knowledge of one. Why make her an accessory after the fact?

Ariel lets go of me and turns her face up. The tenderness with which we kiss surprises me as much as that crack on the bottom had. We clinch for a minute before Ariel disengages.

"I'll be back. See if you can put together a list of things you need. Don't worry about sounding weird if you need to eat strange stuff like peanut butter and lime. I've seen it all." Then Ariel trips up the steps.

Peanut butter and lime? Seen it all? What is she talking about? Who lets a self-confessed criminal into the basement of her mother's house? She doesn't know that I am not the killer I pretend to be. Plenty of women are attracted to thugs, but Ariel does not fit this profile. She usually goes out with heart doctors and antitrust lawyers. Then again, she has rightly anticipated the explosive sex. Ordering me around lit her up something fierce. Why shouldn't women enjoy dominating an imposing man? Most men fantasize about ripping the clothes off demure women. Am I going to end up her sex slave? Am I going to let her do my food shopping?

I doze. Gone are the worries of being in over my head. Gone are the thoughts that my friends are all on the run. Gone are the thoughts that I have no friends. I only dream of Ariel who has lashed me to a pole in the Met's gift shop and spoons peanut butter into my mouth while she drinks Budweiser.

Part II

20

Sushi Rice

The experts have been predicting the death of the mob as long as they've been predicting the death of the novel.

Both hang on because they provide pleasures otherwise unavailable in a homogenized, corporatized world. When you need a whore, you need a whore, just as when you need satire you need Petronius or Celine. There's no substitute in the online pornography or pitiful laugh-track humor from a mass culture that attempts to satisfy the deepest needs with trinkets and pablum.

And if you got inside dope that the Jets' quarterback twisted his ankle in practice, you go to your corner bookie rather than to a faceless, taxable casino in the same spirit in which you read Melville's "Bartleby" to understand how whim and not reason (never reason) is the driver of all important human behavior. To construct a society based on the notion that people always behave rationally and in their own self-interest is an insanity that can only be dreamed up by the most decadent capitalist as he consumes the last remnants of natural resources and pure air on earth. Only reason can lead us to total annihilation.

But all this means nothing. As you can hear, I wake feeling depressed. I have no idea what time it is. From the windows which peek up to the ground, I can see only darkness that announces night. I hear no squeaking on top of me and conclude that everyone is asleep. But who knows when an older woman like Ariel's mother goes to bed? It might be nine o'clock, it might be two A.M. I then put all speculation to rest by turning on my phone. It's eleven thirty. I've slept for only a couple of hours.

Someone clomps down the stairs. I feel sick. If it's not Ariel, I'm fucked.

It's her. A strange shudder of delight thrills me when she appears.

"Good morning," she trills.

I decide to relax, open up a little. "It ain't exactly morning."

"I came down to check on you a few times. You're cute in your sleep. Did you feel me tickling your penis?"

Why shouldn't I have a regular conversation? I won't be giving anything away. And I'm beginning to believe that she won't hold my fucking erudition against me. It would be wonderful to verbalize my thoughts without fear of getting whacked. "I was dead to the world."

"Your penis wasn't. It was all ready to go without you."

This girl makes me nervous. She had seemed fine when I met her. Now that I put myself in her power, she worries me with her insatiability. Something about this situation intoxicates her with arousal. The booze helps.

"Are you hungry?"

I can finally say *yes* to this.

"Wait here." She runs up the steps and comes back with a shopping bag.

Ariel explains as she removes a dozen foil containers, "I got some sushi. You said you liked it. You've had it before, right?"

I love Japanese cuisine. Soba, yakitori, sashimi all delight me.

"You're a large man so I hope I got enough."

She must have bought a dozen rolls and thirty individual pieces. Salmon, tuna, mackerel, eel, a feast for a shogun. She has also brought down a large round platter and she arranges the fish in a very appetizing design. She places the platter between us on the bed. If she's bonkers, she's stylishly bonkers. The last thing she takes from the bag is a smoky bottle of sake.

"Dig in." She puts a small, rectangular plate in front of me for the soy and wasabi dip.

I haven't eaten much in days. My hunger returns in force and I finish four pounds of fish and an equal amount of rice in about fifteen minutes. I wash everything down with swigs of the sake. Toward the end of the gorging I become conscious of Ariel examining me.

I put down the chopsticks. "I'm making a pig of myself."

"No, no," Ariel encourages. "Go ahead. I ate already."

I hesitate. She has no job. She sublets her apartment while she lives with her mother. Yet she spends one hundred dollars on raw fish for a near total stranger. Why this generosity?

"Here," she says. "I'll have this." She drops a slice of a cucumber roll on her plate while keeping her eyes on me. When I reach for a piece of tuna she nods. "I got it all for you."

"Thanks." Does playing out a Jewish-Japanese mother thing turn her on? Does seeing a ruffian wolf down hand-cut fish do something for her? Or is she a witch attempting to fatten me up for the pot? For that she could have gotten more bang for her buck getting chicken from KFC.

Yet I finish everything down to the last speck of wasabi. Then I swallow the remainder of the sake. Sated and disgusted, I drop the chopsticks.

Ariel puts all the take-out containers into the empty delivery bag. "Did you make that list of the things you need?"

"I've been thinking. I can't stay."

A look so stricken crosses Ariel's face that I think she's going to cry.

"I appreciate everything. But I can't put you and your mother in a position—"

"We're in no position," Ariel cries. "None at all. What position are you talking about?"

She knows what I'm talking about. But that's the problem with civilians. They read about all the violence; they see Joe Pesci go psycho on the screen. To them it's all a movie. No one really throws someone into the trunk of a car where he shits himself. No one really shoots someone in the back of the head or puts a meat hook up an ass. All this is fantasy because you see the same dead gangsters in movie after movie, alive and well. As with death itself, people deny the simple fact that so many killers live in their midst.

"The Russians don't play nice," I warn. "They'll hit anyone. Family, friends."

"No one knows you're here. They can't do a door-to-door search."

I sit in frozen obstinacy, but Ariel makes a good point. She knows how to take advantage of having the advantage. She rises. At the top of the stairs, she calls back, softly, "Don't forget that list of the stuff you need."

21

War

When war breaks out, everyone is guilty. Everyone must
take cover. The big shots resort to safe houses, bodyguards,
armored vehicles. Lepke Buchalter, an old time Jew boss in
the 1920s, hid in a Bensonhurst basement for two years while
he orchestrated dozens of hits on suspected rats. During the
Castellammarese war, gangsters carried their mattresses from
house to house to avoid sleeping in the same place two nights
in a row. That battle ended with Lucky Luciano and Meyer
Lansky victorious. They divided the New York Mafia into five
families, set up the Commission to settle disputes, and ushered in a period of Cosa Nostra peace and prosperity that
coincided with the Cold War.

When the Berlin Wall fell, however, ambitious law enforc-
ers started to make their names by busting up the old dago
rackets, especially in the construction unions, while ignoring
the infiltration of the Russian and the Chinese. An Italian
name in the papers always satisfied the atavistic imagination
of the general population.

But what really destroyed the mob were changes in sen-
tencing guidelines. No longer did one get four years for cracking a head open or eight years for murder pleaded down to
manslaughter. The ability of the Justice Department to dic-
tate life sentences for conspiracy made everyone, from the

lowliest soldier to the most influential bosses, flip. Not even the toughest son of a bitch wants to die in prison.

Our little operation here hangs on by its toenails. Vinnie Five-Five's crew consists of his sons, Pauli Bones, and IRA. Associates like Frankie Hog and myself round out the team. Vinnie and his sons are made, as is Pauli Bones. The general rule still holds that you need to do a "piece of work"—murder someone—to get your button.

But even more importantly, you need to earn. Bones, in particular, is a valued employee. He made his reputation as an efficient killer, but his true genius shows through because of the connections he made at pharmacies and hospitals all over the city. Access to prescription drugs is more lucrative and less risky than importing blow or manufacturing meth. Garlic and Double-Down had run the houses and stolen cars for export. IRA peddles counterfeit securities and loan sharks. Vinnie Five-Five gets a percentage of everything and kicks upstairs to Tony D.

Vinnie Five-Five's big problem is that business has been (at least he claims it has been) bad. Tony D thinks that Vinnie is either holding out or is incompetent. In either case, Vinnie is "on the shelf," sent to Coventry, frozen out, by other mobsters. Who knows the truth, but the effect is that we have little backup in this war against much larger forces.

Mostly our corner of the world has been sleepy and all of us have been lulled by the easy life. I have yet to see Vinnie in full battle mode. He never spent his solitary, paranoid moments figuring out whom to whack next.

But he's a gangster through and through and he clips people when the need arises. A punk named Angelo DiMarco, for example, set up a crap game in Vinnie's territory. I knew Angelo, an idiot who thought he was smart. That really is a death sentence if you fuck around with someone like Vinnie Five-Five. Angelo traveled with a vicious little sidekick nicknamed The Turk (actually a Yemenite). They childishly convinced themselves of their invulnerability mainly because they carried large-caliber handguns. Vinnie imported a shooter from Newark who offed them at their own dice game. But Vinnie is more businessman than hitman, never more so than when business is bad. His main headache now is finding replacements for Garlic and Double-Down. He needs to keep his houses running or he'll lose such a large chunk of his revenue that he'd never get back into the good graces of Tony D.

The only reason that Vinnie has not acted on his paranoid hunch about me is because Julius and Gus still like to take me to civilian clubs with them because I attract chicks. In a known mob hangout they do fine because the number of girls attracted solely to mobsters is staggering. In some Bay Ridge places, if you're not connected you have no chance. And if we beat to death some asshole who's bothering them, forget about it. After that, they'll do anything, anything. At these moments, being in the mob makes sense.

On the other hand, when the Russians and Chinese are cutting up your friends' bodies, being mobbed up becomes a drag.

22

The Christmas Box

On the second morning of the war, Ariel shatters the calm when she sits on the edge of the bed. "Hey, sleepyhead."

I jolt awake, eyes wide. She doesn't know how close she came to having her head ripped off. "You shouldn't surprise me like that."

She sings happily, "You are jumpy for a killer."

I yawn and stretch. My body has attracted attention from both men and women since I was fourteen. The men I mostly ignore. Women, however, take any hint of disinterest as a mortal insult. So I don't ignore. Why should I? They pursue until I weaken, though I can generally stay quite strong, a rock, for about thirty minutes.

But if we genuinely connect, the game really begins. This is dangerous work because someone might be injured. Not as badly as with a Glock maybe, but plenty of organ damage can be done by two people who care for each other.

Ariel pushes me back down and lies near me. "I like looking at you when you're asleep."

"You shouldn't sneak up on people. You might get hurt."

"Hoit?" Ariel rolls on her side to face me. "I never thought I'd meet anyone like you."

I had said "hurt." She just imagines the Brooklyn accent.

And I have never, well rarely, met anyone like Ariel. She has done work on three aborted master's degrees, has held an office job for years, and has moved back with her mother to save money after being fired. Who lives like this? Yet Ariel does not otherwise act so rationally.

She has invited me into her house. Has she done this as an act of desperation, because she has nothing to lose? So she adopts a thug. I have no illusions of how I appear to other people. Inside, I may be a person of varied interests and numerous sensitivities. To Ariel, however, I am a dangerous monster in the guise of a handsomish dude with a largish dick. Has she dreams of domesticating me without erasing the primal violence that's so sexy? Can she paper over my cultureless facade with great art that can then be peeled off along with my clothes?

And my feelings for Ariel? What would happen in a more normal situation? Let's say I don't need to hide. Let's say we just meet in a café and I let her lead me around a museum which I have been to a dozen times. Let's say I laugh at her patronizing tone. Would I find her fascinating beyond the initial fuck? Would I think her someone special? Would I find her girlish enthusiasm for life, for adventure, enticing or off-putting? Would I find her wise or naive?

But I can't ignore the circumstances of our meeting. Her actions prove brave and self-sacrificing even if they are spiced with desire, desperation, and stupidity. Ariel is something of a savior and my gratitude at her altruism contributes to my being dazzled by her.

"It's one o'clock in the afternoon," Ariel says.

I pad into the bathroom. Twelve hours of sleep yet my muscles still ache with fatigue.

"Do you want coffee?"

I sit down on the bed near Ariel and put my head in my hands. I feel hung over. I nod, but even that small movement of my head causes a shooting pain in my skull.

She runs upstairs and brings down a mug. I hold the cup tightly, worrying that my shaky hands will spill the hot liquid.

"Are you sick?"

"Don't know," I gasp. The horror of yesterday's whorehouse run assaults me. I'm exhausted by the pressure, by the worries for my family, for Judith. Oh, why did I invite that Ivan to visit? In my apartment, my other basement haven, we got high and talked in near silence of life. And now that conversation can summon death.

It is not difficult to imagine. Vlad would call Ivan to The National, the nightclub on Brighton Fifth Street that Vlad uses as his headquarters. *Ivan, I have a piece of work for you, a job.* I don't know how to say "a piece of work" in Russian. But I'm sure that the Russian mob has a delightful way of saying "murder this cocksucker" just as the Italians do. And I'm sure they have all sorts of institutional mechanisms that ensure people carry out orders. It wouldn't be one of the top organizations in the country if it didn't have strict quality control.

Now Ivan is not terrible. Not this Ivan. He has no amusing nickname in honor of the most effective Russian dictator in history. I don't even know what they call him. Maybe Little Ivan, because he is enormous. Maybe they call him Whitey because of his colorless hair, or Blackie as an ironic comment, though the mob generally limits its irony to slaughtering its own.

Anyway, this Ivan, my Ivan, would be given an assignment. He would be ordered to kill an Italian. Or half an Italian. The other half doesn't matter. We had made no secret of our small friendship. We had been soldiers in parallel armies, so low level that we could act like people.

I had even envisioned an alliance against the Chinese. Ever since Mao broke with Stalin, I figured that the Russians and the Chinese were on a collision course on a number of ideological and geographic issues. I did not take into account the new world order, where the only important consideration is access to resources, money, and the political stability necessary to keep those entrenched in power entrenched in power.

War between nations, rather than just on one's own citizens, is bad for business. Just keep the internal malcontents in jail or dead and all systems function perfectly.

I should have known that our little enclave between the two big powers would go first. I totally misread the geopolitical forces that are so obvious now, as I hide out in Ariel's basement. Even Vinnie had warned me against playing paddleball in Manhattan Beach. "You're setting yourself up," he had said.

But Ivan, like me, understands loneliness. We have many of the same concerns. What had surprised me other than the way he combined ferocity and quickness on the court had been his comprehensive knowledge of Russian literature beginning with Pushkin. He worshipped Chekhov and practically memorized all of Gogol. He could quote long passages from Tolstoy and Dostoyevsky. My own reading, while broader, is not nearly as deep. I had explained to him my system, inherited from my father, of reading every Penguin Classic. He thought it silly until I showed him my library with hundreds of masterpieces. He had said that perhaps one can learn a little in this way. But in the end he thought it disorganized. "You have too much ground," he criticized. "You jump from age to age like blintz on trampoline."

"You must read in the original language," Ivan had instructed. "Otherwise, you think every writer is your friend from down block. Bakunin, this is not a man you know from corner deli. Only original language captures the courage in voice."

In his rough, straining-for-an-original-metaphor way, Ivan has a point. You read a Sumerian epic, go to the French realists, check out Lao Tse, study Livy, and find yourself in Merry Old England with *The Canterbury Tales*. Sure, you learn what some of the gregarious minds thought of their different societies, but because everything is in the most relevant translation, you can't help but think that all literature belongs to the American century.

"If I just read contemporary writers, I'd be stuck in the last 400 years. I can't be tied down like that."

"Motherfucker," Ivan argued, "if your tradition is any fucking good, you should find enough in 400 years to start own universe. Shakespeare by himself . . ."

"I can't tell Dante to fuck off just because he writes in Italian."

We had agreed to disagree. We never considered killing each other. Once, while in my apartment, he suggested that only Joseph Brodsky is worth reading of the twentieth-century poets. I replied that Ginsberg (at his best) can ream Brodsky up the ass. So he stormed outside and kicked in three of my windows, and then I ran out with a baseball bat and smashed his car windshield. But mostly our conversations were models of intellectual decorum.

Ivan last came to my house about a year ago. Maybe he stopped fraternizing because he knew of the coming war. Or maybe he was teaching comp lit at a Midwestern university. His nontraditional background certainly gives him an edge in a job search.

Ariel takes the coffee cup from my hand and places it on the floor. My obvious distraction does not deter Ariel's passion, especially after my hand reaches down the top of her low-cut sundress and rubs against her nipples.

The same automated response that animates my hands operates my dick. It hardens as soon as Ariel touches it. We fondle each other for a minute before Ariel jumps up. "Wait here."

Where the hell would I go?

Because my mind is on other things, my penis deflates as soon as Ariel leaves. And my headache, which had lifted, descends once more. If I go home, I can provide some protection to Judith. But I could also bring trouble with me if they know I'm there.

Ariel comes tripping down carrying a large box colorfully printed with white snowflakes and red stars. It's the kind of box one gets from a loving but sappy relative at Christmas.

She finds me in the same position that she left me, prone on the bed. Well, not exactly as she left me. After glancing at my crotch she says, "I got some stuff that will perk you up."

She plops the box between us and opens the top. "I brought this from my apartment in the city never thinking that I would need it in Brooklyn."

The first thing she takes from the box is a velvet-covered paddle. She whacks it softly against her hand. "It's been awhile." She looks at me. "You can use it on me if you're gentle."

I glance into the box and see a selection of sex toys that includes a dildo with a dozen different vibration settings, a couple of feathers so long that they must have come from extinct birds, a traditional "magic wand" sturdy enough to stimulate a rhino, some satin-covered handcuffs, rope, a nasty wood paddle with holes drilled into it, candy-flavored lubricant, hot pepper lubricant, a butt plug, and four lamb-skin condoms.

I dare not act surprised. "Where did you get all this shit?"

"Here and there," Ariel answers. "People give you stuff. As a joke."

"These ain't no joke."

"No they ain't," Ariel agrees. "But you don't know that until you try it."

Looking at her collection makes me think that one could make a quick buck compiling a Dictionary of Sexual Aids— everything from aardvarks to xylophones. But in another second I realize the scope of this undertaking would be impossible. Given people's varied predilections, there need be more entries than in the Encyclopedia Britannica.

Ariel unzips the back of her dress and lets it fall to her feet. She spins on her heels, giddy as a schoolgirl. "Tie me to the pillar," she commands.

I stare at her for a moment. Then it hits me again. She's hammered. She never gets fall-down blasted but she's buzzed, a little past buzzed, all the time.

I debate. On the one hand, I have no philosophical objections to playing with Ariel. Though never super turned-on by bondage, it has never turned me off either. Men dominated with ropes and gags merely amuse me. A frisson, however, does occur when I view images of bound women. My most recurring sexual fantasies, of course, involve exposed vaginas. I fondly recall all the times I plunged my schlong into warm, moist flesh.

In truth, I never explored the myriad forms of sexual titillation. Maybe this indicates a lack of emotional comfort with my partners. I might have let the macho shit get in the way, thinking that the only manly course is traditional bonking. I had anal sex maybe ten times in my life. Though an outlaw in some ways, rarely do I go beyond the culturally sanctioned positions.

Should I have devoted more attention to paraphernalia and noninvasive procedures? Maybe. Another time and place, I would think Ariel brave and uninhibited, no matter how drunk. I would have dwelled on the cultural and philosophical aspects of violating power taboos and embracing fetish. I would have fucked her any which way she wanted.

But today I have other things on my mind. People want me dead. My family is in danger. Being cooped up with Ariel and her equipment makes me think I am a sexual prisoner, that if I don't comply with her wishes I'd be kicked into the street. No one likes to be coerced into a sexually dominant role. "I have to go home and get a few things," I tell Ariel.

"So? Tie me up. Think of me here, in my bra and panties. I can wait."

The girl is nuts. "How long?"

"Not knowing when you'll be back makes it even better."

Ariel's eyes gleam. When I take the rope she seems dizzy with lust. She leans her back against a beam covered in small brown tiles. "Tie me around my waist. And use the cuffs to lock my wrists on that water pipe."

The ceiling is low and the thin pipe is not even a foot over her head.

I check the handcuffs. Though wrapped in velvet, they're real enough. She would not be able to move unless someone came to get her out of them.

"You don't understand. People are looking for me. To waste me."

"No one's going to kill you, darling. You're too sexy."

She is *soooo* nuts. She stands patiently. I wind the rope around her waist and make a loose knot in the back.

"The handcuffs," she orders.

"If something happens to me . . . you want your mother to come down here to free you?"

The mention of her mother snaps her out of her hyper-aroused state. She reconsiders. Then, more adamantly, she insists, "The handcuffs. Do it. You'll be back."

"It's *your* mother," I mutter. I click the handcuffs closed. Then I put the key into her hand. "You should have enough play to get yourself out if you have to."

Ariel says nothing but her fist closes over the key. She's neither so drunk nor so crazy after all. She's willing to risk a major embarrassment but not a minor death.

Before going outside I gaze on her vulnerable position. Ariel has a juicy body, with round breasts and strong thighs. I see her pubic hair glowing through her sheer panties. She smiles and, saintlike, raises her face to the dropped ceiling. Her wavy brown hair falls onto her bare shoulders. She reminds me of Caravaggio's Saint Sebastian minus the phallic arrows embedded in the flesh. She might even have that painting in mind posing like that. When she doesn't ask me to uncuff her, I run up the steps. My fingers clutch the doorknob when she calls, "Stop!"

No. She can't be left like that. Even the most dedicated fetishist has to see the folly in this. I rush down the stairs and take the key from her.

"What are you doing?" Ariel demands.

"What do you think? I'm going to unlock—"

"Don't fucking unlock anything, you baboon. Blindfold me."

"What?"

"In the box you'll find a black silk cloth."

"*Meshugana*," I mutter as I root around and find what she wants. I don't think I'd enjoy being blindfolded and tied to a pole for an indefinite period, even if I could let myself out. The mortifying prospect of my mother finding me handcuffed to a pipe would weigh heavily, negating whatever sexual pleasure I may experience from being tied up.

But maybe that's what most turns Ariel on.

"You have to come back now." Her serenity is total.

"Do you understand, lady? Shit." Our intimacy recedes with each new request. I imagine Ariel a figure floating away from me and being swallowed by the distant horizon. "There are bad people cruising around trying to kill me."

"Don't be paranoid. They're looking to kill everyone."

"What's the difference?"

"I liked it better when you didn't talk. Touch me down there."

I grudgingly put my hand where she requests. Through the narrow strip of cloth I feel the crux of her is hot and damp.

She hisses, "I want you so much it hurts."

"So—"

"So nothing." She's breathing as in preparation for an orgasm. "Blindfold. Do you know the term *sensory deprivation*? I'll concentrate only on what you will do to me when you get back. I won't move. I'll hardly breathe, but I will have dozens of small orgasms. Do you understand?"

I blindfold Ariel.

"Go," she orders as her pleasure mounts. "Get out of here, you son of a bitch."

23

Packing Up Absurd

My first few seconds on the outside feel like the time I got out of the joint. Anger and fear melt before the fire of freedom. I have spent little more than a night in Ariel's basement, but I had been imprisoned as sure as I had been during that long weekend at Rikers.

I carefully examine the quiet street. An old man drags a garbage can nearly as big as he down his driveway. A squirrel darts to the edge of a limb and leaps onto the adjoining tree. It clings tightly to a wispy twig that shakes as if trying to dislodge it. But the squirrel's grip holds and it scampers to a thicker, safer part of the branch.

The universe is unaware of the war between Vinnie Five-Five and Vlad the Impaler.

Times like these make me wish that I were shorter. I'm not freakish, but in a neighborhood of old Jews and Italians, my bulk sticks out. I'm easily spotted, easily dead.

I should have been a pair of ragged claws scuttling across silent seas.

But outside I need only deal with assassins and mass murderers. Inside, Ariel freaks me out. No one thing is a problem. The sex, the sex toys, the premature trust coupled with unusual demands, each one by itself means little. Everything added together, however, makes for too many layers of weirdness. I have no idea what Ariel is capable of. Maybe not homicide but certainly of making me uncomfortable.

Then I call Judith to tell her that I'm coming. But something is wrong. She chokes out, "Howie. Hide," she breathes.

"I need to get some shit. It's important. Judith, what's going on?"

"Come in the back way. You know . . ."

"Through the alley? Sure. Judith. If something happened to the girls . . ."

"No. Make sure no one is following you."

Sure enough, as soon as she hangs up, I see a yellow taxi roll slowly down the street.

Normally, a taxi on a city street does not inspire terror. But in this part of Brooklyn, the ass end, the sphincter, miles from the big money, yellow taxis stay away. There's no point in cruising this out-of-the-way neighborhood. Drivers hate bringing passengers here because they never get a fare for the hour journey back to Manhattan. All this comes to me in an instant, and in the next second I slither up an alley and force open a garage door. Inside, the smell of oil overpowers. I freeze in the darkness as if the circling killers could see through walls.

After a minute, two minutes, my heart pounding over the danger that lurks in that cab, I reenter daylight. In the garage I have found a foot-long piece of pipe. Its weight feels right in my hand but it will serve no purpose when confronted with the bazookas the Russians carry.

Have I just saved my life or have I acted like an idiot? Only if the occupants of the cab gun down someone else would I ever know the answer. Meanwhile, I continue walking as if in a minefield.

It's cool, and muddy clouds float between the earth and the sun. Still, sweat drenches my shirt. Nothing else raises my suspicion and I get home, to Judith's home, in five minutes via the alleys just as I said I would. If anyone is waiting in a car for me in the front they would never see me enter the storm door in the backyard. In the basement, I stop just to get the Glock and the rest of my money hidden in the ceiling. Then I tiptoe up the stairs.

Judith is standing in the living room holding a towel, gaping in fear as if her executioner has arrived. The towel conceals not a weapon but a dish she had been drying. She cries, "Howard!" and rushes forward to wrap her arms, towel, and plate around me.

I'm not an emotional man, but . . . "Judith, Judith. Everything's okay."

"I'm so worried. When I heard that your friend Julius was found—"

"What?"

Judith releases me. "Didn't you hear? They shot him behind the Waldbaum's on Coney Island Avenue and threw his body in the dumpster like a piece of rotten fruit." Her voice catches and she starts to cry.

The few times Julius met Judith he had been a gentleman. Judith would not think him a thug. And what the hell had he been doing at Waldbaum's in the middle of a war? Getting milk?

Then again, what the hell am I doing wandering the streets when I have the perfect hideout? This leads me to think of Ariel and reconsider the "perfect" part of the sentence.

"Sit down, Howie. Can I get you something? Did you eat lunch?"

The hit on Julius shakes me. Vinnie Five-Five will now fight to the death. Julius, the lesser of the two lunkhead sons, had been his heir apparent, his favorite. Vin will have nothing to lose now, and I expect him to go down in a blaze of nihilistic glory. Now if I run, Vinnie will not hesitate to have me whacked for being a deserter, an asshole, and a potential rat.

Judith brings coffee. I am going to lose my life in this idiotic war. I'm as certain of this as I am of the love of Judith.

She adds details. The hit happened at dusk, about the time I met Ariel in the café soon after our own assault on Vlad's whorehouse.

Judith joins me on the sofa. "What did you get yourself into, Howard?"

"Nothingness."

"It's Dad's fault. Because of his stupid gambling."

"It's all right, Judith. Don't think bad of Dad."

Why blame Dad? He didn't gamble me into the mob. He warned me, in fact, that the life was dying. In the mideighties, federal prosecutions destroyed all the family bosses and the organization's structure. So many people flipped that no one trusted anyone. The rackets fragmented and guys freelanced, with all the lack of security that implies. Emerging market competition, mostly by Russian and Chinese, wiped out half the made guys in the city. By the turn of the century, only idiots became wise guys. On top of that, there were by this time so many legal ways of ripping off people, ways that the government protected you, bailed you out if things went kablooey. Yes, I was a fool to choose the Cosa Nostra even if it regrouped after 9/11, when we got lucky with the emergence of a new foreign-policy hysteria.

"Dad always made his nut," I say.

"Sure, he paid the rent, child support," Judith responds. "But he should have made you finish school. You respected him. Loved him. You would have listened."

I shrug.

Distraught, Judith whimpers, "I hate it when you clam up like this. What are you thinking? What are you going to do now?"

I think of the cozy basement where Ariel hangs from the water pipe. "I got things to do, untie loose ends."

"Untie loose ends? What are you talking about? Howard, where have you been staying?"

"Nowhere."

"These people are crazy. You got to run. What are you even doing here?"

"I left some things that I need."

Judith sinks into the couch's cushions and weeps into her hands.

It only occurs to me now, big dope that I am, that something already happened.

Judith's body heaves a few more times but then she lifts her tear-stained face. "Three men. They came yesterday. They barged in and looked everywhere."

"Was one of them my height with a crew cut?"

"I don't remember. I was alone. I was so scared. I have no idea what any of them look like. Crazy. Thank God, John had just taken the girls to Baskin-Robbins."

This news makes me dizzy. I should have been here to protect Judith. I should have been here with my beautiful Glock and blown those motherfuckers away. "Did they touch you?"

Judith scrutinizes me intensely. In a strong voice uninflected with despair she says, "Don't do anything stupid, Howard."

"Did they touch you, Judith?" I leap off the couch. "I need to know."

"No," Judith answers softly. "Sit down, Howard. Please. One of them just waited with me in the kitchen. The others went through the house. I told them that I hadn't seen you in weeks."

Could I believe her? She would not tell me if they hurt her because she would be worried that I'd go looking for the cocksuckers.

"I need to go downstairs and pack more stuff. You need that apartment."

"You need to get out of here." Judith barely contains a scream. "I'll pack. You hide."

"Judith, I'll be fine. It's you who doesn't seem fine. I don't want to leave you in this state."

"Leave!" she let loose, out of her head with terror. "You get to another state!"

Ivan, that fucking bastard. We had been friends. I thought that our love of literature would protect us from the worst aspects of our society. Instead, it just targets one as weak and stupid. How ignorant and mindless we have become.

Judith clamps her mouth shut and breathes through her nose like an angry bull. She is both furious and frantic. I should stay. I should show her my gun and assure her that the next Russian to walk through that door will get his head blown off, no questions asked. That might calm her down. No, I should help her get the apartment ready to rent. War or peace, she needs money. I also must get back to Ariel. If she hasn't completely lost circulation in her limbs, she'd be in such a state of heightened arousal that it would take all night to satisfy her. I'm tired.

Having to deal with both the tragic and the absurd drains the energy from one's limbs. I sit next to Judith so lost in confusion that I can only babble, "Judith, believe me when I tell you everything will be okay."

She searches my face and shudders.

"I just need a couple of minutes to pack. I have a safe place to stay. Don't panic. Could you get me a bag?"

She disappears into the foyer's closet. After a minute she returns with a suitcase the size of Cleveland.

I can't carry this giant thing through the streets, but I could put most of the things I want to keep, which includes the world's masterworks and the last of my erotica collection. I have owned these magazines since I was eleven, but because of the wonderful cornucopia of online smut I haven't looked at them in years. Yet they have sentimental value. Holding these *Screws* and *Penthouses* allows me to enter a bygone age as dead as the Paleolithic. I know these women's private places as well as I know any of my girlfriends'. And if the text accompanying their spreads is to be believed, they are as open with their thoughts and desires as they are with their thighs and buttocks. Today, a boy enters a sexual frontier where images come and go with a click. You can never develop that imagistic porn intimacy that functions as one's first significant sexual relationship.

The brick of weed I squeeze into the inside pocket of my jacket. The gun I put in my waistband. The porn and Dad's favorite books, the few he particularly mentioned to me, I place in the suitcase. Back upstairs, I ask Judith, "Where should I leave this?"

"Put it in the storage closet."

As I drag the overstuffed suitcase to the second floor, memories of all the times I had kissed Judith's girls good night flood my mind. They wouldn't go to sleep unless I came up. Afterward I'd keep Judith company while John was out trying to drum up business. Mostly he was trying to get laid and succeeding in getting drunk. But with me around, he posed no threat to Judith when he got home.

Judith often advised me to have my own family. Instead I started doing more and more work for Vinnie Five-Five, got heavy into selling weed, and Judith stopped telling me that I should have children.

Judith waits at the foot of the stairs.

"I'll come back and pack the rest of my things as soon as I can."

"NO," she shouts. "Not till this is over. I'll put every-thing in boxes, even the books, and ship them to wherever you want." Judith thinks I keep the great literature, as I do the porn, for sentimental reasons. In fact, she'd be far more shocked to learn what I do with the books than what I do with the porn.

I hug her good-bye. "I'll hide, but I'm not going far. Keep alert. Call me if you even suspect that something is not right."

But Judith doesn't give an inch. "You stay where you're safe. Do not go on the street for anything."

"Sure. Remember what Dad used to tell me about curfew?"

"What?"

"If you're not in bed by midnight, come home."

For the first time in our visit, Judith smiles without pain. "I remember. We used to be a funny family."

24

Tighter, Baby, Tighter

The tense, sad visit relaxes me. Though the same danger exists now as before, I worry less. This war, like all wars, will end. A few survive even the most brutal conflagration. With no supporting evidence, I tell myself I will be one of the lucky ones.

I even conjecture that the hit on Julius will slake Vlad's immediate thirst for vengeance. He might not want to risk his men in our neighborhood now. He might even go so far as to offer surrender terms to Vinnie. Leave town and he won't kill the rest of the family.

Vinnie's response will be a measured, *go fuck your mother when her cunt is momentarily free.*

On the walk back to Ariel I'm vigilant but not crazed. No taxis scare the shit out of me. I appreciate the blocks of tidy houses, the porches with bench swings, the stamp-sized lawns with a single rose bush clinging to a home's brick front. I pass a grandmother pushing a carriage and I say hello. Surprised and pleased to be acknowledged, she returns the greeting. I feel like a prisoner on furlough who gets a glimpse of the free world. Bittersweet.

I arrive back at Ariel's place no problem. I check to see if anyone is following before I slip in the side door and walk down the steps.

Ariel hangs right where I left her. At first I think she's unconscious. Her chin rests on her chest and she isn't moving. But as I get closer she lifts her head and whispers, "I knew you'd come back."

"Yeah. How you doing, baby?"

"I need you." She croaks as if she's dying.

"Are you turned on?" I am curious.

"Untie me, baby. I'm begging you."

"You don't have to beg. I'll be happy—"

"Please, you win. Whatever you want."

She wants to beg. It's part of it. So I go with it. If this is what she enjoys, who am I . . .

I unlock the cuffs. She collapses into my arms. Weakly, she orders, "Help me to the bed."

I reach to take off the blindfold.

"Don't touch that, damn it," she snaps, instantly forceful.

I lay her on the bed. She wiggles her freed hands but otherwise doesn't move. Then, with impatience in her voice, she pleads, "Don't hurt me. I'll do anything you want."

"I could use a cup of coffee."

This is not the right answer. Ariel tenses as if I had slapped her. So I demand, "Suck my dick."

She gurgles with pleasure. "I can't see. Put it in my mouth."

Even without the coffee, the prospect of a blow job arouses me. I have half a hard-on by the time my penis bumps against Ariel's mouth. I expect her to swallow it in one gulp. But she keeps her lips tight.

"What the fuck . . ." I'm annoyed. First she builds this elaborate scenario, and now she refuses to go through with it. The bitch is totally bent.

But it takes only another few seconds to realize she wants me to force her. Ah, the line between foolishness and sexual daring is a fine one.

The other women I banged wanted to kiss and cuddle. We'd feel each other up. Maybe a nip of a nipple brings a gasp or a hard thrust a shriek. Back then, when I had less on my mind, Ariel's imagination would have excited me. I would have happily taken it as far as Ariel wanted.

But in the middle of this war, with Judith on the verge of a nervous breakdown, with Vinnie Five-Five no doubt organizing a revenge sortie, I can't fully concentrate on Ariel's elaborate fantasies. I remember one time a big dude called Nicky Thumbs, because he specialized in breaking said digits in those who refused to pay what they owed, came in and said his new *goomah* wanted him to smack her around. Nicky Thumbs, a ruthless gangster, hesitated. He tells us he never smacked any woman except his wife. But this girl likes it rough, so he hits her, but gently, more pushing around than a beating. Now Nicky Thumbs is laughing when he tells us this. She tells him he's a pussy and that her grandmother used to hit her harder than that. So Nicky cold-cocks her and knocks out two teeth. When she comes to, she says, *Nicky, not so hard.* He concluded. *No fucking way to make these bitches happy, no matter what you do.*

That's the only other story I know that approximates my own situation. Nicky Thumbs found himself a different mistress. I, on the other hand, am not in a position to switch chicks. Besides, Ariel interests me. Her chest alone makes her worth a little aggravation. But she's not just tits. She has soft brown hair with a little wave, large brown, blindfolded eyes, and a trussed body. She's educated, interested in art. She saved my life. Or at least she has made the offer.

She also sees me as her sex slave. Who wouldn't jump at the opportunity to have one? Like all decent people, she has urges and fantasies that terrify her. Onto me Ariel has writ her most outré desires, wishes to live out lifelong scenarios. A chance like this may never come again. I admire her for having the guts to grab it.

Maybe because I'm a gangster she believes I would have little objection even to the most depraved situations. She may believe that being a criminal automatically makes me a subversive in all ways. She doesn't know that gangsters have the politics of hillbillies. No profession is more reliant or supportive of the status quo—merciless to criminals, anti-choice, untrammeled access to guns. It takes a lifetime, short though yours may be, to master the system and find its weak spots. If we lived in a society where any degenerate gambler or restaurateur could get a bank loan, it would destroy the shylock business, the most dependable revenue generator in all of Mafiadom. If prostitution and drugs were legal everywhere, how could some poor street kid with dyslexia compete against corporations armed with marketing professionals and tax lawyers?

Like everyone else, gangsters depend on a consumer society where people sacrifice their lives in order to buy junk they don't need. What good would it do to steal truckloads of electronics, clothes, toys, and in the case of my idiotic uncle, canned tuna, if people were satisfied with what they already owned? In fact, people clamor for this junk *because* it's hot. One guy I know, Sal Gecko, purchased designer knockoffs and convinced people they were the real thing simply by telling them he stole them off the back of a truck. Sal is a great earner, very respected.

On the whole, gangsters reinforce the power structures that they battle to the death. We exist because of money. True hoods are workaholics, looking for new angles, new scams, new suckers, twenty-four hours a day, just as any compliant corporate executive does. Even if I were fully Italian I could never be more than a mook, a hanger-on, because of my suspect attitude toward the dollar. As soon as I began to think that other pursuits might bring more happiness I made myself an outcast. Vinnie Five-Five simply can't understand this while the others, especially the late Julius, had viewed me with contempt. It's really what drove us apart.

So by chance, simple luck, Ariel has hit on the one mob associate who is both eager to question societal norms and also willing to explore the master/slave dynamics erotically. It's only because of everything going on that I can put neither my full heart nor my fully engorged penis into the endeavor. For example, at this moment, my distraction causes my dick to wilt in the face of Ariel's closed mouth.

I pinch Ariel's jaw. This forces her mouth open and releases her tongue. Finally she begins licking my shaft. If she hadn't, I would have wrapped things up, put my schlong back into my trousers and told Ariel to fuck herself, whether that turned her on or not. But her tongue moves smoothly back and forth in wet, gentle strokes. It sends shivers through me. Soon I forget the little annoyances and lose myself in the pleasure. I even shove my hardened prick into Ariel's mouth without a word of thanks.

She loves it. She maneuvers my dick against her soft palate and I grant her a few kind words, "Do it, you cunt. Suck, bitch. Suck."

She inhales, creating a wind tunnel that vibrates around my penis. I'm now kneeling over her blinded eyes and she reaches up to fondle my balls. By the time she sticks her index finger between my butt cheeks I'm coming into her mouth. She releases me and my jism squirts all over her, all over the bed, onto the floor and the low ceiling.

When I'm done, she grabs the back of my neck. "Go down."

Her panties are so wet that I have to pry my hand between the cloth and her skin before pulling them off. Then I gently lay my head between her legs and my tongue rakes the walls of her slit. She explodes instantly. And she keeps exploding, five, six times. She stops for a second so I lift up my head to pick a piece of curly hair from my lip. But she pushes me down again and my mouth brushes her vagina once, twice . . . After another few seconds she begins writhing, breathing rhythmically, and then stops. Each successive time the orgasm becomes shorter. Each time, she grabs my head and crunches it between her legs. After a half-dozen repetitions, she kicks me away and finally removes her blindfold.

Her glassy look slowly, very slowly, dissipates, and is replaced by adoration. "Thanks."

"For what?"

"For playing along."

"Forget about it."

She smiles. "Lie down."

I realize that except for my dick hanging out, I'm still fully dressed. So I kick off my shoes and squish close to Ariel on the narrow bed, nearly pushing her up against the wall. She doesn't mind. She places her hand inside my shirt. "So how's your sister?"

"Fine. Terrified."

"Of what?"

"A couple of assholes stopped by the house. Nothing happened, but they killed Julius. Stuffed his corpse in a dumpster."

Now she leans up against me and touches my cheek. "Was this Julius a friend of yours?"

Gangsters don't really have friends. If you're going to get whacked, it's usually those closest to you who do it. They know your habits, your hangouts, your routine. They don't raise your suspicions despite being angels of death. We still hang out, steal, intimidate, kill, and kibbutz together for almost all our waking hours, for without gangs there would be no gangsters. We sometimes forget ourselves and talk about what we think or, more dangerously, what we feel. But the smartest thugs keep their mouths shut. Secrecy, like surprise in battle, is a devastatingly effective tactic. Why give that up?

"I knew Julius since we were baby punks twenty-five years ago."

"Were you still close?"

"Sure. Blood brothers." I recall his behavior in the car on the way to the Russian bordello. By military or mob standards he acted well. I, however, despised him.

Ariel might not be used to people talking ill of the dead. But then she hadn't known Julius.

"What are you going to do?" Ariel keeps her eyes glued on me as I pop off the bed to pace. "Don't you have to get revenge for your friend?"

This stops me. "What?"

"An eye for an eye. Isn't that like the *Mafia code*?"

That's Hammurabi's Code. The Mafia's code is an eye for a toenail. But like everyone, we enjoy taking revenge if it's easy and involves little danger. Vlad's army poses a problem.

Still, Ariel has a point. In turf wars, all sorts of tit-for-tat slaughters occur. Getting whacked is one of the risks of being a wise guy, just as patent expiration is for drug companies like Pfizer, another piece of shit stock I have the misfortune to own. Its labs couldn't find a pill to stop heartburn, never mind discover a compound to prevent heart attacks.

I start my little march again. No. Vinnie Five-Five will not take his son's death with the equanimity that everyone else who knows Julius will.

He'd reconvene his crew and send us out with orders to come back with the heads of our enemies. I want no part of this. For reasons I can't fully explain, murder repulses me. I doubt I can even use my lovely little Glock.

But why? These are the meanest sons of bitches on the planet. Plus I never held straight society in high regard. Its pieties about peaceful coexistence are grotesque hypocrisies when you consider the savagery it perpetrates the world over, mostly against civilians who do no harm. And this isn't just the United States. Every culture commits atrocities with sanctimonious glee. Why, in the defense of my society, my crew, should I prove any less bloodthirsty? I put some arm on people when necessary. Where cops can never be involved, where others would knock the shit out of you if they could, protecting yourself and your interests is a moral imperative.

On the bell curve that runs from conscienceless killer to mindless pacifist, I always believed that I chart in the middle. Yet Vinnie, a decent judge of character, made me the driver and not the shooter. I'm no shooter. I'm not much of a driver either, but I'm no shooter. I must consider the possibility that along with Quakers and residents of the Upper West Side, I fall in with the outliers on the pussy side of the graph.

"I love you," Ariel says, and then adds quickly, "Not forever, but for this second."

Ah, shit. How absurd.

She laughs and pulls me back into bed. "Don't worry. Whenever I have multiple orgasms with a guy, I always fall in love. It doesn't always last." She rubs my face. "You fucked me blue exactly the way I wanted. So what if your emotions are as frozen as your tongue."

I close my eyes. My mind leaves the Vinnie Five-Five situation. Ariel is a decent, brave, honest woman who not only risks her life for me, but took a chance by letting me into her most primal, and potentially embarrassing, desires. In return, I should not be frightened or ashamed to verbalize. I should have no fear of merging the internal with the external.

But I can't. Not yet. Habits, especially ones that provide chameleon-like cover and preserve life, die hard. Now, Ariel's basement vacillates between a cozy sanctuary and a claustrophobic dungeon. All life is a dualism. Some call this symmetry the essence of beauty. Others call it a pain in the ass.

Ariel goes into the bathroom and I hear the water run as she washes off. She comes back shiny and smiling. "Do I scare you?" she jokes. "Not *scare* you the way those guys who killed your friend scare you. I guess . . . guys get most terrified when a woman says she loves them even in jest. They panic when they realize they have no idea what they feel."

"I like you." Should I say something about my dreams? "Or I wouldn't be here—"

"I know you like me. We like each other. We're different, or at least our lifestyles and interests are. But men are all bluster. You'd be surprised at how many guys wouldn't dare to blindfold me, tie me to a pipe, and leave me hanging."

"Pussies."

"Nothing freaks you out. And that's not just because you're a gangster. I knew right away you'd do anything . . ."

Ariel fishes for my take on the situation. She wants to know if I am going to spank her or do whatever else turns her on. She wants to know if I'm going to stick around.

But she pries no further. She kisses me on the cheek as if she were my wife. "Don't say anything. I know you operate more instinctually than I do, without having to formulate words or probably even thoughts. I'm going shopping for my mom. Maybe I'll see you when I get back. Maybe not."

With that she goes up the steps.

25

The Way it Was

In the old days, mobsters would hide out together during war. Sometimes they'd "take to the mattress," that is change houses every night. Or soldiers would make bunkers out of their own homes. War could never cross a man's threshold. Get caught on the street, go shopping for a tomato, and you would be whacked as it is being weighed. But play cards in your living room and you would be as safe as an infant in her mother's arms.

Also, during wartime, business stopped. Your hijackings, your bookmaking, your shylocking, your whorehouses all need to be put on hold until you could leave your bedroom. Outside guns have to be hired, and mercenaries do not come cheap. Every crew had to kick in for them. The added expenses and loss of revenue ate at the *kishkas* of all gangsters. You build an operation based on muscle and shaded dice, and because of the stubbornness, greed, or just plain stupidity of a few old men clinging to power with the tenacity of aging lions, years of hard work, endless scheming, and life-threatening risks atrophy. Every day that you aren't on the street making collections, taking bets, circulating, your business weakens. So wars ended quickly.

When the Sicilians battled each other, they abided by rules that made the Geneva Convention seem a throwback to

Genghis Khan. But today is different. Now the mob is global. The Russians and Chinese, almost as much as the Feds, pose a grave threat to Italian hegemony. These new guys don't mind bringing anarchy into people's homes. Our women and children might be shot in cold blood. The same is true for the length of the conflict. These newcomers fight with a viciousness that even overcomes their lust for a buck. Every battle is Stalingrad. Retreat equals the Long March. Businesses are set aflame, cars booby-trapped, houses bombed, entire gangs wiped out and still they fight. In Queens, every member of the Grinkovsky ring was hunted down in the course of a war that also led to the demise of Fat Fat Chen, the head of a triad that controlled all the soy sauce going in and out of Flushing.

26

The Second Going

Hours pass. Vinnie never calls. Ariel disappears. Maybe I should have just said that I loved her. Why the hell not? We have all the ingredients of a love story. Cute meeting. An idyllic first date complicated by various conflicts. We made mad love. We both need to overcome demons, mature into self-knowledge, before we could logically end up together. True, she gets off on some weird shit. But she accurately characterized my attitude. Why should I care if she enjoys being tortured, hung from a pole? I'd draw the line, sure, at real injury. But it is kind of exciting to know that a woman spends hours arousing herself in this strange way. I had returned to nipples as hard as diamonds, a labia as engorged as a breadfruit.

Now my penis surprises me. Just thinking about Ariel's body makes me want to wank. She's getting to me. She's gone a couple of hours and I want to slide inside her again.

I decide to take a shower because I'm sweaty and my hardened dick orders me not to count on Ariel's return. Maybe she's angry. I can't take any chances. I've learnt not to rely on the kindness of strangers. So I masturbate under the hot stream and feel that I've taken a step in reasserting control over my environment.

The water cascades down my back and I empty my mind of Judith, Ariel, Vinnie Five-Five, Bones, Vlad, Crazy Bo.

Only the moment matters. I enjoy the tingle of the scorching liquid as it reddens my skin. I shut everything out.

I almost don't hear the halting thud of feet descending the stairs.

Quickly, I turn off the water. That heavy gait is not Ariel's. It's either an assassin or Ariel's mother. There's no time to get out of the shower before I hear an old woman's sigh as she reaches the bottom step. Her breaths come heavy as I stop mine. I remember that Ariel said her mom is losing her hearing so I don't think that she heard the shower running.

Mrs. Hirsch bangs open the washing machine lid. The shower is just a few steps from it but with the curtain drawn, Mrs. Hirsch doesn't know I'm here. The water drips down my body and chills me. Mrs. Hirsch is not a fast mover. She grunts and groans. She complains aloud, "My back, my back, oy."

I'd help the aging lady do her wash except she'd have a heart attack if I walked out of the shower, a large naked man offering to transfer her clothes to the dryer.

She starts the machine. It looks like I'm going to get away with this new silliness when my phone rings. Shit, shit, shit. Ariel's mother walks across the basement. She says aloud, "Oh, my God. Ariel forgot her phone."

I have left the phone tangled in the sheets on the bed.

"I don't see it. I don't see it." The old woman sounds desperate, as if hoping the person on the other end of the line can hear.

The phone keeps ringing as if voice mail has never been invented. Finally it stops. I relax.

But then I hear, "Hello? Hello?"

Oh shit.

"Who?" she yells.

"What windows? We don't need any windows."

A beat. "You have the wrong number. This is Ariel's phone."

Another beat. "No. I am *not* playing a game. You're no friend of Ariel, talking like that."

Do I run stark naked from the shower and grab my phone from an already terrified woman? Ah, just when you think the situation can't get any more ridiculous, it gets dangerous.

"I'm hanging up," she yells. "You have the wrong number."

I slide down the wet wall and sit on the shower's filthy floor.

"People are animals," the mother wails. "Never in my life . . . Ariel's going to be so upset. I wonder why she made the bed down here. Poor girl. Exhausted from all this unemployment."

So the old lady takes my phone. Halfway up the stairs, it rings again. Vinnie Five-Five will view me as nothing less than a dangerous traitor. In war, one's paranoia is as important to survival as one's weaponry. Vinnie could easily jump to conclude that I'm in with the Russians because of my friendship with Ivan. By taking a shower I have signed my own death warrant.

My only chance is to get hold of the phone. I dress quickly. The old lady's senses are failing. I should be able to snatch the phone without being detected.

I tiptoe up the narrow staircase and stop at the door of the apartment where Ariel lives with her mother. Nothing stirs. So I go inside. To the left is the living room. To the right is the kitchen where Mrs. Hirsch babbles to herself. All I can hear is *Ariel*. I sneak into the living room. Knickknacks and picture frames cover side tables and walls like dust. From the kitchen I hear a voice whine: *and she's going to blame me. Ariel is just going to put the blame on me.*

The living room has red wall-to-wall carpeting that muffles my footsteps. I remember such shag carpeting from my grandmother's house. I fervently hope that if I ever own a home, I would keep the decor more current. My eyes, meanwhile, rake the room for the phone.

Pots and pans bang in the kitchen. Mrs. Hirsch is making dinner. If she cooks at the same speed that she launders, I'll have a couple of minutes.

I look behind frames, under snow globes, and between the ceramic figures. I find nothing but hideous kitsch. Mrs. Hirsch must have the phone on her. I'll wait until she goes to the bathroom and then duck into the kitchen to look. Just then, the phone rings yet again.

Oh my God, a frightened voice keens. *Ariel, your phone!* The crazy old bird panics. *What am I going to do?*

I don't have a second to think. I just hit the ground and roll under the sofa as Mrs. Hirsch charges into the living room holding the ringing phone as if it were white hot.

She drops onto the sofa and begins to cry. *It's that terrible man. Who did Ariel get involved with now? What kind of animal? Oh, my God.*

For a second I think Mrs. Hirsch is referring to me. But it has to be Vinnie or one of his messengers who has made himself a persona non grata after just a few words to the old lady. Vinnie must be in a murderous rage. And why not? He just lost his favorite child. His business is being squeezed by ruthless competition. And he himself is the primary target of assassination by two vicious criminal gangs. Such things could put the best tempered into a foul mood.

I'm safe enough under the couch but I might not be able to stay here forever. When the phone stops ringing, Mrs. Hirsch takes it and heads back into the kitchen.

I hear her opening and closing the fridge, clanking glass dishes and copper pots. Ariel had mentioned that her mom is a terrible cook. If so, she goes to great effort in putting together her atrocious meals. And she mutters Ariel's name one hundred times.

It cannot be pleasant for Ariel to be living here.

The carpet makes me want to sneeze. I manage not to move, but I do despair. I'll never get the phone. I'll die by one violent hand or another. If only I could live under the sofa, as cozy as a cat hiding from company.

But I can't. I consider pretending to be a burglar to get my phone back. I could use some of the bondage ropes to tie the old lady up, rummage around for the phone, grab a few other things, and leave by the front door and go back down into the basement by the side door.

The more I think, the better this simple plan seems. No one will get hurt. I'm about to make my move when the front door's lock clicks. Ariel is back.

She comes into the living room schlepping two heavy grocery bags and calls, "I'm home, Ma."

"I'm in the kitchen," Mrs. Hirsch yells back. "You forget your phone and this crazy man keeps calling. What's going on, Ariel? Who are your friends these days?"

Ariel stops in the middle of the room. "What are you talking about, Ma?"

"Hey!" I hiss.

Ariel's head snaps toward the couch but she doesn't see me.

"Get that damn phone!"

She puts down the bags. "Where the hell are you?"

Between clenched teeth I say, "Under the couch. Your mother has my fucking phone."

"How did she get . . . Oh shit."

Her mother stalks into the room and Ariel plops down on the cushions above me. "Ariel, your phone keeps ringing. Such a terrible man—"

Mrs. Hirsch hands Ariel the phone. Her new Samsung looks nothing like my old iPhone. But her mother does not notice the difference.

"It's just some noodge I met. He likes pretending he's a gangster. He actually is a lawyer, a friend of Todd's."

"He's a sick man. You should hear the language." Her mother hands over the phone.

"A lot of lawyers like to think they're gangsters. It makes them seem more manly. I got you the string beans. Three dollars a pound."

This stuns the old woman into silence.

Ariel carries the bags into the kitchen and I wait for the mother to follow.

But the price of string beans has knocked Mrs. Hirsch off her feet. She collapses onto a red brocaded armchair and yells to her daughter. "Are you joking? Three dollars?"

"Two ninety-nine," Ariel replies with satisfaction. "Can you believe it?"

"Thieves and murderers! That's all that's left in this world. Slit your throat for a nickel."

Ariel comes back into the living room. "So don't boil them to death. Use the steamer I got you. That way, vegetables retain their crispness and their nutrients."

"With that stupid thing I just get a face full of smoke," Mrs. Hirsch complains.

"For God's sake, Ma. Don't stand over it the way you do."

And Ariel leads her mother out of the living room and into the kitchen. I wait for a second, grab the phone Ariel has left on the couch, and slip back down the basement stairs.

There, I see that Pauli Bones called. I hit his number and he picks up on the first ring.

He starts off by cursing me and my mother with all the earthy gusto of a Chaucer pilgrim. I let him vent before I politely ask, "What the fuck is going down?"

Bones pants in anger. He snarls, "You heard about Julius."

"Yeah."

Nothing more comes over the line for a few seconds. Then Bones informs, "The cops released the body. Be at the funeral home at eight tonight."

Vinnie Five-Five owns DiPietro's Funeral Home. The crew sometimes meets there.

"If you're not there—"

"You think I'm going to screw Vinnie at a time like this?"

"You piece of shit, you better not." Bones, my best friend in the crew, clicks off.

I put on my shoes. Actually, I like Pauli Bones. He knows nothing about nothing except for the rackets. But within this world, he understands how to handle himself. It's no coincidence that he's the only one left alive from the night Scrunchy got it. If I had to put myself in the hands of anyone in the crew, it would be Pauli Bones.

However, I don't care about Vinnie's business. I don't care about scoring. The only thing I want to do is put my feet up in a cheap motel and read—eating nothing but pizza, drinking nothing but scotch. I'm insane. So what? I don't need excuses for not supporting a war as meaningless as the ones in Vietnam and Iraq.

But this is the situation I was born into. Only when I walk these streets does my father's love still engulf me. Judith, still alive, is here. I can't disappear and never see her and the girls again. And now Ariel. If I weren't in such a situation I could pursue Ariel at my own pace, see how it goes playing at what she wants, get hammered and high and maybe even have a conversation. Ariel went to college, grad school. Perhaps she learned something of interest.

Yet I will fight a war that will needlessly kill many, including me. If life itself weren't such a pointless struggle against unconsciousness, this would be a great tragedy.

The truth is—I don't want to be murdered.

I sit on the bed for a long time before Ariel appears in front of me, showered and changed into a short nightgown whose embroidered hem reaches her midthigh.

She approaches with a smile on her face, a bottle of Stoli in her right hand and a thick leather belt in her left. She puts the bottle on the floor and slaps the belt against her palm, "Ready?"

"What are you going to do with that?" I ask, but feel none of my usual intellectual curiosity, my burning desire to know things.

"We can do a lot of things with this." Ariel sticks out her bottom and whacks it. "It's versatile. I can whip you or you can whip me."

"You're completely loco." I start to get interested. "I'm not going to hurt you."

Ariel sits on my lap and grinds her ass into my crotch. She reaches down for the bottle and takes a swig and hands it to me.

"I'll show you how to use it so you get beyond crazy horny," she says. "You'll thank me for the rest of your life."

Ariel must have thought of me as a sexual primitive, only aware of the most brutal missionary positions. Maybe she grants me a few rape fantasies, but overall, she judges me a caveman, without any idea of the finer points of bondage and discipline.

"You going to hit me, or am I going to hit you?"

"First off," Ariel jumps off me, "we're not going to hit. We're going to strap each other. A set amount of swats in ritualistic positions. I would let you strap me first, but I have to show you how it's done."

"I think I can figure it out." I grab at the belt.

Ariel snatches it away. "No! You'll hurt me. I want this to be fun."

She sees my anger rising.

"Really fun," her voice becomes seductive again. "You won't be sorry. I promise."

She's in the tank already. Most S&M clubs serve no alcohol at all. Only the most sober should wield whips against their loved ones.

I would have been interested in playing if I hadn't so much on my mind.

Ariel sits back down on me. "Are you okay? You know, I have a feeling you're holding a lot back from me. Today, you're even less verbal than usual."

I nod.

"Okay." She loses a little of her girlish enthusiasm. "Was it because of that phone call?"

"I got to do something."

"What?"

"A viewing. Julius. That asshole I was telling you about. The one in the dumpster."

"Vinnie Five-Five's son."

"Yeah. Eight o'clock tonight. Things are going to go down. I might not be back."

Ariel pales. The strap falls from her hand and she leans against me. Her voice shakes, "You can stay here." She picks up the strap and looks at it with longing. But then she pulls out the sex-toy box from under the bed and drops it in. "I don't have to play these games with you, Howard. You think I do this with every guy?"

I have no idea what she does with other guys.

"I get satisfaction a lot of ways. But I trust you more than anyone I ever met. Well, first of all, you're, like, the best looking. Amazing. Another thing. I know you're smart. I can tell that from your eyes, Windows. You can't hide intelligence like you can knowledge."

I snort.

"No, no. Don't be like that. You think I just like you for your body and your brutishness. You might think I exploited . . . took advantage of your situation." Ariel takes a swig of the vodka. "Let me tell you, all that education, all that arcane knowledge, does not make people more open to experience. And not only to kinky sex, but to love itself. Only Todd played a little bit. But I never trusted Todd like I trust you."

"Todd's the lawyer?"

"Yeah. You have a good memory." Ariel tries not to get emotional. "I don't say I understand our connection. You might not be able to express your feelings even to yourself, but you don't have to. You'll never have to say you love me, you'll never have to say—"

"If I get clipped," I interrupt, "it won't be because I don't like you."

"Stop it, Howard. What I'm trying to say is that you're truer than anyone I ever dated. Your emotions, like your conversation, are not tricky, always trying to stay one step ahead.

And you know yourself, even if you're terrified to let other people know you."

"I gotta go to this thing. I have no choice."

"Okay, then come back. There's no reason you can't come back."

"I might be dead."

"You won't be dead. You won't be dead."

Is she a child, thinking that saying it makes it so? Then she gives way to tears. Shit. I'm pleased that a couple of women in the neighborhood would prefer me alive. I just can't make any guarantees.

Ariel has finally run out of words. She buries her face in my chest. I try to think of some literary equivalent to our situation. A million stories of star-crossed lovers and doomed affairs exist. Men hidden by sympathetic women is a subgenre by itself. Women with movie-star beauty and saintlike self-sacrifice dominate World War II romantic fantasy. Here, German barbarity or Japanese cruelty proves to be the main obstacle to marital bliss. None of the stories take place in Sheepshead Bay among *goomba*s and gangsters, where no line between good guys and bad guys exists. And S&M plays almost no role in any of them.

So I must make my own way here. It shouldn't be impossible. I feel confident I can cobble something together from a variety of genres. But before I do anything, I must deal with Ariel, who is kissing me all over my face.

She makes the most of her thin lips. They're silky and Ariel pushes her tongue here and there so my penis hardens on cue. I won't be able to stop now until some part of her swallows some part of me. For someone on the brink I'm pretty horny. Or maybe my impending doom excites my libido. Sex and death give everyone's gonads a *kvetch*.

We roll on the bed now like ordinary lovers. Her breasts fall out of her nightie and flatten onto my chest like chubby babies. She hikes up my shirt and licks my nipples until I squirm away.

"Wait a second." She pulls her magic barrel from under the bed and takes out a skinny, ridge-tipped black stick, about a foot in length, along with a fat jar of Vaseline.

"Nothing complicated. Nothing that will hurt." She's rubbing petroleum jelly on the stick, humming. *Nothing unusual. Just an anal dildo.* She pulls down her panties and lies with a pillow under her stomach. Her buttocks spread and she reveals her whole works without the least self-consciousness. "Have you done this before?" she asks.

"No." I gulp the vodka and place the bottle out of harm's way. This could get messy.

"The key is not to rush. Never be in a hurry." Ariel instructs while pulling her cheeks apart. "I'll tell you when to stop."

I hesitate. She pushes herself up onto her knees. The bottom is luscious and downy pubic hair surrounds her vagina like a cloud. I gently screw the dildo into her waiting rectum. Ariel moans. "A little more. Slow. Remember. Slow." She arches upward and nearly screams.

"Are you—"

"Fine," she screeches. "Turn it on. Turn it on."

"I am fucking turned on."

"Not you, darling." She's now a schoolmarm encouraging a particularly idiotic child. "Turn on the probe. The switch at the bottom. There are twelve settings. Number six is good, better than average."

Okay. I flick up the dial and the wand starts to vibrate.

I hold onto the quivering stick as if it's a thermometer and I am worried about getting a poor reading.

"Let go. Let it go. It will stay."

So I let go. Ariel breathes *ah, ha, oh, oh, yes.* She turns onto her side and parts her legs. I gaze on the glistening complexity of her genitals. "Come on."

I have no choice. I quickly put on the condom. She raises herself a bit so I can squeeze in. It's tight, but, oh, good.

"Yes, yes. Oh, you're big. You'll be okay. Just do what I tell you," she moans in a stream-of-consciousness patter indicating she has created a world in which I am a hulking slave forced into doing my mistress's bidding. I thrust inside Ariel with a savagery that stops her babbling.

Though Ariel convulses with bliss, the dildo sticking out of her ass does little for me. For one thing, I have to worry about shaking it out. Also I never knew a woman who demanded erotic satisfaction with such specificity. I go along because an attractive woman's exposed private parts make me hard. But only when her vagina muscles tighten like a vice do I shudder with any sort of enchantment.

That twitch begins Ariel's long orgasmic spasm and she exhales with the ecstasy of someone being strangled by delight. I come late, which causes her to explode one final time. When she's finished, she falls onto her hip. But she's right. The dildo stays inside her. Ariel removes it slowly and throws it on the floor by the bed. She then turns over, puts her arms around my neck and asks, "Don't I know you from somewhere?"

I lay her back on the pillow and play with her heavy breasts.

"Are you new to the neighborhood?"

"Never left it. Never want to. That's my problem."

"You know, I must have held you prisoner around Easter four or five years ago."

"What time is it?"

"What's the difference? We just had something here. You can't tell me that what just happened was nothing."

"No. It was something. I need to know the time."

Ariel sits up and stares at me. "Why? Stay here. The Russians will get to this Godfather character and that will be it for the Mafia in Sheepshead Bay. You'll be able to start a new life, free of gangster obligations."

I laugh at the idea of Vinnie Five-Five as a Godfather. He's a down-the-totem-pole, on-the-shelf captain. He's a bit slow-witted, lacks the self-assurance of the best mobsters. He's a killer, but people are always on guard against him. A big-time operator knows how to put people at ease before he slips in the knife.

Still. Ariel is onto something. Get rid of Vinnie and the war essentially ends. Maybe, in his grief for Julius, he'll let his guard down, slip. Maybe he'll be the next to get a family discount at DiPietro's Funeral Home.

I say, "Vinnie will kill me if I'm not there." The boss calls, you answer. That's the deal. We have no more right to free will or a conscience than soldiers in any army.

Luckily, Ariel finally realizes that I can't fulfill her fantasies twenty-four hours a day. She sidles into her panties. "It's almost eight o'clock."

So I get ready to say good-bye to my old friend Julius. He had turned into a Guido who threw his weight around, who beat on people for practice, who wrapped himself in a mantle of self-righteousness not seen outside the most incompetent fools of the second Bush Administration. But I knew him as a kid. Together we cut school to play ball and get high. At one time we talked about moving to Los Angeles to get in to the movies. These childish dreams ended when Vinnie's sentiment to pass on his power engulfed Julius. We were taught how to keep book and make collections. He connected us to dope wholesalers and showed us how to run card games. The transformation from an intelligent, open child into a mean, stupid adult can only be accomplished by a good education. Anyway, he had been my friend. Even if Vinnie didn't order my presence I would take a last look at Julius before the ground covers him forever.

Ariel watches me dress. I pull out my Glock from under the end of the mattress.

Ariel's eyes widen. "Was that there the whole time we were making love?"

"Yeah."

"Are you crazy?" she shouts. "On the bed while we're rolling around. You could have blown our heads off."

"No clip in it."

Ariel pants in anger and demands, "Let me hold it for a second."

That's what happens in Brooklyn to middle-class girls. They really think guns are not central to the American experience but only for nutcases and lunatics. Thus, guns become the be-all and end-all of erotic objects.

I give her my piece.

It rests in her open palm. "I don't know how you can bring this instrument of death into my basement."

She turns the gun over and holds it by the barrel, and she slips her finger onto the trigger. Her arm lifts and points at the opposite wall.

"That's enough." I, slowly, take the gun from her and stick it in my waistband.

"Wouldn't it be better if you had one of those shoulder holsters?"

"The cops will see the bulge." I put on my leather jacket.

I don't like carrying, but Bones said to come heavy. Vinnie is so angry that he wants everyone armed to the teeth and ready to kill at every step.

Ariel seems depressed. I have ruined her master/slave idyll by having to take off like this.

She orders, "Kiss me at least." The torture devices not withstanding, she's as sentimental as any of us. And this will hurt her more surely than any rope or gag. We smooch for a bit.

"Text me. Because I think I will go crazy if I don't know."

"If something happens, you'll hear."

"Just say 'hi.' That's all. That will be our *mercy* word."

" 'Hi.' All right."

"You could say more if . . ."

"I'll say 'hi.' That's the perfect message."

27

Hearts of Darkness

This time I pay less attention while on the street. The excess of caution had just made me more anxious.

The breeze coming off Sheepshead Bay brings a whiff of the sea with it, and for a minute I imagine myself in a tranquil New England village. Only the lack of charm and all distinction in the houses grounds me in reality. Still, it pleases me that I again feel slightly relaxed walking these streets, my streets.

The funeral home—in an anonymous one-story building on Coney Island Avenue near Avenue X—conveniently serves as the antechamber to hell. The funeral director, a man named Florian, is a dignified degenerate who had lost his business to Vinnie during the 2000 Subway Series, when the Yankees pounded the Mets. (He bet with his heart rather than his head.)

Vinnie Five-Five often holds meetings in an office grimy with ancient coal dust, a legacy of the building's first furnace. Sometimes a ceremony progresses upstairs. Then I'd hear the funeral in my brain, the mourners treading to and fro. I had always hoped that one day sense would break through. Not for death, which is understandable, but for life, which isn't.

Tonight, Julius will take his turn in the main room.

Coney Island Avenue, a treeless desert dotted with car repair shops and bathroom fixture outlets, stretches like a cement trail from the Atlantic to the Hudson. But it's so ugly that few people, even in Brooklyn, walk it.

When I reach Avenue X, my stomach tightens. Would Vinnie Five-Five now throw what little caution he has into the wind? Would he demand his tribute in severed heads? His only limit: don't get caught. His only concern: being implicated in the massacre.

Stupidly, I'm deep in thought. I do not hear the car creeping behind me like a stalking cheetah. Two pairs of iron arms grab me from behind. One is around my neck and one is around my legs. My head crashes against the car's frame, not once but twice. Black spots come and go before my eyes. I pass out for a second, but I hear a door slam and taste the barrel of a high-caliber gun, maybe a .357, in my mouth. "No sound, motherfucker." These all-American words are grumbled in a proud Russian accent. Then a man cackles.

The gun's tangy metallic taste reminds me of flavored coffee, hazelnut, from Chock full o' Nuts. The monster removes the gun from my mouth and crashes his elbow into my head. I tumble off the seat and onto the floor. The guy starts stomping on my back with his steel-toed boots. I just grunt with pain, though I don't think he's doing any real damage, yet.

Then I start quaking in terror.

The youngest gangsters are taught never to get in a car with people, friend or foe, who may have the least reason to kill you. You have more of a chance of surviving by taking off and risking a shot in the back. Most gangsters are terrible shots. Also, many will hesitate blasting in the street because of the possibility of attracting unwanted attention. Gunning down bystanders can bring scrutiny to other aspects of a gangster's affairs. The original expression—*forgetaboutit*—was coined for the chances of survival when being bundled into a car.

So I am in trouble. I take courage from one insignificant fact. I am not dead yet.

I see the hoodlum in the backseat, the giggler, a little, narrow-shouldered guy with an absurdly stretched-out chin. I'm usually much more scared of these bantamweights, as they constantly need to prove how tough they are. When he notices my looking at him, he exposes his yellowed, crooked teeth in a nasty grin. He then whacks me across the head with his handgun.

The other guy in the backseat, a square-jawed goon with dead blue eyes, glances at me as if I'm dog shit rubbed onto the floor of the car. He puts his foot on my chest while the giggler pulls my hands behind my back and binds me with duct tape. He winds it around my wrists three or four times before he rips the roll with his teeth.

I can no longer hide my discouragement.

You reach a point in these proceedings where one transitions from fighting for your life with the blind fury of a US marine to an acceptance of fate with the equanimity of a Buddhist lama.

I can't decide which state I'm in, but it doesn't matter. The car stops and the driver, the kindest of the group, warns, "We kill you if you give trouble going from car to club."

"You will kill me anyway," I answer back idiotically.

The driver speaks in the same reasonable tone. "I wish to kill you. It will be good to make you dead. But the boss say not kill you."

Ah, if he were only telling the truth, what a sweet fairy tale. Why would the Russians need me alive? To send a message? They could just as easily send one by e-mail or by placing my body in a dumpster as they did with Julius.

The car stops in front of The National. The backseat men force me to walk between them. If any of the million people rushing down Brighton Beach Avenue see me, or see my taped hands, no one dares glance twice. In fact, I catch one younger woman in a wide-eyed moment before she quickens her pace, fleeing from me as she would from death. Then I'm in the foyer of the darkened restaurant/club. To the right is the coat-check and to the left the stairs to the cellar.

In better days, during the détente negotiated by Vinnie's brother and Vlad's predecessor, my friend Ivan had shown me around. On weekends, the place rocks with drunken Slavs and gawking tourists eating seven-course meals accompanied by liters of vodka. There's a floor show of Romanian strippers. Frenzied people gyrate to seventies disco and endless variations of the *Hava Nagila*. During the week, however, only quiet couples and hefty businessmen dine on the *pelmeni* and *shashlick*. There are no strippers.

The basement of The National has achieved a measure of fame equal to the old Gemini Lounge in Flatlands, when Roy DeMeo and his crew murdered and cut up dozens of marks. One cop described DeMeo's merry butchers as the largest collection of serial killers ever assembled in one place. They disposed of the pieces of human at a dump on Fountain Avenue. Here, where his thugs drag me, Vlad has a similarly practical setup, with direct access to the sewers that wash body parts to a filtration plant and then deep into the ocean.

The basement is a dark maze lit only by tiny exposed bulbs. It smells of dank and rat shit. We pass half a dozen closed wooden doors until we reach one at the end of a corridor where my driver knocks. A voice growls from the other side and I'm pushed into a room. Vlad, a giant whose forearms are as big as a thigh, sits at the head of a table and is flanked by two lieutenants, one of whom I recognize as Dmitri, a mug whose hammer-and-sickle facial tattoo alludes to his menacing, if outdated, *weltanschauung*. All three of the seated Russians peer at me with the same disgusted look, as if I have some sickening deformity. This sort of contempt is especially disconcerting when harbored by people who will debone you as they sample the restaurant's excellent tiramisu.

Dmitri finally spits out something in Russian and Vlad laughs. I think the comment has to do with my knees banging against each other.

After his grunted laugh, Vlad stands up. This, as Vlad is aware, is a frightening sight. Thick and broad as a bear, he's also taller than me by a good four inches. Though as pale as a vampire with eyes as cold, blue, and empty as a winter sky, he has the chin and bone structure of a movie star and appears carved from granite. He's the only one in his gang not covered in tattoos, I notice, just as he punches me in the face and knocks me off my feet. His fist has the consistency of a cement block. Blood pours from my nostrils and my left eye swells up so thoroughly that I lose vision.

I'm yanked off the floor. My head wobbles in all directions. The initial searing pain dissipates and a secondary, pulsing ache takes hold. I'm not completely conscious until someone pours a pitcher of water over my head.

This fixes things a little. With water dripping down from my hair, I can refocus on my torturers. Shit, doesn't anyone use his basement for a rec room anymore? Is the administering of pain both the profession and hobby of all Americans—native born and immigrant?

"Listen to me, asshole," Vlad says in clear English. "You tell your boss. One word, even you can remember. I know you are one of the more stupid people who work for Vinnie."

I make no objection. I certainly feel like the stupidest.

"*Finished.* Can you remember that, you fucking idiot?"

I nod.

The thug who has brought me hits me on the other side of my face, without quite the same propulsive force of Vlad, but enough to stagger me and swell my other eye closed.

Vlad says, "Say word."

When my brain settles back into its case, I repeat, "Finish."

My kidnapper punches the side of my head and I go down on one knee. The black spots reappear and gravity forces my head down. I barely succeed in holding onto consciousness. The reason for this last punch escapes me.

"Not *finish. Finished.* You fuck, can't you speak the English. Past tense."

Ah. Ideas come easy, but the rigid strictures of grammar always give me trouble. I get to my feet and mumble, "Finished."

"We get to anybody. Next is his other son. Then him. We give Vinnie chance. We take over his houses, his corners, his gambling, his protection. He goes away. Tell him. Florida with other failures. You, motherfucker, go to hell. You like hell. Not so humid like Florida."

He turns to his boys who break out in laughter.

"You sell one more gram of marijuana here, we cut your balls off then kill you."

"Florida," I repeat before they can knock me senseless again. "Hell."

"We don't want troublemakers in our neighborhood."

With that, someone grabs my collar and pulls me out of the room. My feet churn to keep up. When we get to the steps the guy slows and it begins to sink in that I'm going to leave this place of execution alive.

I may be the first one ever.

Vlad doesn't want a war, even one that he'd win. Why waste the blood and treasure? So he gives Vinnie a chance to surrender, a situation that in gang fights is almost unheard of once hostilities begin.

The car is in the same spot, double-parked in front of the restaurant. I'm thrown onto the seat as if I were a sack of potatoes.

I've had better nights.

28

Maternal Love

Soon enough I'm tossed onto a curb. I hit my elbow on the cement and the pain radiates in all directions so that I don't even know what hurts.

After a minute or an hour I'm lifted, none too gently, and brought into the funeral home.

Someone cuts the tape and frees my hands.

I'm in a back room, away from the visitors and the casket. Through dim eyes, I see Pauli Bones trying to get me to hold an ice pack.

"Thanks," I say.

Pauli backs away and I switch the ice from the left side of my face to the right.

My eyes focus. I take in Frankie Hog, IRA, Gus, Bones, Moron, and the Jew.

Vinnie Five-Five then walks into the room. Wearing a black suit with pinstripes, his slickly shaved face shows no trace of grief for his son. "What happened to you?" he asks in the violent tone he adopts for all occasions.

"Vlad. Met him in the basement of The National."

Vinnie barks, "And you're still alive? What did you give him?"

"Nothing. Vinnie, what could I give him. What do I have?" Even in my addled state, I need to make this clear.

"You're lucky you're nobody. What did the cocksucker say?"

Vinnie is not going to like this. "That he doesn't want war."

"Fuck him. And fuck you."

Vinnie's tone reminds me that he has killed messengers before, particularly ones like me. Still, he waits for me to finish, so I add, "He says he can hit us at will. He wants us out of here. He'll give us some time."

Vinnie stalks out of the room.

His crew sits around. In one corner Frankie Hog's ass is taking up nearly an entire bench. IRA leans against Vinnie's desk. Bones and Moron sit in folding chairs. We are waiting around like an audience in a theater or soldiers in a trench for the show to begin.

IRA can bottle up his psychopathic energy no more. He leaps off the desk and points at me. "You're the luckiest piece of shit who ever lived. You saw the setup at The National." He leans down. "Listen, you prick, can we get to him?"

I lean back and grit my teeth. "Get out of my face, asshole." I want so much to go to bed. Ariel's cozy dungeon comes to mind. There I could be beaten by a loving, beautiful woman who only has pleasure on her mind.

"What's the security like?"

I laugh but immediately regret this. "You're going to hit Vlad at The National?"

"Why not?" IRA demands. "We hit him or he hits us. We'd have surprise on our side, that's for fucking sure."

"To find his office you have to go through a maze in this cellar."

"How many people are down there?"

I don't feel like discussing this. "I don't know."

IRA paces slowly toward me, yanks up my chin with his fist. "How many?"

I bring my foot up into his groin but I'm too slow. His fist cracks against my knee. Oh shit. I'm left breathless again.

The others are looking on with bored expressions, as if this desire for a suicide mission has nothing to do with them.

"How many?"

Every inch of me throbs. "Two lieutenants were sitting with him. Two other punks in the room. But there are a lot of rooms. There could be an army behind all those closed doors."

"How many in front? Before you get to the stairs?"

"I didn't see anybody." My lucidity shocks. I can hold a conversation as if not concussed. "But I don't know for sure. Too much blood dripping down my face—"

"Douche bag," IRA interrupts. "You got down to Vlad's place and you don't look for a way back in. No wonder Vlad let you go. Why not let an idiot go?"

Here I had been thinking that I acquitted myself rather well under trying conditions. I never cried or begged for my life. I didn't give out any information of value. Yet IRA screams that everyone, friend and foe, knows I'm a fuckup.

If true, my clownish reputation has saved my life.

Vinnie Five-Five walks back into the room. IRA's voice takes on a wheedling tone. "Vinnie, we can hit Vlad right in his fucking National."

"Get your ass off my desk."

IRA, eager to murder in nearly any encounter, obeys. "Sorry. It's just, I have an idea."

"Yeah? What?" Vinnie sounds as if he can't despise IRA more deeply than he already does, yet he wants to hear this plan.

"Vlad thinks no one can hit him in his crib. So we charge in, take down whoever's in the front, run down the steps, blazing. Blow everything away—doors, people."

Vinnie pulls out a cigar as if celebrating a victory. But he says sourly, "You're full of brilliant schemes. But somehow nothing except shit comes out of them."

Vinnie blames IRA for the failed attacks on Vlad's whorehouse. Unfortunately, IRA is his chief strategist, so Vinnie must be feeling isolated, surrounded by enemies and dolts.

"This is for Julius," IRA intones somberly.

Yes, I conclude again, IRA is a category-five madman. No one would risk his life for Julius when he was alive, certainly not IRA, insanely jealous of Gus and Julius. IRA's own father, a mean drunk, smacked the living crap out of him without connecting him to anyone important. Vinnie Five-Five is a captain who takes care of business and put his children in positions of power, at least until they get whacked. He is IRA's ideal dad.

Maybe IRA believes that there is now an opening in the Five-Five family for someone over six feet tall. The poor, love-starved killer would do anything to win Vinnie's affection.

Vinnie, with surprising sanity, dismisses IRA's idea. "It sounds like suicide."

"No." IRA inches closer to Vinnie. "I got a secret weapon. A great idea."

Vinnie sinks into his chair and exhibits a moment of total exhaustion. His face turns grey as a cafeteria hamburger and he closes his eyes as if he wishes they never have to open again. But he does open them and stares at IRA. "Stop talking in fucking riddles."

"Night vision goggles. We get into the basement, blow out the lights. But we can see and they can't. Even if they know the terrain better, we'll still have the advantage."

Vinnie buttons his suit jacket. Then he unbuttons it. "Upstairs, all of youze. Show some fucking respect to my son."

Even through swollen eyes I see Vinnie's jutting chest fall in on itself and his shoulders slump as his crew leaves the room. I and Frankie Hog, who has trouble raising his bulk out of a seated position, are the last.

As soon as I get to the main room, I go over to the casket and examine the waxy remains. Julius had a type of dark handsomeness. Now an unnaturally rosy tint feminizes the heavy masculine features. Ghoulish. I back away, almost into the lap of Julius's mother, Rose, Mrs. Five-Five. A tense woman in a black dress and heavy bags under her eyes, she sits on the bench closest to the casket.

"I'm sorry about Julius. He was . . . great."

She wipes her nose with a tattered white tissue. "What happened to your face?"

"You know. An accident."

Tears leak down the channels created by wrinkles and irrigate her pallid cheeks. But she maintains a stony expression. "A lot of accidents around here."

I say nothing.

Rose Five-Five grabs my arm and pulls me down onto the bench. The tears end up at the tip of her nose and drip off. "Howie, how much more? Am I going to see my whole family dead? Is everyone I know going to be murdered?" She loses the Rushmore cragginess and her face crumples into the balled, ineffectual tissue she holds.

Her body shakes as she speaks. "My life ended up in the dumpster with Julius. I have nothing left." All the tough sons of bitches sitting on the benches stop their low conversation. Mrs. Five-Five might or might not know that the floor is hers. "Julius never wanted to hurt anybody. He did business, but he told me, *Ma, I never harm nobody if nobody harms me.*"

"He was a good man," I lie.

"He was a boy! He lived at home."

True, as far as it goes. But he was, like his brother, Gus, in his thirties and a killer.

She hiccups now with grief. "I should have stopped it, Howie. I gave the boys my soul, but I didn't protect them." She talks so loudly that everyone hears.

Someone tells Vinnie, who comes upstairs.

Without him having to ask, I get off the bench. Before I walk away I hear Vinnie saying, "Rose, please. We can't blame Julius's work. His goals . . . He took on responsibilities."

From a couple of benches back, I see that Rose neither touches nor looks at Vinnie. And he doesn't dare touch her. They've been married a long time. She hates him.

Besides our crew, there are a dozen soldiers and associates from the family. This death, it seems, has taken Vinnie

Five-Five off the shelf, at least momentarily. But Rose's bitterness would get back to the bosses. Maybe they'd worry that the wife would turn on the husband in revenge for getting their child into the life. This could hardly help Vinnie get the backup he needs to hold on to his territory.

Rose calms down. I've known her, Mrs. Spoleto, my whole life. She always struck me as background, silent and indispensable. A mother. When very young she loomed large. Afterward, we ignored everything but her veal Parmesan.

Vinnie waves to IRA and the others to come back into his office. I go too, but Rose calls me back.

She grabs my hand. In a tone low with urgency she tells me, "I didn't see . . . this is not forty years ago . . . the life today . . . the Pistones didn't let their boys near the business. Michael Pistone is a podiatrist. Michael. Could you imagine what Julius could have been?"

I knew Michael Pistone. As a teenager he gangbanged, a punk like any of us. But after he beat a heroin rap he got his GED. From there it was only a small step to podiatry. In my imagination, even in a topsy-turvy alternate universe, Julius could never have reached the heights of a foot doctor. I think of him maybe as an EMT, someone who enjoyed using his vehicle to scare pedestrians.

I lean over and whisper to the grieving woman, "Julius could have been a surgeon."

This snaps Rose into a dreamy reverie. "A surgeon. Yes. A heart man. That's what he told me when his grandpa died of a myocardial infarction."

I agree, though I have only mentioned surgeon because Julius liked to cut people. I remember him telling me that a man with a knife can close twenty feet and slit a man's throat in 1.4 seconds. Being good with a blade, Julius had contended, made you far deadlier than someone with a crappy handgun.

"I gave my life for Julius and Gus." Rose Five-Five speaks in a monotone drained of all anger, all energy. "Vinnie took it all away. I fought him, but not hard enough. Gus is next."

"Nothing will happen to Gus," I assure Rose. "Vinnie will make sure of that."

"How? By starting a war? That's some funny way to keep your son safe." Her grip tightens on my hand. "You think we will turn back the clock by killing a few Russians? Howie, your mother was my friend. Everyone with Vinnie is going to end up in the garbage. He's going to take his people with him. That means you too. I'm talking now for your mother's sake. Get out. In one piece." She speaks with the same nihilistic fury that now animates Vinnie Five-Five. Both react to their son's murder as if they have nothing more to lose.

Too bad neither could do anything constructive, like leaving this killer neighborhood. I don't even see Rose Five-Five leaving Vinnie, though she wishes him dead.

Still, Mrs. Five-Five flabbergasts me. I have always known Rose as the quartermaster for Vinnie Five-Five's army. She did the food, the cleaning, the laundry. Neither Gus nor Julius mentioned her much. When we ran wild as teenagers, we turned to Vinnie to bail us out. That Rose saw her whole life in her kids, that she battled her husband for control of their destiny, shocks me just as much as Rose's warning to get out, to betray Vinnie during this war.

But maybe Rose's reaction should not have surprised me. In grade school, both Gus and Julius were good students, far better than I. They did homework I never dreamed of touching. I saw their mother hover, urge them to study, to get control of their tempers. Rose fought to keep her kids out of the business with her only weapons, love and nagging. By erasing herself for them she hoped to win them to a safer, saner life. All this comes to me suddenly and I grieve for Rose. She lost to powers far stronger than maternal love.

What happened? High school. Vinnie sometimes used his twins, who had morphed into wide-shouldered, contemptuous kids, as bagmen. He never objected if I tagged along. He tipped well. Then he hooked us up. Soon we went to school solely to sell drugs to the other kids.

Rose's total defeat occurred when her sons started meeting girls who knew Vinnie Five-Five's position in the community. Suddenly, they were not short, lunkheaded punks. Once, a girl named Brenda needed a favor. This guy was hassling her as she walked home from school. He waited on his mother's porch on Ocean Avenue and Z, and followed her all the way to Avenue T, feeling her up no matter what she said. She asked the boys, as a team, to talk to him.

I, a tall, strong kid, the perfect build to debate with this man, went with them.

That Monday afternoon, we trailed thirty feet behind Brenda. I recognized the guy. He used to be part of a gang called the Stompers. He was badass, but two of his crew went down for manslaughter, while two others went down by getting manslaughtered. This cat, when not hassling high school girls, spent his time lifting weights and taking steroids. He cobbled together a living by stealing cars, moving a little junk, and keeping on the lookout for the odd score. But he was with no one now—no gang, no girl.

When Brenda passed his house, he strode down the steps. "Hello, beautiful."

"I'm in a rush, Ray."

"Come on. You have a minute for Ray." He put his arm around her shoulder.

He was running his hand through her hair when Julius crushed him with a metal garbage can lid. The rest took about a minute. We talked good. A punch in the face meant a broken nose, a couple of kicks translated into a cracked rib. And something that was said early on, maybe by a few links of a chain, led Ray to conclude with a concussion. Overall, we explained that a sack of shit pasted to the sidewalk should leave a girl alone when she requests this.

Brenda had not stuck around until the end of the conversation, but later, giddy and on fire, she thanked both Gus and Julius by cleaning their pipes. Her gratitude extended even to me. I was beginning to discover that the initial stages of relationships with women would not be a problem for me, whether I was in the life or not. For Julius and Gus, this was less the case. Lovely Brenda, in fact, was their first. But as soon as they realized that girls would do anything if they beat someone up, Rose lost. Cash and pussy combo knocks out maternal love every time.

Rose only managed to save her daughter, Tanya, by getting her to go to rehab in California and by warning her never to come back.

Mrs. Five-Five, meanwhile, holds both my hands and stares into my messed-up face. "I liked your mother. Did I ever tell you that?"

"No."

"She wanted for you what I wanted for my kids. But your father . . ."

"He was addicted to the action. But he never pushed me into the life."

"He was a good accountant."

"With someone like Vinnie, honesty pays."

Pauli Bones is standing over us. "Mrs. Spoleto," he begins. "I'm so sorry about what happened to Julius. He was my best friend. I loved him like a brother."

Rose nods. While hardly true, Pauli delivers this little speech with impressive earnestness.

Rose finally takes her flaming eyes off me. "For your mother. Find a way out of this."

I stand with some pain. My lungs hurt and my head aches worse than ever. Being a gangster is as painful and dangerous as being a professional football player. And our pension plan consists of dying young.

IRA demands, "What was the old lady telling you?"

"Nothing. That she wasted her life."

"Bitch. Gives Vinnie more trouble than the Russians and Chinese put together. Come on. Let's see Vinnie."

The back room is now crowded with soldiers and associates who have come to Julius's viewing. All the chairs are taken and I lean against the wall. A guy who I only know as Charlie Ear, an ex-boxer, looks up. "You okay? You look like shit."

My head hangs and I rub my forehead. "I'm fine."

"You look like shit," he repeats with satisfaction. With his spread legs he takes up the whole couch as he sinks into its soft cushions.

The pain kneads into my tissues. If I had a home I would go to it.

Vinnie clears his throat and orders, "Turn on the music."

Gus moves to the stereo and cranks up on an old Snoop Dog album.

"This was Julius's favorite song," Gus yells.

The noise will interfere with the listening devices that the Feds enjoy planting like so many spinster gardeners. Everything will be mentioned in code, but Snoop Dog will add another layer of static.

"Thank you for coming," Vinnie mumbles. "It's a sad occasion, fucking tragic, but we have a problem. We need it solved and we have the people now to do it."

These new guys, most of whom I don't know, are trouble in tailored jackets. But when I reexamine *our* crew (not as well-dressed, I notice) an insight, which had been staring me in the face for years, finally hits me. We have survived this long because, like the old DeMeo crew, our gang is made up of a half-dozen serial killers. All crews are violent, but IRA, Bones, Gus, and Vinnie form a nucleus of sociopaths who lack not only remorse but also all fear of punishment. This species of bravery, a type of madness, has kept us in business despite the competition. Even Vlad the Impaler, until now, has trod carefully. Maybe that's why he offered us terms of surrender. It's only the Chinese backup that gives Vlad the courage to make any move at all.

Vinnie continues, "Here's the proposition. We'll eat at The National tomorrow. It will be dark, but we'll have glasses. An early dinner. Meet back here at six and we'll go together."

Then Vinnie nods and the new shooters leave the room.

So Vinnie has decided. All-out war. I don't think much of IRA's dopey plan. It might, *might* work with people trained using night vision goggles. But I can't imagine it's easy.

Along with his books, I inherited my father's fear of tools, whether a hammer or night goggles. I'd just put them on backward and shoot myself in the head.

Vinnie then signals for me to approach his desk. I limp over. "Get some rest," Vinnie orders. "It looks like an elephant crapped on your face." In this way, he warns me to be ready for tomorrow night or he'd cap my ass.

The others stay. I don't like this at all. Normally, you can expect people to talk about you as soon as you leave a room. But if those people are trigger-happy assassins, your ears don't just burn. You need to make a will.

On the street I'm dizzy with pain and sick with worry. I don't care about killing Vlad. I certainly don't want to be killed doing it. Nor do I want to get clipped by IRA. I can hear him wheedling and begging Vinnie for the chance. Gleefully would he hog-tie me and drive to the Gowanus Canal, where he would dump my body into its corrosive waters.

I stumble by Judith's house. John's car is in the driveway. John, no W. Buffett, often taunts, "You can't even rip off people with any consistency."

He blames my books. I think too much. Such men are not dangerous.

He's right. Not that it's easy to fleece people. Most stay on their guard, remain cautious, hand out cash only under extreme duress. That's why I like selling pot. You can make money without strong-arming or cheating anyone. For the best weed, people line up. By dealing I provide a necessary service and I take pride in my quality control.

That I'm not more successful has as much to do with my lack of ambition as with genuine incompetence. But John thinks that an unsuccessful gangster is doubly cursed. He risks prison and death for nothing.

John himself had dreamed of being a wise guy. Lacking the guts, he overcharges for roofing and thinks he's badass. In fact, all he got was a badass reputation, which is why he has a lousy business.

I don't feel like seeing John, so I text Ariel. *In the area.* What I should do is get the hell out of here, come back in fifty years when other woes will lay waste a new generation.

29

The Bomb

Halfway to Ariel's, blaring sirens suddenly startle me out of my reverie of 1920s Paris. (I had been telling Sartre about my nausea.) Fire trucks and police cars zoom down Nineteenth Street. Has the war started? I had thought it would wait until tomorrow night.

My instinct is always to go in the opposite direction of the authorities. No situation is so dire that it couldn't be made worse by the arrival of the cops. But all the screaming vehicles are heading in the direction of Judith's.

I have to keep myself from running. The fire trucks have stopped in front of the house. I mingle in a crowd of people who are in bathrobes. Some hold umbrellas for it has started to drizzle. I push through to where the cops are holding people back. Judith's two street-facing windows have shattered and the metal frames have twisted. Bricks have tumbled onto the porch. Judith is holding both the girls, each one sobbing into her housecoat.

John is behind her and he sees me. His eyes radiate bolts of loathing. But he knows enough to keep his mouth shut. Neither Judith nor the girls appear hurt. There is nothing I can do to help, so I fade back into the crowd. Then I fade farther, cross the street, go up a driveway and into a backyard, where I climb over a low fence and walk down that driveway, emerging onto a quiet block that never heard the phrase "Molotov cocktail."

This calamity happened because of my friendship with Ivan. But why? Has my defense of reading widely in the great books somehow pissed off not only Ivan but Vlad?

Whatever the reason, Vlad has decided to scare Vinnie by terrorizing me. Families are not off-limits he wants to say. The men of the Cosa Nostra betray every rule they hold dear—don't deal drugs, give your boss a taste of everything, don't whack your captain. But they keep the wives and children out of it.

The Russians, however, have no such deal. They live in armed compounds and their kids travel with bodyguards.

As I calculate my next move, figuring all the angles of staying or going, of hiding or fighting, I somehow find myself crouching behind rusting garbage cans in an alley between an apartment building and a doctor's office complex on Avenue U. The stink of shit seeps from the cracks of the poorly soldered cans and two rats scurry across the apartment building's glass-strewn courtyard.

I forget about calculating anything. I'm overwhelmed with grief and terror as I imagine what might have happened to Judith and her girls. Lisa, the younger, is six and just lost her front teeth. Her lisp makes me crazy with love for her. I'd take Jessica, the ten-year old, to Coney Island where we'd hold hands and comb the beach looking for mermaids who sing each to each. That they do not sing to us doesn't matter.

That I brought this misery into their midst rakes at my intestines. When I got into the business all I had to worry about was avoiding arrest. How did the pillars that supported the universe collapse, the rubble about to bury everybody I love?

I finger my phone. It dings with a text. Expecting more disaster, I open it with shaking fingers. It's from Ariel. *Call immediately.*

I press her number and she says, "A friend who lives on your sister's block tweeted about an explosion. Was it that? Your sister?"

"Yeah."

She whispers. "Are you still in the neighborhood?"

"Where else? Why are you whispering?"

"Can you come here?"

I don't answer.

Ariel adds, "No more games."

"The games are not the problem." What I don't say is that I need to evaporate, eddy into the firmament. I want my unhappy soul to dissolve into the forest glades that reverberate with the nightingales' eternal song. Barring that, I think I should whack Vinnie and end this.

Someone's coming. I remove the gun from my waistband.

"Howie, are you still there?"

I shut the phone. The super has pushed open the metal door and stands in the courtyard smoking. He's tall, wiry, in a sleeveless undershirt. He tilts his head back and gazes at the starless sky. He takes two steps toward the garbage cans but he can only see the dark night.

My gun rests on my knees. All the Russian supers are connected to Vlad.

The guy stubs out his cigarette. After a final glare in the direction of his trash cans, he goes back inside.

I take out my phone and call Ariel back. "Listen, I can cause you big trouble. Look what happened to Judith."

"Everyone knows you live with Judith. No one knows about me."

"You're willing to risk your mother?"

"It's not a risk. We're invisible. Please, I won't ask anything of you. You'll owe me nothing." She sounds frantic.

"Why are you doing this?"

"Because we have something. You know it and I know it. And courage is not only sitting in an office day after day doing work you hate."

"This is not a test, Ariel. It's fucking life and death." Maybe she gets off on being a savior. It sounds far-fetched, coming from a dedicated masochist, but who knows? Fetishes can overlap. "I'll be over in ten minutes."

I rise from my crouch and press my back against the wall of the building. I peer into the street, though what I really need to do is peer into the future. Will Vinnie Five-Five keep to his plan when he finds out about the bombing? Night vision goggles my ass.

There's no pretending now that I'm paranoid, that no one is after me, that I'm too insignificant.

Though I see no people, cars cruise down the street at regular intervals. In each one, I notice death is driving.

So when a lull in traffic occurs, I jog out of the alley, head down. When I can, I cut down driveways and backyards and, in eight minutes, I get to Ariel's house. She hears me coming up to her door and she pulls it open. I dive in and she instantly slams it shut.

"Your face," she gasps.

Her deaf mother has heard. "Ariel?"

Ariel calls back. "I just needed a breath of air."

"Don't forget to lock the door."

"Don't worry."

"What do you mean 'don't worry'? Who knows what kind of maniacs are running around out there?"

"For God's sake, Mom. I locked it."

"That's all I ask."

"I'm going to work downstairs. Just go to sleep."

"Good night, sweetheart."

Ariel comes down looking grim. "I need a job. I need to get out of here. Did I tell you that Joan, my subletter, moved out? I'd love to move back in myself, but . . . So you don't want to talk about your face? The black eyes? Top secret?"

I say nothing. I begin to believe that once I start talking, I'll never shut up.

I press Judith's number. She picks up immediately. "Howie."

"Are you okay?"

"John told me he saw you. We're at his mother's. The house is a crime scene."

"I'm so sorry."

The dam breaks. Judith sobs, "When is this going to end? We'll all be dead."

"No. It'll be all right. Can't you get away, take a vacation?"

Judith wails, "John hasn't had a job in weeks. We barely made the mortgage payment. Now we have to fix the brick-work and replace the windows." She hesitates but then adds, "John says he wants you to pay for it since the bomb was really meant for you."

That cocksucker. "Of course, Judith. Don't cry. As soon as I . . ."

"I can't have you and John arguing." She gets control of herself. "I can't take it."

I think we have more serious headaches than family bick-ering. But Judith maintains some normalcy by focusing on these tensions rather than the tsunami of history that swamps us all.

"Stay at your mother-in-law's until all this blows over. It shouldn't be long."

"The girls are watching TV," Judith sobs. "I need to put them to bed. And please, please, please, don't do anything else stupid. Just stay alive."

Though we're as close as a brother and sister can be, we don't go around expressing deep emotions, other than advising each other not to get murdered.

So Judith will stay at her in-laws'. I don't tell her where I am and she doesn't ask.

Ariel stands, looking distressed. Maybe seeing my shat-tered face has finally brought home the reality to her.

You can't unilaterally withdraw from the mob without being executed. The exception, of course, is if your crew is wiped out and there's no one left to kill you. IRA's plan strikes me as particularly dumb, suicidal. But Vinnie knows that he'll lose a battle of attrition. Both the Russians and the Chinese will pick off his crew one by one. Risking everything on an all-or-nothing strike is his only chance. One gang of brutes exterminates another gang of brutes.

Then once Vinnie's bigger headaches pass, he will kill me. How do I know? I know. The deepest truths are arrived at not through reason but through feelings.

I regret not bringing some philosophy. Reading it relaxes me.

"Can you get me some other shit that I need? I have something on, but I'm not sure it will come off as planned. I might have to hole up here for a while."

Ariel comes toward me. "Whatever you want."

Should I bet my life that Vinnie doesn't survive another twenty-four hours? Do I dare chance that whoever else runs this neighborhood will forget about me if I stay hidden? Your allies one day are your enemies the next. At all times, someone will prefer you dead.

"I don't even have a pen."

Ariel goes to her desk and gets one.

If I'm going to transform into a mole, I'll need to anesthetize myself with liquor and some special works, books that I have been pushing off reading until the right moment. I'll also need some snacks. I keep the list short.

1. Johnny Walker—Red Label
2. Peanut Butter—the chunky kind
3. Crackers—Ritz
4. *The Nicomachein Ethics*—Aristotle
5. Candy—Almond Snickers
6. *In Search of Lost Time: The Fugitive* and *Time Regained* (vol. 6)—Proust

I examine the list. Reading Aristotle always makes me hungry for a Snickers Bar. The Nico of Nicomachean is Aristotle's son, to whom Aristotle dedicated the work. It's about how to live a good (moral) life. My father, who never other-wise talked philosophy, did mention this. Now I have time to give the work a close reading.

The Proust I've been working my way through for years. If I remain holed-up, I'd finally finish.

Ariel laughs. "Do you need help? What are you writing so much?"

I give her the list.

Still smiling, she peruses it. After a second and then another second, her face whitens. "What is this?"

"What?" I snatch the list out of her hand and look at it closely. "Fuck." Right away I see the problem. I have spelled *Nicomachaen* incorrectly. I change the *i* to an *a* and hand the paper back to Ariel.

The list drops from her hand and floats to the floor. "Who the hell are you?" Her voice rises in panic and fury. "And what the hell is wrong with you?"

Part III

30

The Poetics

We stand glaring at each other as if hoping for a director to call "cut." But even after a minute of very uncomfortable silence, we stay put.

As time passes I begin to relax. My shoulders, which have tightened, return to their normal tension and my facial muscles slacken as if I thought better of making a joke.

Ariel senses that I will not take up her challenge to explain. The one thing I truly learned, the one thing that has allowed me to survive on the peripheries of organizations peopled by violent lunatics, is to say nothing about nothing. Almost always, it's not what people do that gets them killed; it's what they say.

But that never stops the toughest sons of bitches from plotting, confessing, boasting, and shooting off their idiotic mouths. The Feds have the tapes to prove it. If you can overcome the unbearable urge to blather, you can live forever.

My father was the only other person I know who barely said a word.

True, he was not a great success, but he died leaving us with the impression that there was nothing wrong. Cancer and nothing else killed him. Once, on a beautiful summer day a few months before he died, emaciated and in pain, he shocked me by mentioning that he just missed hitting the trifecta at Belmont. The way he bet I would imagine that that race cost him one hundred g's. His illness must have weakened him because just two weeks later he opened up again, saying that his second round of chemo made him as sick as a pooch but left his tumor in tip-top condition. He died without bringing it up again.

Even among the closed-mouthed Italian peasantry, this kind of reticence is unusual. Among Jews, it is blasphemous, anti-Semitic, outlawed in Germany and Canada and barely tolerated here in the United States. Though he would never say so, my father didn't give a fuck.

As expected, Ariel gathers her forces to attack. But I have to grant that she does not go overboard. "I think you're an asshole. I thought you were an asshole before, but for other reasons. Now I just think you're an asshole."

Ariel leaves it this cryptic in order to draw me into the conversation.

Instead, I pick up the paper with the list. "If you can't do it, don't worry about it."

She grabs it out of my hand. "I didn't say that. But you lied to me."

"I did?"

"You told me you . . . you can't express yourself. You told me you were virtually illiterate, through no fault of your own. And now . . ." Ariel works herself up, her face purple with anger, "And now you're reading Marcel Fucking Proust and you don't have two words for me! How dare you even know who Proust is when you spend your day punching people in the face?"

I would like to answer Ariel, but I don't know where to begin. First of all, and I can check my notes on this, I do not recall telling her I was illiterate. I may have left the impression that I am capable of violence, but I make time for other things.

Faced with what she views as my intransigence, Ariel turns and stalks up the stairs. Even though we just had our first fight, I still appreciate her ass so delicately sausaged into her jeans.

I sit by her computer and check the price of GE. Down another twenty-seven cents. Shit. I check Pfizer. Down a dime. I shouldn't be playing with things I know nothing about. I just thought that one day I would have a portfolio like my dad had, tiny and useless. We Fensters will never live off dividends. I should learn a trade, or better, how to trade. My father sometimes talked about this. Done right it's a way to mint money. Just get connected to an organization. Small-timers have no chance.

I hear Ariel running down the stairs. I think something is wrong and I dive for my piece.

She nearly falls down the last steps. She catches herself and straightens up. When she sees the gun in my hand, she shrieks.

Her mother, this supposedly deaf woman who hears everything, calls down. "Ariel, what's the matter? What happened?"

Swallowing, Ariel calls back up, "Nothing, Ma. A spider. I killed it. Go to sleep."

I stick the gun in my waistband.

Ariel orders, "Don't you dare leave. Just because . . . You're going to talk to me. Not now because I'm too angry." She turns and marches back up the stairs. I barely have time to sit back down when she returns. "Are you planning on leaving? Tell me the truth for once."

"Ariel, I will explain everything to you. But I have to do some things which would be suicide to talk openly about."

Ariel gapes. I have lost the gruff working-class accent and switched to more polished cadence. Still in shock, Ariel manages, "All right. But after tonight, we talk just like this."

I nod.

"And stop doing that!"

I keep my body totally still. When one is in the mood to misinterpret, the most innocent twitch can cause offense.

She can't contain herself, "I have to know . . . have you read a lot of Aristotle?"

"Some. His thing on poetry."

"The *Poetics*?" Ariel seethes. "You read the *Poetics*? You jerk." And with that she stomps back up the stairs.

It's hardly my fault. Not only is Aristotle the second most influential philosopher in history, but his name begins with an "A," which means he is one of the first writers my father bought in his alphabetical attack on the Western canon. He's been on the shelf my whole life.

With Ariel gone again, I consider whether she has a point. Had I tricked her? Maybe unconsciously. No harm done. She appreciated the opportunity to school me in the ways of the sophisticates.

Meanwhile, I need to decide about Vinnie.

We are all soldiers. We see ourselves as warriors who happen to be trapped in a feminized, corporatized age where the poets no longer celebrate certain types of mano-a-mano vicious-ness. Small tribes battling for micro territory is considered an annoyance by the global players who see only continent-wide domination a true measure of manhood. Backstabbing, fear mongering, and access to a nuclear arsenal have replaced courage in the face of fire for both leaders and followers. Any schnook on the front lines is treated with contempt by the Vinnies in political office and the Vlads on the general staff.

Back to Ariel. Never go to sleep angry at your lover so I debate going upstairs to apologize. What the hell is the matter with her? So I read the fucking *Poetics*. So what? Aristotle, as far as I know, belongs to world culture, not just to those who lord their intellectual superiority over others for a living.

But before I can make a move I hear Ariel coming down the stairs again. I'm mollified. Pleased. Maybe she even set up this fight so we can make up with some bloody sex. I think of the ropes and paddles and dildos. I just hope she doesn't want me to cut her. Once a girl asked me to slice her breast and I turned her down flat. Call me a prude but I don't like blood, even the blood of cute chicks. Yet right now, if Ariel gives me a blade, I'll slice her in half if she so desires.

But when I see Ariel, I realize that if she did have a knife she'd use it to gut me. She grabs the vodka from under the bed and stomps back upstairs.

I watch her go and tell myself that under no circumstance can I ever discuss Montesquieu. If she finds out that I enjoyed the *Persian Letters* she'd never forgive me.

31

Makeup Test

I fall asleep contemplating the French Revolution. That often happens when I'm under pressure. I think of the great Enlightenment Philosophes and wish I had lived during that time—not in France, where the Reign of Terror and the verb conjugation would have killed me. One either participates in the terror or becomes its victim. I have enough of that in my current life. I would like to have lived in England and contemplated the instinct for political freedom and self-determination à la Edmund Burke from a safe distance. People who like to be at the heart of the action have never been at the heart of the action. Our most pointless wars are fought under presidents who have never served in the military.

Anxieties of being a great coward gnaw me awake.

I would die for causes in which I believe. Maybe. I used to knock people around when they didn't come up with the necessary payments. In those situations I sometimes stopped my partner—an efficient gangster like Pauli Bones—from committing permanent harm to the mark. (And he let me stop him. I sometimes think Pauli Bones might not be as crazy as he lets on.)

I care about too many things, including my victims.

As a kid, callow, I gave no fuck. It's only after I got into my father's books that I developed this tic, this hesitation.

It doesn't matter that the novels I most enjoy are skeptical and allergic to sentiment. They still make me homesick for times and places in which I never lived. (As if I don't have enough headaches by being so stupidly attached to this asswipe neighborhood.) Is it possible that a moral education actually makes you moral? How can that be? The Nazis worshipped Beethoven and Heidegger loved Hitler as much as he did Plato.

Can empathy hit one like a sledgehammer descending from the clouds?

I check the time. It's two in the morning. I slept for two hours, long enough for insomnia to strike for the next five.

In circumstances like these, I always enjoy doing something stupid. So I put on my jacket and slip out the door. The streetlight in front of Ariel's house is out and there's no moon, making the darkness comfortingly thick. I pull a joint from my pocket. Just holding the skiff between my fingers relaxes me. I've been getting high since I was twelve. The bud never disappoints. Like a good mother, it quiets whatever cruel demons are poking at you.

I start feeling better. Whatever happens, happens. If I survive, things will work out. If I die, than nothing else matters. Calmly, I dream of killing everyone—Vlad, Crazy Bo, Vinnie. I'll kill Pauli Bones and IRA and my friend Ivan the Slavic Chauvinist. My homicidal musings stop short of my family and Ariel, but not of myself. A Glock 9 and a thirty-round clip can accomplish much in a very short time.

Time stops as the cannabis circulates in my system. Why suffer the slings and arrows? Over the last 400 years we have answered the question that so baffled the Bard: it's not worth it. There's nothing out there. Yet this powerful insight doesn't help. One still hallucinates oneself into meaning and purpose. But on nights like this, when the dogs of war bark, when pity is frozen in every heart, when intellectual disgrace blots every face, a general slaughter makes the most sense.

"What are you doing?" Ariel purrs.

I drag on the joint and offer it behind me. She still has not shown herself.

Ariel takes it and I hear her inhale. "Wow."

For personal use, I only roll the most medicinal hydroponic product. It never fails to blast one out of his/her shoes.

"You must be standing in the dark and answering the big questions: the nature of time, what happens after death, what is this phenomenon we call reality."

"You're drunk," I tell Ariel.

"You bet your psycho ass," Ariel replies. "What else have you read that you haven't told me about?"

"Nothing."

"Bullshit. Liar."

"Why ask me if you're just going to get angry? If things work out like I hope, we'll have plenty of times for long, intelligent discussions."

"I need to know the depth of your deception." She waits before she asks, too loudly for this quiet night on this quiet block, "Have you written anything Mister Philosopher Gangsta? Have you connected the disparate parts of your life into some hard-boiled intellectual tract?"

"Do you really think I'd put something down on paper? Risk everything for what? Not that anyone reads anymore, but still . . . Let's go inside." I turn and see her standing barefoot on the cement. She's wearing nothing but the sleeveless nightie. Now the belt she wanted me to whip her with is stylishly cinched around her waist.

I sweep her off her feet and carry her inside. As we're entering she pulls the joint from the edge of my mouth and flips it away. "My mother can still smell like a bloodhound."

I put her down on the bed. The nightgown rides up and I stare at her red thong. She spreads her thighs and mutters, "Come on. I don't care if you've memorized all of Kierkegaard."

"You're too drunk."

"So? You're too educated. Much more unforgivable."

"I never finished high school," I defend myself.

"It doesn't matter. I always knew you had secrets. But I thought it had to do with putting bodies through meat grinders, not familiarity with the classics."

"I'm sorry."

"It's not really your fault," Ariel sniffles. "I'm just a fool. No matter how many times I'm wrong, I still think I'm a good judge of character. Why do I attract these . . ." She sobs, "Why did you let me make such a dope of myself?"

I feel for Ariel, this mostly naked girl lying down with her knees bent apart. I kneel on the bed and push the G string away from her crotch. It takes another second to pull my dick from my pants and gently penetrate. For the first time we use no condom.

We move in rhythm from the start and soon she comes with an explosiveness that almost rivals the time I tied her up for an hour. But she orgasms only once and then she pushes me off.

After her breathing returns to normal she says, "Don't tell me you didn't use a rubber."

I don't respond. She knows I hadn't.

"Wonderful." She reaches under the bed. "Where the hell is the vodka?"

"You took it upstairs."

"Oh."

"Why do you drink so much?"

She crawls into my arms. "Because it helps control my drug use. And if I did nothing, I wouldn't fulfill a single fantasy. I trade my liver for erotic fulfillment."

"So you have your own secrets," I say. "You pretend to be totally straitlaced, but you're really an outlaw. By the way, can you get pregnant?"

"Why do men always ask the same stupid question? I am a woman. We're usually the ones who give birth. But we should be okay."

Our fight recedes and our relationship strengthens. Ariel leans her head on my shoulder. "Technically, you know, we have more in common now than we did before."

"Yeah."

"Not *yeah*. Yes. We do. And I'm not saying it's a good thing. But we have to explore each other anew."

"Sure."

"Not *sure*. I'm serious. You're more of a person. I just can't have you whipping me."

"Why not?"

"Because I can't." Ariel falls back on the bed and begins a half-drunken weeping. "Maybe it's not you. It's me. I just don't know myself well enough to allow . . . for this . . ."

I no longer fit into the fantastical dream world Ariel created from mannerisms and hair gel. I'm not the savage retard that originally so aroused her.

I really must get going. But I have five minutes. "Lie down with me."

She topples onto the pillow and we scrunch together on the narrow bed. She falls asleep with the bare bulb burning over her eyes. I make a note to myself: my girlfriend is an alcoholic.

32

Mother Fucking Courage

The Saint Valentine's Day Massacre. 1929. Al Capone took over all the bootlegging in Chicago after whacking seven leading lights of Bugsy Moran's gang. The lucky seven were lined up by men in police uniforms and machine-gunned in a warehouse. A few years later, Lucky Luciano, in a single glorious slaughter, whacked the entire old guard of Mustache Pete in New York and ushered in the modern family structure that propelled New York to the top of the rackets. The five-boss Commission has ruled over every aspect of wise guy life ever since. Sure, the power of each family waxes and wanes, but extremely organized crime will be here as long as people are people and corporations are people.

But will the Italian Mafia survive? In Italy, sure. Despite competition from recent immigrant groups like the Serbs and the Albanians, the 'Ndrangheta and other Sicilian gangs are well entrenched at every level of law enforcement and government. As much as the Italians hate the Italian Mafia, they hate the foreign gangs worse. Like good citizens everywhere, they feel if they are going to be terrorized, let it be by *paisans,* homegrown boys who themselves are deeply dedicated to keeping Italy Italian.

Here in America, however, immigrants change the face of the nation every generation. One wave swamps the previous one. Italian migration receded decades ago, leaving only the restaurants in its wake. A few holdout ethnic neighborhoods exist, like here and in Bensonhurst. But we're islands in a sea of Russians, Pakistanis, Chinese, and Dominicans. Like immigrant groups before them, many barely speak English and aggressively huddle in their neighborhoods. They have unity and the profound contempt of authority so necessary for criminal activity to dominate an economy.

Vinnie Five-Five and his little crew are ruthless enough gangsters, but only a tiny segment of their community remains behind them. Despite the century of Cosa Nostra tradition, we are out on a limb without the necessary societal approval that gives us the resources, not to mention the confidence, to fight off the Feds and the newer gangs.

So why am I going to die for this marginal character?

Ariel snores gently but loud enough to disconcert. I imagine her a bit older, a bit heavier, a bit drunker. The gift of daintiness is not given to those careless of it.

She needs to move out of her mother's place. Maybe she should come to the end of the world with me.

I rearrange Ariel on the bed and cover her with the blanket. Her breathing lightens and she mutters a sweet, happy nothing.

I go to the computer. I will not spend my last night surfing financial sites or porn. I do, however, check *night vision goggles*. Just as I suspected, it takes experience to use them correctly. It seems like Vinnie is doing a Jonestown, giving his crew night vision Kool-Aid.

I slip out again. More than anything I want to see Judith and her girls, but I dare not go to her in-laws'. John poisoned that well a long time ago; they see me as an insane fool who brings only trouble on the family.

They are right about everything.

On McDonald Avenue the elevated F train tracks loom. My father hated this train. "Takes forever to get into the city. Who needs it?" Why the hell did Dad place such an inordinate premium on having quick access to Manhattan? His bookie worked out of the corner candy store and his job took him no farther than Midwood. Had he seen our elevated lines as underground railroads to freedom? Had he, too, dreamed of escaping the rackets, the accounting, his gambling addiction? Like so many misfit Brooklyn boys of his generation, he imagined a life of the mind, elegant, full of art and argument, beauty and passion. He would have delighted in the disappointment of knowing the wisest men and wittiest women in the land. In Manhattan he could escape the prison of his destiny.

So why hadn't he ever acted? Was he worried that he wouldn't be able to take us with him? He loved his kids; that I know. And my mother, his wife, would have found nothing of interest outside the places in which she spent her childhood. She went into Manhattan twice a year, exclusively to shop at a Macy's sale. Or maybe Dad didn't give a flying fuck about the city and he just had a stupid, pointless subway obsession.

You can never know about these things.

I touch the Glock under my coat. Its metallic solidity comforts me. Where am I going? On the corner of Dahill Road, I see a red neon sign that blinks *Bob's*. It's a bar, but metal shutters cover the window. No wonder. It is three A.M.

Farther into Bath Beach the buildings turn smaller, less forbidding, more residential, with one exception. I have reached Vinnie Five-Five's house. We call the place The Fortress.

Vinnie could have moved to New Jersey. His relatives would have let him keep his rackets, given him more territory. But for some reason he chose to stay in a place that his grandfather moved to in 1945. The outside of the house hasn't been altered in seventy years.

It's a strange house, built to be a bunker. It sits in the center a triangular plot of land. The wall facing the street is solid stone. The only opening to the wider world is a slit in the attic room where one can watch the entrance while aiming an M-16 at the street below. In the back, the windows face a garden that Vinnie's wife cultivates with Voltairean zeal. A ten-foot cinder block wall keeps neighbors from appreciating all the energy Mrs. Five-Five puts into her azaleas.

Here is the seat of the Five-Five Empire. Here Vinnie's grandfather plotted, unsuccessfully, on becoming a captain in the Bonanno family. Here Vinnie's brother Gregory fulfilled his grandfather's dream before suffering from the unfortunate experience of being whacked. And here Vinnie runs the operation.

I stare, somewhat amazed at having materialized in this spot. It seems that I just wandered over, but it is impossible for that to be true. One doesn't aimlessly arrive at The Fortress. Nor does one examine the building with a ferocity of gaze that alone could incinerate it.

We played here—Julius, Augustus, me—all the time. Video games, cops and robbers. As long as the cops were killed, we had the run of the house. I ate dinner here a thousand times: ziti, meatballs, Mrs. Five-Five's veal. I was watching TV with the twins when Vinnie shot Chris Cupcake in the back of his head as he went to check out Vinnie's new hot water heater. Vinnie thought he was a rat. Murdering people in your own home is not standard practice, but it does have the advantage of convenience.

Twenty years ago, I learned a narrow tunnel led from the basement to the garage. Using the logic acquired from years of serious reading, I deduced that the same tunnel led from the garage to the basement.

Of course, as a nonfamily member, as a nonmade guy, as a half-Jew and as wholly ambivalent, I was not supposed to know about this. But ten-year-old boys with stunted imaginations can never keep secrets. Both Gus and Julius, separately, led me to the tunnel. They had stumbled upon this entrance by crawling around some built-in cabinets in the basement while looking for a good place to hide in ambush. They liked doing that, bursting out of the closets with fake guns and real fists. Eventually, after discovering that they both told me about it, we incorporated the tunnel into our games as long as Vinnie was not home.

Now Julius is gone. Now Gus is a stranger. Now Vinnie doubts my reliability. But the tunnel remains.

In the left corner of the garage's back wall, secreted in what looks like solid cinder block, is a hinge. A simple push and the fake cinder block pops up and creates a space large enough for a grown man to slip through. An enterprising gangster with a car stashed nearby could be fifty miles outside of the city by the time his enemies realize that he is not hiding in the house. The whole setup is a miraculous feat of Mafia contracting.

Before I do anything I check if anyone is watching. Of course I can't tell a thing. Then I go to the back of the garage. Even in the dark after all these years I find the stone that's not a stone—the piece of wood covered in plaster and painted to look like stone.

The part of my heart not pounding my brain to smithereens gladdens. I push.

Nothing happens. Had Vinnie replaced the fake with the real? Had he known that his system had been compromised? I kneel and get my weight fully into my shove. The hinge must be rotten from disuse. Then I hear a squeak. And then a squeal, long and loud. I stop pushing. It takes all my strength not to run for my life. Enough noise has been made to attract every capo in the tristate area. I imagine that Vinnie has gotten a shotgun and is waiting for me inside the garage. Do I want to die reliving my childhood?

So I die. So what? Suicide by gangster. Annoy a wise guy enough and he'll pull the trigger almost as quickly as a cop. I push again. The squeaky hatch lifts. Was the opening always this narrow? Could Vinnie Five-Five's gut get through? Impossible. But he always believed the tunnel would save his life at least once.

Meanwhile I slither into the pitch-black garage. I stand utterly still. I listen carefully for movement, breathing, the cocking of a gun. No. I'm alone.

My eyes adjust. A bit of light filters in from a small window covered in chicken wire. Julius's Mustang is parked two feet away from the tunnel.

Vinnie must have given up any thought of using his elaborate escape mechanism. Maybe after all those years he started to feel safe. Maybe he got too fat to crawl for his life.

I can go back the way I came and no one will be the wiser. I look at the stone. It has stayed in the up position. They would be the wiser. So I make another stupid decision. I pull up the trap door.

I lower myself into the tunnel. It's tighter than I remember. I crawl through it. My clothes blacken with grease, my face streaks with grime. I think of the scene in *Apocalypse Now* when a mud-encrusted Martin Sheen rises out of the swamps. I hum, *This is the end / my beautiful friend . . .*

A decade of dust rises from the floor like a toxic event. I'm going to sneeze.

Three quick bursts. Tears leak from my eyes. Snot runs from my nose and drool flecks the corners of my lips.

As kids, we had flashlights. Now it is dark as a grave, so I have nothing but memories to light my way. They're enough to find the metal ladder banged into the dirt and I climb into the basement. (The only time Vinnie used the tunnel was to put Cupcake into the trunk of his car without any chance of the neighbors seeing him carrying a corpse.)

This is the most dangerous point. If Vinnie has an office down here, if he has retreated to plot strategy with his soldiers, I'm dead. There's nothing I can do about that.

It's quiet, however. I suspect Vinnie is asleep. Often gangsters gad about most of the night. When things are going well, we party, enjoy the hookers, dine with mistresses. Vinnie Five-Five has a dark-haired, dimpled Pakistani *guma,* about twenty-two, whom he takes to the finest restaurants where he meets other middle-aged gangsters with other post-pubescent lovers. He goes to meetings at strip clubs all over the city. A gangster's work is never done.

But tonight, in the middle of the war, in mourning for his son, with the need to psych himself up for the coming bloodbath, he might very well be contemplating his affairs, maybe even talking to his wife, though in the mood I saw her, I doubt she wants to talk to him.

A deep weariness now overcomes me. I want to crawl behind the boiler and go to sleep. I also need to take a dump. I half expected this. Many housebreakers experience loose bowels. The burgled come home and are often more disturbed, horrified, by the pile of poop in the middle of their living room than by the missing silverware. The emptying of bowels is taken as a definitive "fuck you," a personal level of contempt that docs more to violate a victim's sense of self than the emptying of her entire living room.

In reality, it's a combination of nerves and adrenaline that makes thieves drop their pants where they stand. It's nothing personal.

After another minute the pressure dissipates and the need passes.

The basement seems to have fallen into disuse and has become filthy. By now, I have enough grime on my body to apply for a Superfund grant. So what? It makes me invisible in the night.

I pull the gun from my waistband. This action and the solidness of the weapon calm me. Afterward these sentences somehow assemble themselves: *My decision to hit Vinnie is both stupid and suicidal. Thus, it is the only ethical course.* I try to think more profoundly but those words lie at the bottom of my brain as if they are a desert carcass and my consciousness a circling vulture. *Ethical, stupid, suicide, justified,* light up in neon and then fade like the phosphorescence in a firefly's ass. At one point I fall against the back wall. But in seconds my eyes open and I'm floating in a tranquil sea. My chest rises and falls in lightly heaving waves.

Why am I doing something so risky? The days of individual heroism ended in the eleventh century with the "Song of Roland." Why buck a thousand-year tradition of cowardice?

Even this thought doesn't stop me. The third stair is warped and I step over it. I have so much experience sneaking into and out of basements that it seems I do nothing else.

At the head of the stairs, I hear nothing. I enter the kitchen and push through the swinging doors into the living room. I see that Mrs. Five-Five has kept all the plastic slipcovers on the furniture. They gleam evilly, reflecting ambient light and bad taste.

I go into the den: large-screen TV, La-z-Boy armchairs with attached cup holders. Here is a narrow spiral staircase, metal, that Vinnie installed years ago so he could get directly to his bedroom. It will not creak as I climb it.

I listen. Vinnie snores the snore of fat men. I assume his wife is also asleep. I hold the gun, its safety off.

Even if Vinnie awakens, the story will be over.

The key to a successful hit is the willingness to pull the trigger. Once the hurdle of conscience is overcome, you could murder one or a dozen or a million. Just weaponry limits you.

The bedroom door is open. Vinnie and his wife lie in separate double beds. I'm not surprised. Even in his sleep, Vinnie probably throws his weight around.

If the night had been dreamlike before, it turns positively hallucinatory. I'm me but not me. I'm acting and also hovering on the ceiling watching the action. Events that take forever to unfold then occur quickly. I grab the pillow out from under Vinnie's head and just as his eyes record a second of recognition, I cover his face, press the barrel of the gun into the pillow, and pop him three times.

Though the pillow muffles the noise, Mrs. Five-Five bolts up in her bed. She doesn't recognize me right away, blackened as I am, and she shrieks, her hand coming up to her face just as in the Munch painting.

Must I pop her too?

My hand is still pressing the pillow into Vinnie's face. Blood seeps through the pillowcase. Mrs. Five-Five sees this too.

"Howie?"

She has made me. Not that surprising since she's known me all my life.

I point the gun at her head while I nod in greeting.

"What did you do, Howie?" she asks with only a trace of hysteria in her voice.

I let go of the pillow. She knows exactly what I've done.

"You should leave this house, Howie. You should leave immediately."

I keep the gun pointed at her head. She now gazes at me frankly, not the least bit frightened.

"Howie, where are your shoes?"

Without even realizing it, I left them in the basement.

"You should have taken my advice and run before all this."

My head hangs. I'm embarrassed by my stupid miscalculations. "I should have done a lot of things."

"That's right." Mrs. Spoleto gets out of the bed and puts on a bathrobe that's thrown over a chair by her toilette table.

The gun taps my leg. I don't know if I need to kill her.

"Howie, you have a cigarette?"

This surprises me. I never saw Mrs. Spoleto smoke. But from my pocket I pull out a plastic bag. "Nothing. Just some pot."

"All right." The old middle-aged lady opens the table's drawer and removes a bone-stemmed pipe with a purple glass bowl. Her hands shake as she takes a pinch of cannabis out of the bag and stuffs it into the bowl. "Do you have a light, Howie?"

I pat my pocket. Horrified, I realize that I have lost my lighter.

"Go into the cabinet above the stove and bring the matches."

When I get back from the kitchen, Mrs. Spoleto has applied some lipstick and is examining her face in the mirror. She must have concluded that at fifty-eight she looks seventy because she frowns and shakes her head in disbelief. She lights up. "I'd offer you the pipe, but even your lips are covered in crap."

"Don't worry about it."

Mrs. Spoleto holds the match to the bowl and inhales. She takes close to thirty seconds to exhale. "That's very good, Howie. Thank you. You got in through the garage tunnel."

I nod.

"I told Vinnie to blow it up. I told him that someone would find it. He said only the contractor and he knew about it. And the contractor got whacked years ago."

"We found it when we were kids."

"Really? I told Vinnie . . . it doesn't matter what I told Vinnie now, does it?" She points to the bag of pot. "Do you mind?"

"Please. Go ahead." I still don't know if I'm going to shoot her.

Mrs. Spoleto stuffs the pipe again. "In college, you know I went to college?"

"No."

"Brooklyn College. I tried to go to Tulane where my friend Mary went, but my parents wanted me close to home. They worried I'd marry a black guy. Kids back then did those things."

She's babbling.

"I should never have let Vinnie into my life. But my parents liked him."

"Vinnie had his good points."

We both looked at the bed. By now a large brown stain spread from under his pillow.

"I shouldn't speak badly about the recently dead." And her nose reddens and she starts whimpering. But she quickly gains control of herself by sucking in as much weed as one could in a single breath. "Thank you for this, Howie. I used to smoke a lot. Maybe too much. It calmed me down enough to stay with Vinnie. And now everything's turned to shit. You know he was smart and handsome. Everyone knew he would be a captain. I came from a family that believed working your way up in the Cosa Nostra was a decent career path. There were risks, of course, but every business has risks. Joe Bananas was my mother's cousin. He lived until ninety."

"He was the exception."

"Everyone thinks they're the exception. Do you think you're an exception, Howie?"

"To what?"

"To the run of the mill. To the inevitable consequences of your actions."

"Who knows?" A murdered husband brings out the philosopher in everyone.

Our eyes again drift over to Vinnie's body. Fifteen minutes ago he was the kingmaker in south Brooklyn. He commanded a private army and had the power of life and death over his subjects. Now he is a piece of meat, as defenseless against his wife's criticism as he is to the maggots that will pick his bones clean.

"I would have left him when the kids were young but he would have killed me," Mrs. Five-Five says. " 'The Spoletos,' Vinnie told me, 'do not believe in divorce.' "

33

The Carpet

All her life she fought him. She had nearly pulled Julius from the pit. She got him out of high school and accepted into Fordham. (Gus's achievements would have been limited no matter what.) In the end, Julius never made it past his first semester. Vinnie won because he offered the quickest route to a powerful identity. A lot of people think they're tough guys. However, knowing yourself to be genuinely fearless— above the dread of pain, beyond the terror of death—is a rush. Taking the safest route to contentment is too full of risk to be worth it.

"I tried," Mrs. Spoleto continues to insist. "You remember how I used to make them do homework. Vinnie wanted them to clip that hoodlum Rocky Monk." She sighs at the memory. "Vinnie and I, we were never on the same page about those kids."

This leads to a longish, meditative silence in which Mrs. Five-Five slowly packs another bowl. After taking a hit, she asks, "Are you going to kill me?"

"No."

"Too bad."

"I just wanted to stop the war. I also think Vinnie planned to whack me."

"He certainly did," Mrs. Spoleto confirms with sickening certainty. "You're a good boy, Howie, even if you aren't all that . . . even if you don't thoroughly think things out. Killing one man doesn't always do the trick once the wheels are in motion."

Mrs. Spoleto speaks with the confidence of one with inside information. First she knows that Vinnie had enough of me. Had Vinnie already made the arrangements? With whom? Gus? I understand now what murderers of every rank know. Once you start, the killing never ends.

"What do you plan on doing with Vinnie?"

"I did it!" What the hell more can I do to the poor fool?

"Relax, Howie. All your life in the rackets and you still don't realize that the hardest job is getting rid of the body. You have to clean up after yourself. On that Vinnie and I were in agreement."

I stare blankly at Mrs. Spoleto. If I hadn't whacked her husband I would never have guessed what a wit she is. "I was going to kill you both and then wait until Gus found you. He'd think that Vlad got you."

"I'm still here."

"I never thought you would be okay with . . . I thought you would be upset about Vinnie."

"You did? Even after our conversation at the viewing?"

"I knew you were angry, but I didn't know that you and Vinnie were . . ."

"Bitter enemies?"

"I didn't know how deep the hatred ran."

Mrs. Five-Five murmurs, "Deep. I never found the bottom." She looks into the mirror. "Was I really that invisible? I see myself in the glass. How come no one else does?"

It becomes hard to imagine how a woman with character this strong had all the impact of a benign ghost on her family's destiny.

She snaps her head away from the mirror. "Since you left me alive, it would be better for both of us if Vinnie vanished."

I wait for Mrs. Five-Five to finish. I'm tired of thinking.

"You can take him to the usual place."

"You know—"

"Howie, I know everything. I'm a human wiretap. That's what happens when your husband thinks you're deaf and dumb."

"You know about Loch Sheldrake?"

"Exit 21 off 17. There's an old carpet in the basement. Roll him up in it and get him to the car through the tunnel. Take the same trip as Cupcakes."

"You know about—"

"HE WHACKED HIM IN MY HOUSE. The son of a bitch. Go now. Then I'll call Gus and tell him that his father never came home. That might put off the raid on Vlad's head-quarters. I can't see Gus leading the charge. Or I can't see anyone following him."

I can't stop myself. "How in hell did you know about—"

"Get the carpet. It's in the rec room."

I run down the stairs. Before I even hit the lights I recognize the place from its sour, smoky odor. Here the twins and I whiffed on anything that could be rolled. When Mrs. Five-Five came down to stop us, we laughed in her face. Yeah, we were real tough guys.

I search the room for the rug. The pool table stands where it always had, the felt worn away in the same places. Gus got good enough to hustle all over Brooklyn. It was the one thing in which he surpassed Julius. Julius got so aggravated at Gus's skill that he stopped going to bars with us. Then Gus, who played pool only to annoy Julius, stopped hustling too.

There is the TV with an old Nintendo, the one we had as teenagers. The heavy punching bag still hangs from the ceiling, as does the speed bag. This is a museum to my child-hood. I see Julius sitting on the ratty couch, no rattier today, rolling a joint. Gus practices a bank shot. And what am I doing? I'm quiet. By then I had learned enough to keep my mouth shut and channel surf.

But I'm happy. I'm with my brothers. Even before pubescence, we had the sense that we were special, that people would not fuck with us. To a boy, this is as intoxicating as the sweetest weed, as the purest blow. It changes one's brain pattern. It allows one to step into a lion's den with a pair of night vision goggles to hit the deadliest animals in the world. It gives one a heady sense of power, significance, and invulnerability. It allows us to savor the present. Like soldiers off to the front, gangsters live for the moment, relish food, pussy, and soft fabrics more deeply than the most heedless, straight epicurean.

I can't help myself. I plop down on the couch. I never want to leave this room, never mind the neighborhood. Here in this half-finished basement I had reached the apogee of human communion. Our youthful plots to conquer the world achieved a specificity far more satisfying than any reality. The shadows and I can live here in peace for the rest of time. Reading the old masters is useful for when you find yourself disgraced in fortune and men's eyes. But it is not human communion or even the memory of it.

But time puts an end to love as surely as the bullet put an end to Vinnie Five-Five.

"HOWIE, what's going on down there? Did you find it?"

Ah, shit. You can go home again, but just for a minute, long enough for you to mourn the inability to recapture the best times of your life.

My eyes scan the room. In the corner, leaning up against a folded Ping-Pong table is a carpet tied with string, heavy and stinky with mold. More dirt attaches itself to my face. I've been tarred and feathered.

The carpet weighs a ton. I can't imagine how we're going to roll Vinnie's 250 dead pounds into it and then schlep it to the car.

I lug the carpet up the stairs. Mrs. Five-Five still sits smoking at her table.

"Good boy," she says as I push the rug into the room. She throws me a pair of nail scissors. "Cut the string. I'll help you move the body."

After I snip the cords, another toxic cloud releases into the atmosphere. Both Mrs. Five-Five and I cough out the particles.

"Terrible," she says.

Mrs. Spoleto goes to the bed. "Get the sheet from that side and we'll wrap Vinnie in it. There'll be bloodstains so we'll have to flip the mattress. Eventually, you'll help me get rid of the bed. I won't be needing it anyway."

I grab the inert torso. "One . . . two . . . three!"

Mrs. Five-Five pushes the legs off the bed. The corpse lands with a thud on the carpet.

It's not that hard to roll it up with Vinnie inside. Then Mrs. Spoleto gives me some duct tape to bind the carpet. Vinnie will not escape.

"Now we have to get him to the car," she says. "We can just push him down the stairs. But getting him into the tunnel and then up into the garage won't be easy."

She can't lift the carpet an inch off the ground. Sweat drips off me just going ten feet.

"This is not working," I say as we reach the top of the steps. "We need help."

Mrs. Five Five's face is red. I worry that she is overstraining.

She regains her breath. "And who do you think you can call at this moment?"

"I have a girlfriend. Another pair of hands."

"She'll be an accessory. Do you want that? How long do you know her?"

"A couple of days."

"Howie. Don't be an idiot. Not all your life."

"She'll do whatever I want."

"Hardly the point." Mrs. Five-Five sniffles. "Did you know that Julius was seeing a nice girl? Studying to be a nurse at Kingsborough. She could have saved him." Saying this sets off Mrs. Five-Five. So cool up until this point, she collapses now into hiccupping weeping. "I told her not to come to the viewing. I didn't want her to see all the . . . Vlad could have hit . . ."

It takes a few minutes before Mrs. Five-Five gets hold of herself. So I sit on top of the carpet before I remember that Vinnie is rolled up inside. I jump up, but then I sit right back down. The old lady has curled into a ball on the floor and sobs uncontrollably. I put my hand on her shoulder and her bony fingers grip my hand.

I say nothing. At the end of the *Illiad,* Priam, the king of Troy, travels to the Greek encampment to beg Achilles for the body of Hector, whom Achilles has killed. In a poem that spends most of the time glorifying the heroic deeds that can only be accomplished by soldiers gutting one another, Achilles and Priam weep over their wasted lives, the wasted lives of their families, and the pointlessness of their murderous endeavors. Then they immediately go back to the Trojan War, where they finish the job of annihilating each other.

I don't know how long Mrs. Five-Five cries for the waste of her life. But her grip on my fingers loosens and soon her uncontrolled weeping changes into a soft animal whimper. I dare to glance at her. It is not a pleasant sight to see an older woman in a nightgown lying in a fetal position on the floor. Here is a picture of unrelieved and inconsolable misery. Her life, indeed, has gone up in smoke, her transcendent purpose discarded in a dumpster.

I help her up. I lead her back into the bedroom where she can cry with dignity. She only protests when I put her into the bed.

"I'll take care of everything. You're in shock and you have to be strong not just for yourself, but for . . . Gus."

She looks at me with dry-eyed sternness. "Howie, you can't take care of things yourself. If you could . . . This is a two-person job. And if this is shock, I've been in it all my life."

I have no idea if she's bullshitting. Her older son is dead, her husband has been murdered in front of her, and all that's left to keep her out of the pits of hell is an inarticulate goon who popped out of her as an addendum to the primary event and a junkie daughter on the West Coast.

"Where's Vinnie?"

"Where we left him. At the top of the stairs."

"We're going to do this. And we're going to do this now and we're going to do this right. I can't have Gus finding out that you capped his dad."

She leads me out of the bedroom and goes directly to the carpet where she picks up the part with the legs. "Just push it onto the steps."

It gets stuck a few times, but we're able to kick the body to the first floor.

There, a reinvigorated Mrs. Five-Five helps me get the carpet down to the basement and to the mouth of the tunnel, where I get my shoes. The next challenge is pushing a 300-pound stuffed carpet through the tunnel and then lifting it into the trunk of the car.

But nothing now daunts Mrs. Five-Five. "On three," she says.

By lifting, dragging, pushing, pulling, and yanking for the next forty minutes, we get the carpeted corpse to a point right below the door leading into the garage.

But now a sheen of sweat covers Mrs. Five Five too. A trickle dribbles down her cheeks. "I told Vinnie that he should lose weight. Wait here. I'll get Julius's keys."

So she trudges back into the house. While she's gone, I'm tempted to just leave Vinnie in the tunnel until he rots.

Actually, I conclude, not a bad idea. Why take him all the way to the lake when we could get some quick lime to mask the smell? No one remembers the tunnel is here except for Gus, who wouldn't think for a second that it's being used as his father's grave.

I hope that Mrs. Five-Five cannot find the key.

But she returns with one dangling off a Taj Mahal key chain. I remember going to Atlantic City with Julius when he got that key chain, a promotional item given out to whoever got an ace of spades blackjack. Julius hit one right away, and this then became his lucky talisman no matter how many thousands he subsequently lost. My God, memories can annoy you as much as the stupidest person.

"Let's go," Mrs. Five-Five says.

Mrs. Five-Five stands in the garage while I get down on my knees and put the carpet on my shoulder and climb the ladder with it. Atlas must feel like this, supporting the world on his back. The old woman helps me maneuver her dead bastard of a husband in a way she never could during his life.

Finally, Vinnie is in the trunk. I get behind the wheel and wait for Mrs. Spoleto to say something, some last words like, *He wasn't much, but he was my husband.*

She can't even say the first half of it.

34

The Diving Board and the Mothballs

I stare out the windshield as if trying to pierce through the garage's wall. What a woman this Mrs. Five-Five turned out to be. I had no idea what strength the deepest loathing can engender. Powerful. Far more powerful than love, its sickly sibling.

And what the fuck did *I* do? The crime flashes before me. The pillow, the blood on the sheet. I gasp. His face, Vinnie's face, floats before me. The jowls quiver. I smell his putrid breath. The vision fades with a scowl.

I've known Vinnie since I was a kid, since before he wanted to kill me. He gave me my first job, a hijacking of a tractor-trailer full of toys. For my sixteenth birthday he took me to his whorehouse. True, he got half of everything (except for the clap) which over the years added up to a lot more than I got from him.

I only began to dislike this gig because I cultivated other interests. And I became allergic to violence. At least, like a lot of people, I thought I was allergic. What did I know? I whacked the bastard totally on my own initiative. He would have whacked me, sure, eventually, but that's no excuse.

Suddenly, something explodes at my window and I leap out of my skin and crash my head on the roof of the car. I duck onto the floor and pull my gun. I'm about to fire through the glass when I see the vague outline of Mrs. Spoleto.

She's yelling, "Howie, Howie, roll down the window."

"Why?"

"I have to tell you something."

She spooks me so that I think I need to kill her.

"Clean up."

"What?"

"Take a shower. Change your clothes. Before you go upstate."

I step out of the car.

Mrs. Five-Five continues, "What happens if the cops stop you? You look like a chimney sweeper. You can't drive one hundred miles with a dead body in your trunk while in black face."

"I really want to get this over with."

"You can't. Ever."

She's right.

"I'll find clean clothes for you. I'll see if Julius has something."

I am six inches taller than Julius had been. But it's the only option.

I follow Mrs. Five-Five back through the tunnel. By the time I get back into her house, I'm looking forward to this shower, and not just for metaphorical purposes.

"Go inside. I'll get you towels."

My clothes stick to me as if glued. The grime streaks my chest, dick, and legs. I turn on the shower and appreciate Vinnie's connections with the plumbing union. For such an inconspicuous house on such a dead street in such a marginal neighborhood, he has water pressure fit for a mogul. The showerhead is one of those gigantic, bristly ovals that shoots needles of hot water that hit my body like a purifying scourge.

The world narrows to the breadth of the bathtub. My eyes are open but I see nothing. Then my hand brushes something hard. I look around. Nothing. Then another touch of iron.

Suddenly, my penis floats into view, stretching from one end of the shower to the other.

I examine it with interest. You think if you know one thing, it is your own body. But even this surprises again and again. Usually, the surprises are unpleasant, as you become ever more aware of your slow disintegration. For no reason a limb aches. Your eyes weaken. Your digestive tract goes to hell. You eat less but gain weight. You can't run as fast or punch as hard. You are in a constant state of mourning for the passing of your powers. But occasionally, unexpectedly, you are surprised by joy. The life force must be circulating heavily for my penis to pulse so. I push the shaft down and it springs back like an Olympic diving board.

My mind casts back, though it need not cast back that far, to Ariel. Her body appears before me, especially her own dark and juicy genitals. I bet she wishes she were here. I envision the water dripping off her engorged nipples. Rubbing soap on my hand, I begin stroking my prick.

This relaxes me further, until the thought that I just killed someone assails me. I should not be masturbating in his shower. I was never this crazy. I have always viewed myself as cautious and prudent. I told myself never to do something that is utterly irreversible. And I have violated this. I will be hunted by both the lawful and the lawless. Every day will bring new threats of exposure. I will not have, nor will I deserve, a moment's peace.

Ariel returns to the shower as soon as I close my eyes. She's wet and sticky with desire. I pump my soapy penis gently, no rush, I will stay here; my testicles tingle in anticipation—

"Shut the water, shut the water."

My eyes pop open. Mrs. Spoleto has yanked open the fiberglass shower door and she takes in the scene. She stops her urgent shouting and whispers, "What are you doing, Howie?"

"What does it look like? Showering. The dirt caked into my skin . . . do you mind?"

The old woman doesn't take her eyes off my erection. "Gus just pulled up."

"Fuck."

"Put this on." She hangs a black tracksuit on the towel rack. "And wait for me in my bedroom closet." With that she picks my dirty clothes off the floor and rushes out of the bathroom. From outside the door she calls, "You have ten seconds before he's in the house."

Gus. I played pool with him for hours. I encouraged his solitary talent as if it mattered. In some ways I had been closer with second banana Gus than I had with Julius. Of course either would blow me and his mother away for what we've done.

Besides the tracksuit, Mrs. Five-Five leaves a pair of underpants that I imagine are an old pair of Julius's. I try not to think of the grossness of the situation. I just take everything and duck into the bedroom as the front door opens.

As much as I want to hear what Gus tells his mother, I take her advice and hide in the closet. I must fight my way through three rows of pantsuits before I hunker down in the farthest corner where the smell of camphor assaults me. She must keep her woolens back here.

I gag. My maternal grandmother smelled like this but no one else I ever knew. Mrs. Five-Five struck me as traditional and old-fashioned, but she never stunk of mothballs.

What is Gus doing here at four in the morning? Sitting on the floor of the closet, I grip my gun and think of Molière, his play *Tartuffe*. Hidden in a classic French farce with slammed doors and lecherous groping is a powerful challenge to doltish authority, a call for a revolution against stale ideas that keep happiness at bay for no sensible reason. One particular fool is told to wait quietly, not to jump out of the closet too soon. But of course he does, for he wouldn't be an idiot if he could contain himself. And he nearly ruins everything.

This comes to me because I am being pulled out of my own closet by unseen cords. What I need to do is whack

Gus. Because after Gus, no one would care about avenging Vinnie Five-Five. Tony D in New Jersey might make some desultory inquiries, but he'd be happy to let the dead bury the dead. Why look for war against the Chinese or the Russians? He'd probably make a deal with them for a piece of Vinnie's old action. Why not? The Russians and the Jersey Italians do plenty of business together. Like businessmen everywhere, gangsters make goodwill gestures if it will ultimately profit them.

But if I hit Gus, I'd also need to hit Mrs. Spoleto. For her reasoning behind helping me with Vinnie is to save Gus. Now Gus would not have been the first one in the lifeboat, if Mrs. Five-Five had her choice. Maybe Mrs. Five-Five believes Gus will one day overcome his powerful tendencies toward dimwittedness.

I hear footsteps approaching and I click my piece's safety. The closet door opens and Mrs. Five-Five whispers, "Howard?"

I crawl out from behind her dresses. "Is he gone?"

"Come on. I have to talk to you."

Even outside the closet I still feel immersed in a dream. First, the new clothes bother me. The T-shirt Mrs. Five-Five has given me barely reaches my waist. The tracksuit bags around my middle. The socks fit.

Mrs. Five-Five leads me to her kitchen and sits at the table. I've always liked the Spoletos' kitchen. The walls are painted a sunny yellow. The black granite countertops are mirror shiny and contrast nicely with the cabinets' deep mahogany. Looking at this kitchen one would never get the impression that the people who live here are forces of darkness, sociopaths who pride themselves on their deep immersion in the pieties of the striving middle class.

"Gus came here to tell us that they found IRA's head and legs by the bus stop on Coney Island Avenue and Z. In trash cans catty-corner to each other."

I lower the gun. Finally, some good news. Wonderful news. "Just now? At this hour?"

"Gus got a call. So he and Pauli Bones drove over. And now I told them that Vinnie never came home. Gus left thinking that they got Vinnie. I told him to do nothing stupid until the morning."

"That's a long time for him."

"Gus is a good boy." Mrs. Spoleto wipes her eyes. "He idolized his brother and father. Maybe he'll blossom without them. He may not be the idiot everyone thinks."

"He is as tough as anyone," I say for I can tell that Mrs. Spoleto is trying to convince herself that her surviving son is not hopeless.

"He could be something," Mrs. Spoleto is crying openly. "We have to convince him that Vinnie is in hiding somewhere so he doesn't go after Vlad. You could do that. Just tell him you got a call from Vinnie, from an undisclosed location and he said to lie low— "

"Why would Vinnie call *me* to say this? He'd call Gus. Or you."

"Me?" Mrs. Five-Five wipes her cheeks and chugs a beer. "Would Vinnie call me? We stopped talking years ago . . . but I can tell Gus . . ." Mrs. Five-Five's face now lights with pleasure. "Yes. I'll say that Vinnie ordered Gus to get out of harm's way. You know Gus loves the Southwest. New Mexico. Santa Fe. Taos."

"I know. Julius kept trying to get Vinnie to expand into the Sun Belt."

"That wasn't Julius's idea. It was all Gus."

"It was?"

"He went out there to . . . on business. He painted such a beautiful portrait of the climate and landscape that Julius fell in love with it just from Gus's description."

"Gus painted a verbal portrait? Just using the words fuck, shit, cunt—"

"Howie. Please. Haven't you heard of hidden depth? Aren't *you* a little smarter than you let on?"

"No. Actually, I'm stupider. If you just knew what I think about—"

"Get rid of Vinnie's body. Now. Then we'll worry about stopping the attack on Vlad."

"What about Gus? If he comes back and notices the car missing—"

"He won't be back. He and Pauli are going to a motel to get some sleep."

Of course, Aeschylus's *Oresteia* immediately pops into my mind. I try to stop these uselessly cascading thoughts, but the story rolls out with the uncontainable fury of cognition itself. Gus Spoleto would play Orestes and Mrs. Spoleto Clytemnestra. I'd be Aegisthus, even though I've never been Mrs. Five-Five's lover. Vinnie is the doomed Agamemnon. In the original, Clytemnestra kills Agamemnon, her husband, for sacrificing their daughter Iphigenia. Orestes, their son, then kills his mother and her lover. The Furies hunt Orestes down. But Apollo decides to save him by setting up a trial. He gets the goddess Athena to be the judge, and, ultimately, Orestes is exonerated. Mercy prevails. In our case, the ending would be different for pity does not exist 3,000 years later in a society as primitive and bloodthirsty as ours.

"Howie, are you still with me? What's the matter? Why are you . . ."

Why can't I stop my mind from spinning in these endlessly useless circles?

"Can you do what you have to? Can you drive upstate?"

"Yes. It's just . . ." The great books haunt me worse than Vinnie's ghost. I check my pocket for the keys. "I'm ready." I go to the stairs that lead to the basement and Mrs. Five-Five stops me. "We can go around the front."

Outside, the cool air envelops our faces. It's nice not to be crawling around like a hedgehog.

35

A Day at the Lake

I pull out of the garage and drift slowly into the street. I can't afford to attract the least attention so I repress my desire to floor the accelerator. I glide onto the BQE. Ninety minutes later, the last scuds of night still envelop the world. Luckily the people around this lake know enough to keep silent if they see strange men rowing around with a package wrapped in a carpet.

I've made this run twice. Once, after Vinnie clipped a made guy with the permission of the Commission. Another time Vinnie asked me to dump a metal box that contained I know not what—a hot gun, a large scrotum. In any case, he told me to treat it like a dead body, to leave nothing to chance. So I took a rowboat, a few always dot the shore, to the middle of the lake where I watched the box sink below the surface.

This current job would be identical. My only problem would be lifting the load into a rowboat.

The shore is deserted. Adrenaline pumps power into my muscles so I lift Vinnie's body from the trunk with no more difficulty than I would a shopping bag. I work quickly, slinging the carpet over my shoulder. I half waddle, half run over the wet ground where my feet sink into the mud. Even this doesn't matter. I get to a boat and push it into the water.

The lake is at 3,000 feet and it's much cooler here than in Brooklyn. The sun begins to rise and its rays streak the sky cobalt and yellow. In a few minutes, I stop rowing. The boat bobs and the dawn reveals a terrible beauty. Fir trees line the far shore. Purple mountains rise above them in the distance. Ducks quack overhead and slide onto the water near the boat.

I glance at the carpet in which Vinnie is rolled and think that it wouldn't be the worst thing to change places. I've had a death wish on and off for most of my life, though I only allowed it to overwhelm me that one time, in the Seventy-Ninth Street subway station. But I have a gun. If I use it on myself, I will never have to worry about someone else killing me.

Then I imagine a life with Ariel. We'd get a place above ground, copulate in weird ways, maybe have a strange kid. Both of us could, eventually, be good earners. Buy a house. Travel. Read. Find an inner life a little less tormenting. Everything would come together perfectly. That's the moment I will get it in the back of the head. Why live in this unbearable state of heightened anxiety when I could evaporate in this lovely spot?

With the last of my strength, I push Vinnie over the side. The carpet floats until it absorbs enough water to turn it into an iron chain. It sinks. Only if the last drop of water is drained from the lake will Vinnie's bones ever come to light.

If I'm not going to kill myself, there's no point in hanging about. Why ask for trouble? I bring the skiff back to shore and, unseen as far as I can tell, take off.

Without the body weighing me down, I speed down the highway helium high. I have accomplished something. What, I'm not sure. Have I finally matured into a conscience? Have I finally learned that it is not enough merely to think? One must act. Have I eliminated a vicious predator who should have suffered this rough justice years ago? Or am I just another self-justifying killer? I have gone through life believing myself incapable of killing. Ridiculous.

At this hour, this far away from the city, the roads are quiet even of cops. A few cars disappear in my rearview mirror. I pass a few trucks. The car's rocking motion lulls me. Usually, it is not a good idea to close one's eyes when driving sixty-five miles an hour unless you want to . . . I pass on yet another opportunity.

The car slows as I pull into the parking lot of a Giant supermarket. It's only dawn but the lot is half full. My only risk is that I meet other wise guys on their way to the lake. But because of the war, most regular business has been put on hold. These days, bodies lie where they fall.

While I sit with a coffee I call Mrs. Five-Five, who picks up on the first ring. She sounds extremely clearheaded when she demands, "Where the hell are you?"

"Having coffee."

"Really? Howie, I never expected this of you."

"Coffee?"

"You always struck me as—"

"Incompetent?"

"No. A good kid."

This night has gotten to Mrs. Five-Five too. "I was never a good kid."

"You were suggestible. That's what I mean. I thought you'd just go to your death like the rest of them, guns blazing but without much of a fight. You never looked too deeply into things. Howie, I always liked you." Is the old lady coming on to me? She continues, "Of all my boys' friends, you were the one I thought might be able to do something else. You were never the utter thug that Julius and Gus usually played with."

Mrs. Five-Five sounds out of her head. The weed might have worn off, but she's in that truth-babbling, life-threatening stage. "Mrs. Spoleto, just go to sleep. You sound exhausted. Don't talk on the phone anymore."

"It's been a long night, hasn't it, Howie?"

"Yeah."

She purrs, "We need to talk, Howie. We're in this together."

"Of course." Never have I been more alone.

And she *is* flirting. This revolting development arrives out of nowhere, like everything else that ever happens. So why does each idiotic surprise shake me anew? Why can't I see anything coming? I can't scorn this woman. I can ice her, however. I just hope she has another unused carpet lying around. "I should be at your place in about an hour."

I take the coffee to the car. If this be worth doing, it be worth doing now.

Because I have murder on my mind, I keep the car under the speed limit.

Mrs. Five-Five meets me in the garage. As soon as I get out of the car, she melts into my chest. She murmurs, "Howie, Howie. We did it. You know, you probably saved a bunch of lives. Certainly yours."

I slip the gun out of my pocket. Mrs. Five-Five's arms encircle my waist. I hear her panting. If I kill Rose Spoleto then I'm just another gangster willing to justify any murder as self-defense. I will gain my life but lose my soul. Rose is not Vinnie.

Rose tilts her head toward me. I don't know what she expects. She has fine bone structure. She is also so transported that she does not notice that one of the arms hugging her is holding a gun.

"Put the gun down, Howie." She disengages, but still grips my arms. She does notice. "You're not that kind of killer."

"What kind is that?"

"The kind that kills. Vinnie brought devastation to whatever he touched. He needed to die like a plague rat."

As a kid, I always believed that Vinnie and Rose were quite the traditional couple. She kept house and he murdered enemies. Go figure.

"Come in the house," she says.

I have parked the car away from the tunnel entrance. We pull the door up and climb down into the narrow space.

Mrs. Five-Five says, "I'm going to blow the tunnel up after this."

"You might disturb the neighbors."

"I'll do it quietly. I have my own connections in the building trade."

Back in the house, Rose goes to her fridge and pulls out some covered Pyrex dishes. "What do you want? I got some lasagna, meat balls, and . . ." she sticks her head deep in the fridge and takes out half a salami and a block of cheese. "Or I can make you a sandwich."

If I'm not going to kill her I should just go.

"Howie, I got emotional. Don't think about it."

Rose's face relaxes to the point that I can make out individual features. I see she has a small nose. Pert. Never noticed. When she was younger she was a mom, as ancient as any. Once in a while I'd glance at her chest. Even as a kid I appreciated matronly. But her face had been composed of dark lines and a worried expression. Her features remained vague.

But now the nose. Maybe because someone finally whacked her husband she feels comfortable enough to showcase her extremities. Her ears, too, I can see, are nicely rounded. They peek out from under the curtain of dirty blonde hair. Yes. The hair, too, I just notice. Up until a minute ago I thought it had been grey.

Next, I dare look at her eyes. They're blue. Not a clear sky blue, but a cataracty, smoggy blue that veers into purple and brown. Mrs. Five-Five may be Sicilian, but Northern European crusaders raped at least one of her ancestors.

"What are you looking at?" she asks as she bows her head.

"Your eyes," I say. "They're blue."

"You know me thirty years," she retorts, angrier with me now than when I pointed the gun at her temple, "and you just this minute—"

"Sorry. I didn't mean anything." I continue to stare as new facets of Mrs. Five-Five's countenance come alive. Her cheeks are doughy but her forehead curves into her hairline at the right nanometer. Her lips are nicely colored . . . I turn away before I infuriate her further.

The microwave beeps and Mrs. Five-Five removes a plate of lasagna and puts it in front of me. "Eat this," she orders.

I slice the thick slab in half. Steam rises and brings the aroma of tomatoes and beef to my nostrils. My mouth waters. I am starving. I chew a piece and it's the best thing I ever ate. The juice from the meat combines with the tangy sauce. "This is really delicious."

I take another bite because I can't help myself. But after a third mouthful I put my fork down. No matter how tasty the food, I really can't eat the leftovers of the man I murdered.

Luckily Mrs. Five-Five has also sliced some salami and cheese. This I can eat.

"Howie, I've thought of a variation on our plans. Now I think it's better that you go to the funeral home and act like you know nothing about Vinnie's disappearance." She plays with her coffee mug. "Gus has gone crazy. He is going to carry out Vinnie and IRA's plan. Especially now, in honor of them being gone or some such bullshit."

"I thought the whole point—"

"Shut up. You have no choice. If you jump ship now, either Gus or Tony D will find you. Survive the attack on Vlad's place, and there's a chance you can get free of all this. Everything."

I'm impressed. Mrs. Five-Five is just another gangster, a good one. She does not, I believe, want me to leave Vlad's place alive.

"Do you understand what you need to do?"

I turn back to Mrs. Five-Five who stares with ferocity. For a second I think she's going to whack me. She does not want her part in Vinnie's death known. For her revenge to be pure, she needs to get away with it.

I pull myself together for the final part of this denouement. I must leave Mrs. Five-Five with the impression that I'm not going to fuck this up. "Okay. I will demand retaliation against

Vlad with such demented force that Gus will think I'm as nuts as Pauli Bones."

A smile lights Mrs. Five-Five's face. "Exactly. You seem to understand things if they're explained simply. Go home and get some sleep. You need to be fresh for the performance." And with these words, the vision of Mrs. Five-Five recedes into the ether. The hair, the forehead, the eyes, the cheeks, the lips, the breasts return to their undifferentiated form. She becomes the black widow mom of the living and the dead.

36

Reconciliation

Maybe a smarter person would know what to do from here. A genius would intuit a redemptive conclusion to this entire unholy mess. He would leave behind friends, family, fear, and aggravation and be reborn into a sensible and blood-free existence. In this new identity he would drink good wine and become a churchgoer. His sex would be confined to the most savagely basic. He would learn to enjoy driving.

But I am not that clever. I would always hate driving and forever enjoy simple bondage and discipline. Violence, to be truthful at last, solves some problems even if it creates ten new ones. Must I join the battle at The National? I text Ariel, *coming over.*

In a second I get her answer. *Hurry.*

Fifteen minutes later, I'm at the side door. I turn the knob. She has left it open.

In the basement. Ariel is wearing a yellow T-shirt and white panties. Her hair is uncombed and stray strands stick out like needles. Self-consciously, she runs her fingers over her scalp.

But then she remembers to be shocked at my own appearance. "Where did you get those idiotic clothes? That tracksuit? It doesn't suit you at all."

Even after cleaning up at Mrs. Five-Five's I can't camouflage my wrecked condition.

"Where were you all night?"

"Nowhere." And this is, in fact, the entire explanation I can give her.

"I understand perfectly. I should mind my own business. Fine. No problem. What gives you the right to do this to me? Answer me, you stupid mute. I know you can talk in the same way I know you can read."

"I said I had to do this one thing and that I couldn't talk about it."

I say this forcefully, but without anger, and Ariel turns away, abashed. "Sorry."

"You've been drinking."

"It's the only way I can contain my anxiety while you're wandering around a battlefield thinking . . . thinking something. I know you think even though you've never actually said a single interesting thing. You lie even about being ignorant and uninteresting. And you lie about being nowhere." Then her anger dissipates. She turns to me and rubs my cheek. "This is new." She means it is not one of the bruises I got in the beating when I was kidnapped. "It's raw. Who did this to you?"

"No one did anything to me."

"Howie, you're not a fighter. You're certainly no killer. So why hang around with them?"

I shrug.

Ariel begins licking my face, like an animal trying to heal a wound.

I must have chafed my cheek raw against the rough carpet while lugging Vinnie to the boat. Now that Ariel has pointed it out, it begins to burn. Her tongue is certainly no help and I tilt my head away from her.

Ariel picks up my hands. "And your fingernails are black. What have you been doing?"

"Nothing." Grease covers the whole nail like polish.

Indefatigable, Ariel lifts my shirt and runs her fingers down my chest until they reach my waist. She gets down on the floor and yanks the legs of my pants. I close my eyes in anticipation of some sort of pleasure.

37

The Longish Good-bye

When I awake, I'm lying on the bed, covered with the blanket. Ariel is not in the room.

I look up at the window but can't tell if it is night or day. I control my rising panic. If I miss the rendezvous at the funeral parlor, Gus and the others will think I'm a deserter, or worse, had something to do with Vinnie's disappearance.

Just obscenities fly through my head, interspersed with the word "dead."

I hear footsteps and I stop moving. I wait. Ariel walks into the room.

"You're up," she says.

"I missed it?"

"Missed what? Oh. The blow job. Sorry. I don't fellaciate sleeping men. Do you feel like getting some Chinese food? Unless you want to finish what we started . . ."

I glance at my phone. It's almost six o'clock. With great relief, I go to my gym bag and pull out a pair of my own pants. A look of deep disappointment crosses Ariel's face.

"I have an appointment."

"Where? With who?"

Whom. But I don't correct her. Instead, I get another clip for my gun. I will have to dump this piece after tonight no matter what. Too bad. It really is the first gun I owned that has the gravitas necessary to kill someone.

Ariel continues her doleful observation of my every move.

I give her this much. "I just have to do this one last thing. No one will get hurt."

"That's exactly what people say right before they go out and get themselves killed."

I put on my jacket. "I'll be fine."

"You look terrible."

There's a scummy mirror in the toilet. I strain to see through the foggy reflection but I can't tell if I look any worse than I did before the Vinnie thing. I am glad, however, that Vlad beat me up. It's hard to tell the old bruises from the new.

Without saying anything, I take the steps two at a time. I hear nothing more from Ariel until I am out the door. There, heavy breathing makes me turn just as Ariel jumps me.

She hangs onto my back and at first I think she's playing. I laugh and twist around, but then her crying and cursing break through. "You bastard. You fucking bastard! Where are you going?" Her nails dig into my neck and she pulls my hair. "You're supposed to be hiding out."

The last thing I need is attention. Carrying a loaded piece is a mandatory three years. And the most dangerous place in the world would be Rikers, where Gus could have me clipped for two or three g's. So I try to peel Ariel off gently, but she holds tight. In the end, I throw her against the wall of her house. She stays on the ground sobbing loudly into her hands. If anyone has seen this bit of business, I'm fucked. The cops have probably already been called.

So I start running, thinking things couldn't be worse until I realize that Ariel is chasing me.

What happened to the ultraconventional girl I met in the pretentious café? The one with the mom, with an education, with artistic sensitivities, with a minor drinking problem, with no plans to destroy herself. Does unemployment really drive regular people insane? Where has this sprinting lunatic come from? I turn the corner and race toward Coney Island Avenue.

But Ariel must be some world-class sprinter because I turn my head and she's gaining on me. This, again, does not look good. A frantic woman chasing a six-foot-three thug with a bruised face might make even Brooklyn cops drive over to investigate.

So I stop.

Ariel comes up to me. Her makeup is smeared on her face like war paint. Furious, she explodes, "WHERE ARE YOU GOING?"

It will only take one punch to knock her unconscious. But that might also attract negative attention. So I keep my voice level. "It's better if you don't know."

"Tell me," she spits. "I don't give a fuck. You know I stopped drinking."

"When."

"Just now. I've been sober since you woke up."

I calculate. It has been about fifteen minutes.

"And I don't plan on drinking anymore. Not if we can be together." Her voice regains its normal pitch. "Those books. Did you really read them?"

"Not now." I don't want to reexcite her.

"Is that all you can say? I'm risking my life for you, Howie. So I can be with you."

It all becomes very touching and very silly. "Go home, Ariel. Please."

She looks down at her stocking feet. "I have no shoes."

"You got here fine."

"I stepped on something." With that, her knees fold and she collapses onto the ground. There, cross-legged, she pulls off her sock.

"It's a piece of glass." And she wrestles a shard the size of a large thorn from her foot. This unstops the puncture and blood trickles down her sole. Maybe it started hurting suddenly or maybe the sight of blood freaks her, but Ariel begins moaning. "I can't walk. Please, Howie."

I don't have time for this. "You might need stitches. I'll call an ambulance and they'll sew you up in the emergency room."

In a soft voice, she begs, "Can you help me home?"

How do I get sidetracked like this? These ludicrous subplots will cost me my life.

"For God's sake, Howie, say something already." On the ground, she sways back and forth as if in terrible pain. "Now that I can't get drunk, we must talk to each other. Converse. What else will replace alcohol in making things bearable?"

I regret Ariel's teetotaling. "The booze certainly let you make the sex interesting."

"Thank you for saying something." She grimaces. "I expect articulation, if nothing else."

Gangsters could be as punctual as garden-variety neurotics if the situation calls for it. I can't stand here arguing for or against sobriety. "If I don't get to where I need to go, I'm dead no matter where we run to."

Ariel picks herself off the ground. "You know, if you really read all those books, you should be able to think of something clever."

"Call the ambulance. A doctor has to check you out."

Ariel hops away like a bunny. "Go," she calls without turning around. "I'll take care of myself."

"At least disinfect the cut as soon as you get home," I yell to her back.

Now twenty feet away, she screams, "I'll hate you forever if you get yourself murdered."

So now I can head toward my fate. About time.

38

National Massacre Day

From the outside, the funeral parlor appears empty. The heavy wooden doors are locked tight. No light emanates from the two small windows facing the street.

But I go around to the back and knock on an industrial steel door. It's yanked open by the skeleton of Pauli Bones. He holds a sawed-off shotgun, barrel up.

"Don't stand there like a dickhead," the emaciated ghoul grunts. But his voice is almost gentle as he examines me, as he weighs the cost of letting me live.

Inside, ten people are crowded into Vinnie's office. Of course, neither Vinnie nor IRA show up, nor will they ever again.

Of those I recognize, only Frankie Hog comes over to me, and without his usual hostility.

"You heard?"

"Fucking tragedy. We'll take care of him today." I make as if checking the room. "Where's Vinnie?"

"Not here yet."

I say nothing more. The situation must develop.

The office fills. Moron and the Jew nod at me. Gus hasn't come yet. I circle the room, trying to find the best spot to make my stand. In the process, I accidentally kick someone's leg.

"Sit down, bro," says a smooth-faced, gel-haired kid, nineteen or twenty but one who glows with the aura of an up-and-coming maniac. He rouses himself from leaning against the wall. He's nearly as tall as I, and his muscles stretch the fabric of his black Lycra shirt.

I worry that my nerves show. So I look at the guy and try to formulate an appropriate apology. I begin by giving him one of my patented shoves that sends him flying across the room.

I stand my ground confident that others would grab him before he reaches me.

And that's exactly what happens. In fact, it's Pauli Bones and Moron who hold his arms. I straighten my shoulders and stand with my hands clasped in front of me. "Let the punk go."

The kid's smooth visage changes into its natural dark volcanic fury. He doesn't strain against the people holding him, but if left unchecked, he'd beat me to death.

"Fuck you, cunts." Gus enters the room pushing a dolly with an open wooden crate. Inside are Uzi machine pistols and other automatic weapons. "Save it for fucking later."

We all crowd around the box. The kid glares at me but the sight of heavy weaponry distracts him in the way a box of colored blocks does a three-year-old.

"Don't grab, you fucks," Gus admonishes. "There's enough for everyone."

I take an M-16 assault rifle.

"Hey, Windows," Pauli Bones demands, "you know how to use that?"

"I've fired it at the range."

Both Gus and Pauli give me hard looks.

"Friendly fire can do a lot of fucking damage," Bones says.

"Where are the night vision goggles?" I ask.

Gus answers, "IRA was supposed to bring them."

At IRA's name everyone stops moving. He may not have been popular, but his death brings home one's vulnerability. If they could detach the head and feet of a hypervigilant psychopath like IRA, a man who craved human flesh and thirsted for human blood, not one of us is invulnerable.

"So how are we going to see in the dark?" the Jew asks.

"We'll tape flashlights to the barrels. Shine the light into the Russians' eyes. Avoid blinding each other."

Silence takes over as we digest this. Though using the night vision shit had struck none of us as an intelligent solution, it now seems as elegant as E=MC^2, compared with the jerry-rigged flashlight idea.

Finally, someone realizes we are captainless. "Where's Vinnie?"

Gus rises to the occasion with a bravado display of mindless contempt and arrogance. "None of your fucking business," he shouts at the guy, an older gangster with wavy white hair halfway up his skull. "If Vinnie wanted you to know, he would have fucking told you."

This question lingers unasked: who's going to lead the attack?

Because Gus has lived for so long in the shadow of his father and brother, and because of his reputation as a fool, the experienced hands cannot imagine Gus in command. Yet the chain of command leaves Gus in charge. We have to follow.

I must admit, Gus looks less stupid than usual. He has just put together a few coherent sentences that move beyond his exclusively obscenity-filled vocabulary. *Henry V* comes to mind. Could this cement-brained thug become a leader of men? Would he be able to fuse this motley group of freelance assholes into a single cohesive anus? Could he deliver a speech to rival the Saint Crispin's Day oratory and, like Henry V, inspire his army to take on the superior forces lying in wait in the cellar of The National?

Everyone's checking their weapons, grabbing extra clips. Though we lack formal military training, we've been soldiers our whole lives. We've all handled automatic weaponry. We follow orders. And most of all, we feel justified, indeed righteous, blowing people to hell. We tell ourselves we are protecting our friends, our culture, our territory. Few people risk everything. We are the heroic few.

Gus clears his throat. He's going to do it. I already hear echoes of Henry's powerful rallying cry. *We few, we happy few, we band of brothers, for he today that sheds his blood with me, shall be my brother, be he never so vile, this day shall gentle his condition.* On and on it goes, more bloody nonsense than I can ever remember.

Meanwhile, Gus says nothing.

Like dolts, we stand around looking at each other. I am not the only one who expects a monumental power shift.

Gus peers back at us. He clears his throat again. Finally, he begins and with enormous self-possession states, "We'll order some fucking pizza."

"What?"

"Might as well eat while we wait for Vinnie. We can't do this without Vinnie."

A great relief spreads through the crowd. No one, not even Gus himself, wants an idiot to lead us despite Henry V's unexpected victory at Agincourt in October 1415.

I conclude, however, that Gus gave the best speech he possibly could. He follows up by confidently ordering a pie with anchovies and two with onions and sausage.

Frankie Hog stands next to me and mutters between gritted teeth, "I don't like this."

At first I think he means the toppings. But I realize that Frankie would eat anything including the cardboard box. He means the situation. So I respond, "You don't like anything unless it's covered in cheese and tomato sauce."

"Shut the fuck up. Vinnie would not be late for this if he were . . . able to come."

This comment loosens my intestines, but I stay on the offensive. "You worried about hitting The National?"

"Fuck you," Frankie says. "Vinnie should be here." He shakes his head but brightens when the pizza arrives. Grabbing slices from both boxes, he alternately bites giant chunks. My stomach is knotted but I eat just to show people I'm fine.

Frankie Hog comes back to me and barks, "You know something."

"You have no idea, big boy."

"Where's Vinnie?"

"Fuck off."

Frankie examines what remains. He lifts the lone slice out of the box. "The smelliness of the fish does not complement the mozzarella."

I see his point and go to the bathroom to discreetly puke.

In the office, the thugs are milling about dangling their weapons. A few have red sauce staining the corners of their mouths, except for Frankie Hog, whose whole face is schmeered with a layer of oil. He's licking his lips.

I think of Ariel and her secret weapon in life. How can I do this without being drunk or high? Long ago I decided not to say much, and never anything in public. Going on the record invites trouble. But I need to go on the record now. "Gentlemen, I don't think we can wait any longer. The shape-up at The National will be over and we'll lose the opportunity."

The milling stops. People who have been hopping from foot to foot freeze in midhop. Those stretching now slacken their muscles, and those who have been whispering shut up.

My voice shakes as I announce, "Cry 'havoc!' and let slip the—"

"What are you talking about," Frankie Hog interrupts, "you fucking dick?"

"Shut up, Frankie," Gus orders. He turns to me, "What the fuck are you talking about, you fucking dick?"

"Did anyone ask you a fucking thing?" Frankie Hog continues.

"Shut up, Frankie. And you," Gus points. "I don't want to hear another word from you, especially not what . . . you were just fucking saying. It's so fucking stupid that, that . . . you fucking cunt."

So everyone returns to form. Nerves and fright become immediately obvious when you start quoting Shakespeare on war or death. It's an ugly tic I have. Still, I have expressed myself publicly for the first time. That's something. I modulate my voice but even now don't totally retreat into goonspeak: "I just mean that we can't lose the element of surprise. After today, Vlad will whack us one by one."

Frankie Hog sums up his faction's position. "We need to wait for Vinnie."

Gus, I can see, is momentarily confused. Maybe this epiphany excites his few working neurons: *I am unprepared for the burden of leadership.*

Frankie growls, "Vinnie's not here for a reason. Maybe he's at a sit-down with Vlad."

"Wouldn't he fucking tell me?" Gus asks rhetorically, though we all know Vinnie would not necessarily tell Gus a thing.

"Windows is right," Pauli Bones says.

This shuts everyone up. I may lack the heft to convince a mosquito to bite a juicy ass, but Pauli Bones is a killer and a bona fide madman. His word is respected. I see Armageddon unfolding, hell opening. Bones will carry the day.

"Pauli," Gus says, "Vinnie will kill us if we act without his go-ahead."

"He gave us the go-ahead. This is his plan."

"So where is he?" Gus shouts.

"Where do you think?"

Gus deflates. His small power of command deserts him and he says softly, "Motherfucker." His complexion turns ashy as he admits to himself that his father is dead.

Bones looks around the room. No one has a thing to add.

Through the fog of nightmare I hear Bones make reasonable points. "Vinnie is not at a sit-down with Vlad. Not after Julius and IRA got snuffed. Besides, everyone he would bring to the sit-down is in this room."

There is no more debate. Instead people begin taping flashlights to the ends of their guns.

The irresistible current of events pulls me along. But I don't panic. Because of my own reckless and irretrievable actions, I'm benumbed, dead inside. Outside, my gun is ready to go.

By the time we leave, the desire for revenge awakens Gus and he asserts himself more strongly than at any other time in his life. "We have three cars outside," he says. "Four men to a car. Guns under the seats. No speeding. Nothing stupid between here and The National. We pull up together, we get out together. We go inside like all we want is borscht. Blow away anyone who tries to stop you. It's Tuesday, the slowest night. But they'll be there, We're in and out. Empty your clips. Do damage."

Bones adds, "Shoot the lights and bust down doors. Anyone with a flashlight is one of us."

People nod, each convinced that he will be the sole survivor.

We put the guns in our coats as we make our way to the cars, which have been stolen for the occasion. I'm with Pauli Bones, Gus, and Frankie Hog. Pauli drives.

We are attacking our neighbors so the drive is short. In five minutes we pull up in front of The National.

Getting out of the car, not a single literary allusion comes to mind. A few film clichés flash by—the final scene in the *Godfather,* something with actors playing Luciano and Lansky—but these only annoy me.

I need to focus on the moment. No matter how rich my inner life, no matter my hesitation about this work, I can no longer pretend I'm only half a gangster. No, I am a vicious outcast, a Nietzschean jerk. Killing Vinnie seals me into this identity whatever my motives. Death and destruction continue unabated and I'm part of this. I should just let myself be killed.

So I find myself on point, first into the club. But it is Pauli Bones who opens fire and hits two surprised crew cuts standing in the foyer. I see them fall and I hear screams coming from the dining room.

We charge downstairs. In the dank low-ceilinged basement Pauli Bones hits the lights. Flashlights beam here and there, creating monstrous shadows on the wall that dance and fall. I hear the thuds as bodies hit the ground. The Russians can't see. Lights shine in the heavy faces of gangsters armed just with handguns. Chaos. Something socks me in the ribs. I don't know if it is a bullet or a fist. But I keep moving forward.

In the same second I realize I'm in the room where I got that beating. Vlad, here too, stands to his full six foot seven. And while his underlings are emptying .22s and .38s, he's blazing away with an AK-47.

Lying prone, I feel the whoosh of bullets flying over my body. I open up on Vlad. He shoots back, but another burst sends him diving behind his pillar. My gun clicks. I have emptied my clip. The light now serves as a beacon for my death. Vlad shouts Russian obscenities and I'm frozen as much as any animal who knows the game is up. But right before I die Pauli Bones and Gus burst into the room and catch Vlad in the chest. The monster is wearing a bulletproof vest so he's merely knocked backward. He raises his gun just as a headshot blows his skull into a thousand fragments.

The first thing I do is feel my urine. Lovely. The dead smell nothing.

Gus and Pauli Bones are laughing as I sneak out of the room. No point in publicizing my little accident. In the hallway there's no more shooting. We have killed every Russian. This should go down in the annals of mobdom. But then I hear a burst of fire. I lunge back into Vlad's office. There, Gus lies in a pool of his own blood.

Pauli Bones swings the gun, and the flashlight at the end of it blinds me. "Vlad got him."

"I need to use the bathroom."

"You saw Vlad get him."

"I'm not blind, Pauli. Gus died a hero."

Pauli Bones lowers his weapon. "Change your diaper. Clean up. Then get out of here."

For a moment, I freeze, shocked. Pauli Bones is letting me go. I know what happened, yet he's not going to shoot me. Our friendship? Is that what Pauli and I have? Or . . . no explanation fits, but for the second time I leave Vlad's charnel house still breathing. That must be a record. But Gus. Vlad, my ass. I saw Vlad's brains drip down the palace walls while Gus and Pauli high-fived each other. Pauli Bones took out Gus. He would not have done that to Vinnie or even Julius, but Pauli Bones was never going to serve under Gus Five-Five Spoleto.

For some reason, calm overtakes me in the toilet. I remove my underwear, wash my thighs, dry my pants the best I can. Pauli Bones. He's a good earner, a decent manager, a stone killer. But I never thought him a boss with the vision to run a wide-ranging business. Again, it is I who lack vision.

I try not to leave any DNA behind. In the trash can is a plastic bag which I use for my soiled underpants. I have no choice but to slip this mess into my pocket.

By the time I leave the bathroom only dead bodies litter the floor. I drop my guns near one and head up the stairs. The stolen cars are still in front of the club, but my people have scattered. No one is in the restaurant or the lobby. I hear sirens. The cops will be here in a minute. I take one more quick look. We did something here. We, including me, smashed a gang that had been bigger and stronger than we were using a ruthless guile that I never believed existed outside of books.

A bit stunned, I walk into the night.

39

Say My Name

I head to the boardwalk. Even here, in Brooklyn, the waves wash in and out with the regularity of a Caribbean paradise. At the edge of the water, I try to lose myself in this oceanic moment. Ah, nature. Its comforts are just one more sentimental illusion, like the attachment to this neighborhood that blights my life. I throw my urine-soaked underpants into the sea.

Old Russian men stroll by, shooting hard, suspicious glances. I have no weapon but so what? Let them take me out. I can't think anymore. I walk back toward Sheepshead Bay and text Ariel, *coming over.*

Ariel responds with one word: *hurry.*

Thirty minutes later, I'm in her basement. She's waiting for me at the foot of the stairs, her eyes open so wide that she eats me with them.

I say, "Give me a minute."

"Why?"

"Privacy. Fuck. Please."

Without saying anything she walks up the stairs. But she immediately runs back down and says, "You don't have to say 'fuck' every other word. It's just an affectation."

And with that she charges back up the stairs.

I remove my clothes and get into the shower. The more grease and shit and blood I wash off, the filthier I get.

Hours, days pass. Suddenly, Ariel rips back the curtain, "Are you okay? You've been in there for twenty-five minutes."

She's wearing a white T-shirt that is getting wet and showing her nipples. But she's not trying to be sexy. She has bandaged her foot. She's ghost white. Poor girl.

I shut the shower and she hands me a towel. With the latest gore wiped clean, I go to the bed. The towel is still wrapped around my waist. I brush back my wet hair. This impresses Ariel.

"You have great hair," she says.

I kiss her now and tug at her shirt. A sappy desire to touch her breasts overtakes me. I'm pulling her jeans down when I sense resistance.

"Howie. Not before we talk. You know I stopped drinking."

"So? Do you need to start again?"

She sighs. "Without alcohol . . . I can't have sex with you every time. I hardly know you."

"You fucked me like a cheap whore when you knew me even less."

"I thought I knew you. With the 'fuck this' and 'fuck that.' With the gangster stuff. The gun. I loved an unselfconscious brute. Boys like you in high school . . . you know, like nerds despise and salivate over cheerleaders. My situation here. Nothing going on. My mom. The booze. You tempted me with your killer attitude. Remember how you went out the bathroom window at the café to avoid those guys. That was thrilling. You know the rest. Now the only thing I know is that you're no killer. So stop acting like one."

This little speech annoys me, but not enough to shrink my painfully engorged dick. I say nothing but I rub her crotch. A moan escapes her and I wheedle, "I need you, baby."

"I haven't slept in two nights, Howie."

I pull the towel off and when she sees me fully loaded the color returns to her face. "Blow me. It will take a minute. Then we can talk for the rest of our lives."

She accepts that until I get my rocks off I won't be coherent. So she gently swipes her tongue along the base of my shaft. When her lips enclose the head of my dick I explode. She cups my balls as pleasure racks my body.

She says. "All right? Can we talk now?"

My breathing quickly returns to normal. "Sure. What."

"Howie . . . why did you pretend . . . I'm furious with you."

Is this significant? In a few days we traveled through the five stages of relationships. We liked each other. We craved each other. We became annoyed. Then furious. Soon we will become violent. Typical. I thought it cute the way she desired to educate me. Rembrandt. Sushi. Sadomasochism. She surprised me with the bondage—not that she enjoyed it but that she had the nerve to explore it so deeply. Her tits also provided a nice jolt, hanging off such an otherwise petite body. That she had been drunk almost the whole time had hardly decreased her appeal.

Sober now, Ariel acts like everyone else.

"Say something."

"What?"

"You have words besides 'blow me.'"

"I read a few books. So what? Does that mean you can abuse me?"

"I'm not abusing you. All I'm asking is that we have a conversation. It's no longer acceptable to merely grunt like a gorilla. Gorillas don't read . . ." She pulled the crumpled list from her pocket, "The *Nicomachean Ethics*. Do you think you are oh so clever?"

"I am who I am."

"You made a fool of me. Maybe you think I'm the idiot because I never read the *Nicomachean Ethics*."

"How could I know that?"

"Because no one reads it! Maybe dopey undergrads. Don't play these games, Howie."

"So only your games are legal."

She stares at me with monumental resentment. After a few moments she runs up the stairs and slams the door to her mother's apartment. The last thing I hear is her mother's high-pitched whine, *Ariel, is that—*

I begin packing.

I put all my things in the gym bag. This really isn't a good time to be walking the streets. Though we struck a decisive blow against the Russians, stragglers who hadn't been in The National could be roaming the streets looking for revenge. I did not see, for example, my old friend Ivan among the dead.

Ariel returns. "I got this for you." She hands me a paper bag. Inside is everything—the booze, the snacks, the Aristotle, and the Proust. Oh. Not everything. No Snickers Bars.

I put it all into my gym bag.

"Howie, please don't go."

"You don't want me here."

"That's not true. It's just that we seem to have things in common that you kept secret."

"I'm trying to be more open. But my interests make people not trust me."

"I trust you," Ariel says.

"That's not what you said a minute ago."

"I said I was furious. You can be furious with someone you love."

"Over a book?"

"It's not about a book. It's that you made believe—"

"I didn't make believe shit. You assumed I was a savage. I'm not. You're disappointed."

"Why did you give me that list if you didn't want me to know about you?"

She's right of course. Why did I do that? "It was stupid, a mistake. My father's goal was to read every Penguin Classic. I inherited his obsession. It's a fu— curse."

"Every one?" Ariel blanched. "There must be hundreds."

"One thousand, seven hundred and forty-eight. So what? I'm starting with the most interesting. I hope never to make it to the 'Faerie Queen.' It's famous for being the most boring poem ever written. I'd like to be dead before I get to it."

Ariel replies in a stricken tone, "We need to adjust the relationship. I also have intellectual interests I don't talk about all that much. You'll see. I just never wanted to read every classic. Why? What would be the point?"

No point. Ever since I started on this stupid reading, I've alienated everyone I know. Truth and beauty bring out the worst in so many. Only Ivan understands me, is simpatico, and he firebombed my house.

Even Ariel of college and grad school holds my erudition against me. She's thrown by the juxtaposition of my abs and my library, my gun and Aristotelian ethics.

I grab my bag off the bed and take it to the stairs. She follows. "Where are you going?"

"Underground."

"You're already underground," she says, desperate.

"I'm a sick man. My liver is diseased." I walk up the stairs toward the street.

"Howie, don't. Let's go to the city. We can stay in my place there."

I believe Pauli Bones will let me live if he never sees me again. "Has your renter left?"

"My tenant moved out two days ago. We can stay there until we figure out what to do."

As much as I hate driving, I could get my car and go out west, the far west. "I need to get farther away. Wyoming. Montana. I have enough money, credit, and pot to survive for months."

Ariel follows me onto the street. "Let's go together. We're finally starting to talk normally."

"There are people hunting me. They see you with me, you're dead too. Go inside."

"But you never did anything. You're innocent of everything except for reading Proust."

"They'll clip you without a thought."

"I don't care."

"You say that now. You won't be so sure with a few extra holes in your head." It's not that she doesn't care. It's that she doesn't believe me. She still thinks that murder happens to other people.

"My therapist says not to catastrophize."

"What?"

"It's unhealthy to always expect the worst scenarios to materialize."

"Being shot in the head, Ariel, is the best scenario. It's quick."

"Say my name again."

"Why?"

"Because it makes me feel good. You only used my name when we first met."

I can't believe this shit. "Ariel. Ariel. Ariel, get your ass inside your house."

She stands there, her nose reddening. I finally grab her hand and drag her to her door.

"Howie. Stop. Please, you're hurting me."

"Go inside. We should not be seen together. Trust me on this."

She shoots me a wicked look, her squinting eyes reminding me of a snub-nosed .38. I'd be dead if they were. But she finally goes back down her steps.

40

Two Plus Two

I go get my car, which is parked in front of Judith's house.

First, I check my blue Mazda for wires, anything suspicious. While the Italians dismiss car bombs as ostentatious, the Russians, for whom too much is never enough, favor them. They like the idea of being nowhere near the hit. If bystanders are hurt, well, luck runs out for all of us. A properly installed car bomb leaves no trace of the perpetrator or the victim. I duck to examine the vehicle's underside. It looks clean and so I jump in and turn the key, bracing myself. Nothing happens. So I pull into the street and drive toward Ocean Parkway. I'd pick up the Belt Parkway and head to the Verrazano. I'll keep going west until I run out of continent.

But at the Prospect Park Expressway, I find myself exiting and doubling back. I really am a shade condemned to haunt the streets between Coney Island and Sheepshead Bay.

In another twenty minutes I'm circling Ariel's block.

If she were in the car, could I leave then? Would having Ariel break the spell?

She wants to be with me. She thinks one day we might have a conversation.

Unfortunately, the little I've said so far has annoyed her. She likes me best when she knows me least.

I pull into the driveway and Ariel comes out, wearing a short, stylish suede jacket and pulling a rolling suitcase.

"What took you so long?" she asks as she gets into the car. Her face is elegantly made up.

Maybe she does know me. She knew enough to get ready. I just say, "I have to say good-bye to my sister. We might not see each other for a while."

"Good. I'd like to meet her."

"You'll stay in the car."

Ariel doesn't push.

It's not the right time to introduce a whole new element into the situation.

Judith's in-laws live in a solid brick house on Court Road, a quiet dead-end street hidden between Avenues S and T. It's too close to Brighton Beach for my liking, but there's nothing to do. It's late, almost midnight, and I text Judith that I'm coming over.

I hear nothing back and I pull up in front of the house. John's father is a successful mason and his home is set back behind a gated front yard. Judith likes it here. There's plenty of room for the girls. John's mother dotes on her grandchildren.

We wait in the parked car.

"Is she going to come out?" Ariel asks.

I hit her number. I have little hope that she'll pick up until she picks up.

Judith whispers, "Howie?"

"Did you get my text?"

"I was putting the girls to sleep. They have nightmares."

This rips into my guts.

"They'll get over it," Judith reassures inanely when she hears my silence. "Give it time."

"I'm parked outside. Can I see you for just a minute. Can you come to the porch?"

"I'm in my nightgown. Do you want to come inside?"

"I don't think John will appreciate—"

"John's watching TV in our bedroom. I'll open the door. We can talk in the den."

"If you think it's okay."

I say to Ariel. "I'll be back."

Ariel nods.

Judith opens the door and peers into the night. I slip inside and we hold on to each other for a long time. Then she says, "Is someone else in your car?"

"No one. A friend."

"Is that a woman?"

"Never mind." I absorb her familiar, worried features. Under the pale creases, however, I still see the gentle, open-faced woman that Judith had been when she eagerly married John. She really thought that she'd create this loving circle unencumbered by cares or Molotov cocktails.

I have been no help to Judith at all.

"I'm going away," I say. "This time for real. The neighborhood is just too hot."

"I heard something happened at The National."

"Really? What?"

"A massacre. Guys came in and shot the owner and a bunch of the workers."

Judith is not fishing for information. She certainly doesn't want to know if I was one of the gunmen. She's telling me that she understands the reason I must go.

In the next second she's crying on my chest. The sobs are low because she can't risk disturbing John. What Judith does say is, "At least you're not alone."

"Thanks. I'll always know that you're with me, Judith."

She picks her head up and wipes her cheeks. "Not me, silly. The girl in your car."

Right. Ariel. "I don't know her that well."

"She's in your car at a moment like this. Cherish her, whoever she is."

"Sure."

"I've packed up all your stuff. What do you want me to do with it?"

"Nothing. Dump it."

"The books?"

"Especially the books."

"They were Dad's."

"Yeah. Well, you read them."

She laughs.

"Why not?"

"I don't know. I'm busy. They don't mean much to me. Dad gave them to you for a reason. I can send them to a post office where you can pick them up."

"It's not going to work. Knowing anything can be dangerous."

"I think of you every time I come across those orangey bindings. Any orange reminds me of you. I see a box of tangerines and I want to ask, *Howie, what's going on?*"

I'm causing my own sister to lose her mind. "When are you moving back to your house?"

"John's father is going to start fixing the bricks as soon as the war is over."

"The war is over. For now. Pauli Bones . . . the war is over."

This surprises her. "Then why are you leaving? If the war is over and you're still . . ."

"I have to leave. It's my chance. And someone would get me sooner or later if I stay."

"But why?" Judith can no longer contain herself. "What did you do?"

"What the fuck—" John materializes into the little entrance foyer where Judith and I are tearing each other to emotional shreds.

"Hey, John."

"Fuck you, punk. You son of a bitch." He advances on me with fist clenched. Because he's so angry, he thinks he could take me. The idiot.

Judith steps between us. "Go, Howie. John, please. He's saying good-bye."

"Not before I kick his ass." He begins shouting, "Because of you my family—"

"Let him go, Judith," I say softly. Why not rip John's head off? Besides my own stupidity, he's the main source of Judith's misery.

Once more in a choked voice Judith begs me to leave. I really do want to kill John before I go. This is one way I know Judith will be safe. But I leave. Behind me, the door slams and I hear a bang, as if someone has been shoved against it. I charge back up the stairs and kick the door. It shudders on its frame. As I lift my leg to kick it again, Judith's voice rings out, "Howie, please. I can't take this anymore."

I keep my head down as I walk to the car. I wonder what Ariel thinks of this display, but then I don't give a damn.

I pick up my head and glance into the passenger seat. *Shit. She's gone.* Then, out of the corner of my eye, I glimpse Ivan clutching a chunk of Ariel's hair, jerking her head back. I don't see a piece, but I have no doubt that a weapon is pressed against Ariel's spine.

It never ends.

"Hello, motherfucker," Ivan greets me with what I hear is genuine friendliness.

"Hey, Ivan. Let her go."

Ariel is too terrified to do more than whimper.

"Let me see your hands," Ivan says.

I lift them palm up and say, "I'm not heavy, Ivan. I dumped the gun."

"Leave hands high."

There are times that Ivan could pass for a human being. Today is not one of them. The scar that runs down his face appears blood red against his pale cheeks. His eyes have disappeared into slits behind the ridge of his forehead and his lips are translucent. Without a drop of makeup he could play a zombie. On the other hand, he has not killed Ariel or me yet. So this could be a cry for help, a request to just talk.

I venture, "Ivan, listen to me. I had nothing to do with what happened at The National."

He jerks Ariel's head back with force. I imagine Ariel's neck snapping.

Only a low-pitched moan emerges from her.

"Where are my friends now?" Ivan screeches in a voice so full of fury and pain that he shocks me back into the world.

"We're free now, Ivan."

"Free? I have no one."

This dumb Russian fuck is as sentimental as any of us and this will be our deaths. The *friends* he mourns had never been his friends. I'm sure Vlad considered whacking Ivan as often as Vinnie debated clipping me. They let him beat up people because they were too lazy to do it themselves. That was the extent of their affection for him.

"Do you know what freedom is, Ivan? Freedom is the right to say two plus two equals four."

He spits on the ground. But this comment arouses his interest and slows him down.

I continue, "Vlad could force you to believe any bullshit, no matter how false. He was your connection to the old country, but he was never your friend."

"Where you read *two plus two is four*?"

"In Orwell. *1984*. Also in first grade."

"I got better one. Freedom is saying two plus two equal five. Dostoyevsky. *Underground Man*. Fuck the Crystal Palace. Fuck the mathematicians. Ha ha. Two plus two equal five because that is what *I* want. *I* make rules."

"I don't know if I agree."

"Orwell sucks cock. Informer, rat for secret police in England."

"Dostoyevsky stole from his wife and was a degenerate gambler with the math skills of a mosquito."

Ivan raises his gun. "You know about degenerate gambler from father, right?"

"Son of a bitch," I leap over the car's hood and Ivan pulls down on Ariel's hair and she screams in pain. He levels the gun at my eyes so I freeze.

Suddenly, the night turns totally silent. The streetlamp illuminates the three of us like a spotlight. On this dead-end street the babbled confusion that so infests my brain finally silences itself. The fogginess that normally shrouds people and events lifts, and the scene comes sharply into focus. I welcome death. I hope Ivan pulls the trigger.

Ivan releases Ariel, who's too stunned to move an inch. His scar pulses like a neon light. I myself feel embraced by the damp spring night. The breeze nips at my cheeks and nose, and cools my rushing blood.

Despair can easily overtake you, but a death wish has no real staying power. If you don't die at the right moment, the force that drives flowers upward also yanks you back from the brink.

I laugh.

"What's so funny?"

"I love Dostoyevsky's work."

"So why you talking shit?" Ivan finally lowers the gun. "Orwell is not bad."

Ariel stumbles and collapses. She lies at our feet as our discussion continues. "You know," I tell Ivan, "my father who never made recommendations gave me *The Gambler* to read so it must be special."

"Orwell hated Stalin dictatorship. So I understand why he become rat. Also, his essay on politics and language is best."

"What are you going to do now, Ivan? You're free of our ancient attachments, free from blood, from tribe. You finally made it to America."

"I have family. Kids are in school."

"I could talk to Pauli Bones for you."

He sneers in a way that only Russians can sneer, with such endless contempt that it causes vertigo. But Ivan's right. Pauli will whack me before he does me any favors. Knowing what I know, I'd be lucky if Pauli Bones just lets me stay disappeared. I ask Ivan, "Can't you take your family to somewhere until things settle down here?"

"People there will kill me. People here will kill me. Seems no one wants Ivan alive."

"And you're far from the worst of us."

Ivan shrugs. "This business eats people young. I need to be on the street here."

"Yeah. Listen, I should pick Ariel up and put her in the car."

"Sure."

Ariel has risen to one knee.

Ivan pockets his gun and watches me go around to the driver's side. His eye sockets twitch. I tell him, "You can light out for the territories, too."

"I'm not so American like you. I stay here with my people. I just want to say good-bye."

I wedge myself between the open door and the driver's seat. "What makes them your people? A love of Pushkin and vodka? Because you live with them?"

"Because I will die with them."

"That's a hell of a philosophy. You can die with anyone, no problem."

"Yes, it makes no sense."

"Find a nice town. Spend your days selling dope and reading in a clean, well-lit café."

"Wouldn't that be pretty," says Ivan. And with his huge shoulders hunched, he walks into the night.

Ivan will never leave Brighton Beach, Little Odessa, for any place in the universe. He has convinced himself that it's here that his destiny must play out. Maybe he'll be okay. Maybe Vlad's successor will enjoy his national literature and will not treat Ivan as a dangerous aberration. Maybe Ivan will expand his own pharmaceutical businesses to the point where his literacy will not infuriate his superiors.

Probably, however, he will remain the same outcast in his world as I had been in mine. A small-time dealer should never have as much perspective. On the outside he will appear like every other thug, but once he opens his mouth, no matter how much he fumes and curses, Ivan will give himself away, alert the gangsters to a broadness dangerous in the closed world of moneymaking enterprises. The broader the perspective, the less tied to your group on the ground. Reading anything beyond a sports magazine raises issues of loyalty.

I fold myself into the driver's seat and glide the car out of the spot. I don't glance into the rearview mirror until I turn a corner.

Ariel straightens up in her seat and asks, "Is he gone?"

"Yes."

"Where are we going?"

"To the other end of the world."

At this hour there is little traffic into Manhattan.

"You're not going to regret this," Ariel says, her energy returning in powerful currents. "We'll have a life together. Regular sex. No games this time."

"I told you a hundred times, I don't mind the games."

Ariel's hand gently lands between my legs. "You're so sweet. But I've played myself out for now. Why don't you believe me?"

Is that possible? Can a woman who took such pleasure in extreme masochism really renounce this type of eroticism as if it were no more than a childish interest in princesses? Well, can I tell myself that I'm not really a violent person? Can she lie about what turns her on? Never mind the mystery of others. People have little idea about their own selves.

Her warm hand feels good rubbing my jeans-encased penis. I ask Ariel if we should take the FDR or the West Side Highway.

"It's the same," she says.

"Come on," I tell her. "I can't do this by myself."

"Then go up the east side to Houston. Take a right on the Bowery and a left at Bleecker."

We make it to the end of the world in twenty minutes.

"Pull up in front of the white brick building, the one with the green awning."

Ariel walks in slow motion to her door, awed by the possibility of a new life. She says, "I never thought I'd make it back."

"Don't get used to it. We can only stay a day or two." I grab my bag from the trunk. It contains everything I need but feels weightless.

In her still awed tone, Ariel adds, "I haven't been in my apartment in a year." Then, frowning, she concludes, "I'll have to get an agent to sublet it again."

The elevator creeks up to the fourth floor. The hallway is odorless, like one in a hotel. People in Manhattan don't cook.

"The apartment might be in terrible condition," she warns. "Don't be shocked."

I'm so tired that I'd sleep on a bed of broken glass.

She opens the door and flips on the light.

"I told you. It's nothing much."

Ariel is not wrong about this. The living room couldn't be more than fifteen by fifteen, with one wall painted peach and two windows facing south. I go over to them and peer onto Thompson Street. It's good to have a street view, to be able to see what cars are pulling up in front of the building.

"Let me show you around," Ariel says.

Besides the living room that has a couch, a rug, a television sandwiched between two bookcases, there is a bathroom and a bedroom, neither worth describing. I check out her bookcase and she has an eclectic mix of masterpieces and shit. She must have been into Thomas Hardy at one point because she owns five of his novels; at another time she searched the Chicken Soup series for spiritual enlightenment.

"Nice place."

"Thanks," Ariel says. "At least Joan left it clean."

There seems to be nothing else to do but to have sex. I start to remove her clothes when she pushes me away. "Wait. I need my suitcase from your backseat."

"Leave your shirt off."

Downstairs, I pull her bag out of the car. It's five times as heavy as mine. In the elevator I open it to peek inside. On the top there is a thin layer of underwear, jeans and T-shirts. Underneath are the sex toys—creams, feathers, ropes, cuffs, dildos, paddles. She hasn't brought her whole collection, but there's enough stuff here to spice up a de Sade orgy.

Back in her apartment, Ariel pulls me into the bedroom. We sit on the edge of her bed and she orders me to wait. "We're starting new," she says. "I don't have to drink to stay sane or use instruments to get me off. And you don't have to use *fuck* every other word."

I judge that she finished her little speech and I remove her bra. Her breasts spring free and I gently bite her nipples. Ariel moans. "Do me a favor."

I lift my head off her chest. "What?"

"Get the nipple clamps from my bag."

I hesitate. Ariel explains further, "This way I can go down on you while I'm still being stimulated."

"Sure," I say. "It's an engineering issue."

I rifle through her bag for the tools she needs. The clamps look nasty, like metal clothespins. But Ariel gasps with pain and gurgles with pleasure as they go on.

She sucks me dry. Then she lies on her stomach and I go down on her. My tongue rakes her quivering cunt. As soon as we finish, Ariel jumps off the bed and unclips the clamps.

"What's the matter?"

"Nothing."

But she's agitated. She wants a drink.

"Let me show you around the neighborhood."

"It's almost midnight."

Ariel crawls onto the bed and looks down into my face. "You *aren't* a killer, are you?"

"Why do you ask?"

"Because you can't be. You're the most gentle man I've ever been with."

"So what are you worried about?"

"Nothing. I just want to know if my instinct is right."

"With instincts there is no right and wrong. You just follow them."

"You're not going to tell me?"

"There's nothing to tell." ·

She lies parallel to my own body, stiff and cold. "If you don't tell me," she says with a fierceness that the alcohol used to cut, "I'm going to get a drink."

"I never killed anyone. I couldn't do it if I wanted to."

Ariel buries her face into my chest. Her muffled voice bounces up, "I knew it. I knew it."

41

A New Beginning

The morning brings the first spring day without a hint of winter chill. We walk to Soho and breakfast at Balthazar.

On the way we talk about how we're going to get by. It's a tense conversation. We'll leave New York, at least until things cool down, tomorrow. Ariel doesn't want me to sell pot because my suppliers might give me up. After the Ivan incident, she now believes me when I tell her that my acquaintances play for keeps.

At the restaurant, our first time outside together fully clothed since the day we met, Ariel pretends we're a normal couple, "So what are you reading?"

I sip the coffee. No one had actually ever asked me this before. "Still the Aristotle."

"Tell me about it."

"There's nothing to tell. What is good? How does one live a good life?"

"Important questions." Ariel keeps the conversation going despite strong headwinds. "So what does Aristotle say?"

"Search for truth. Appreciate beauty. Avoid assassination. Respect others. Have oral sex at least twice a week and strive to please the gods. It's an ancient formula and I don't know how much relevance this has today."

"The old masters knew everything. A little updating," Ariel encourages. "That's all."

I say no more. The waiter puts down our omelets. Before he walks away, she asks him to bring her a Bloody Mary. She concludes, "This is going to take awhile."

"Fucking A," I respond.

ACKNOWLEDGMENTS

Writers, like all criminals, need aiders and abettors, safe houses, and connections. So I'd like to acknowledge Shane Solow, who fenced this manuscript to Martin. Also, thank you to Michael Popkin and Betty Engelberg, who blackmailed me into continuing writing with their decades of encouragement (and who also made sure I had paid work). And to Ira Elliott, who stuck his editorial knife into the soft underbelly of what I had judged impenetrably great. Only by his locating these weaknesses could the writing become stronger. Finally, Randi Priluck, whose love and support for a megalomaniac baffles all who know her. I love you too.